Bolt Action Remedy

"Crime writer J.J. Hensley deserves readers' attention and trust, because beyond his ever-stronger prose, he brings his ex-badge carrier's street smart eyes to this hard world we live in. Put him on your READ list."

—James Grady, author of
Six Days of the Condor

"In Trevor Galloway, J.J. Hensley has given us a deliciously flawed hero whose unique gift makes him a phenomenal investigator, but also leaves him teetering on the razor-thin edge of genius and insanity. Hensley weaves a captivating tale while providing an authentic voice and a dash of ironic humor."

—Annette Dashofy, *USA Today* bestselling
author of the Zoe Chambers Mysteries

"Fast-paced and funny, *Bolt Action Remedy* is an action-packed thriller that will keep readers guessing until the final page."

—Rebecca Drake, author of *Only Ever You*

"*Bolt Action Remedy* is entertaining as hell."

—Andrew Pyper, International Thriller
Writers Award winning author of *The Damned*

"The welcome return of J.J. Hensley's trademark blend of breathless action, haunting atmosphere and sly wit."

—Gwen Florio, award-winning
author of *Montana* and *Disgraced*

"Strap yourselves in. This author guides you to the conclusion through twists, turns, and drops that will leave you so engrossed, you lose track of time."

—Lucie Fleury Dunn,
Movies in My Mind Book Reviews

Praise for *Measure Twice*

"It's about time somebody gave Hannibal Lecter a run for his money. J.J. Hensley's *Measure Twice* is up to the task."

—Gwen Florio, award-winning
author of *Montana and Dakota*

"A finely crafted story of redemption, *Measure Twice* will keep your adrenaline pumping."

—Tim Green, bestselling
author of *The Forth Perimeter*

Praise for *Resolve*

"J.J. Hensley's debut novel is a lean, fast-paced, suspenseful murder mystery—told with style, intelligence, and wit."

—John Verdon, bestselling
Author of *Let the Devil Sleep*

"This artfully constructed mystery makes effective use of the third-rate-college setting and of Pittsburgh"

—*Publishers Weekly*

"One of the 10 best books of the year."

—Pam Stack, Authors on the Air

BOLT ACTION
REMEDY

J.J. HENSLEY

BOLT ACTION REMEDY

A TREVOR GALLOWAY THRILLER

Down & Out Books
3959 Van Dyke Rd, Ste. 265
Lutz, FL 33558
www.DownAndOutBooks.com

Cover design by JT Lindroos

ISBN: 1-946502-04-9
ISBN-13: 978-1-946502-04-9

For Kasia and Cassie

"Every mile is two in winter."
—*George Herbert*

PROLOGUE

Centre County, Pennsylvania

It was a suicidal snowfall. The flakes were bunched together and fell heavy, rather than yielding to an angelic descent. Peter Lanskard exited the black Chrysler, stood with his face to the sky and inhaled while letting the frigid dampness invigorate his sixty-five-year-old lungs. The ride from the regional airport had taken less than an hour, but Lanskard had been anxious to reach his property. He longed to stretch his legs and allow wintertime amnesia to erase memories of stuffy meetings in dusty Southern towns that had once been exploited for coal and were now being explored for pockets of natural gas. Even with the cloud cover, he had to squint to allow his eyes to adjust to the white Pennsylvania hills surrounding him.

"Sir? The perimeter alarm," reminded his head of security. "We should move indoors."

Lanskard exhaled a disappointed puff of vapor into the air as reality was once again intruding upon the serene.

"It's been a hard winter, Brady," said Lanskard. "The deer are going to be restless until spring. We should just turn the thing off for the season."

Brady Mason didn't respond. He didn't have to. Both men knew the perimeter alarm was going to stay active and would be tripped periodically by the wildlife as long as Lanskard insisted on not fencing in his acres. If it were up to Mason, a web of alarm sensors would cover most the grounds within the perimeter, but the security man knew he was lucky his employer had agreed to the basic system that was deployed along the property line.

Lanskard turned to the security man and said, "Who's heading out there?"

Mason shifted his weight, uncomfortable with his boss's procrastination, and said, "Mark took a four-wheeler out to the eastern boundary. He should be there in a moment."

The landowner took in more fresh air and slowly exhaled, watching the ghost of his breath fade into nothingness. He couldn't help but grin as he watched Mason's growing agitation. The driver emerged from his side of the car and asked if everything was okay.

"We're fine, Jason. Thank you," Lanskard replied as he watched Mason scan the tree line and bite his lip.

The alarm notification wasn't unusual in itself, but Mason didn't like the timing. The call had come just as the car was entering the property. He had turned from the passenger's seat and informed his boss that an external alarm had been tripped, and that they should stay in the vehicle until the alarm had been cleared. Predictably, the owner of Mountain Resource Solutions stated that he was in a hurry to get inside the house. That Lanskard now appeared to be *anything but* in a hurry to get out of the open was driving Mason crazy, and the owner of MRS was enjoying every minute of needling his trusted guard.

Sensing he had exhausted the security man's patience, Lanskard laughed and said, "You're good people, Mason. But I sure love being a pain in your ass."

Mason maintained his stern expression, kept his eyes on the woods, and replied, "As always, sir, you are exceptional in all that you do."

Lanskard leaned back and roared an echoing laugh and

patted the shoulder of the man he considered more of a friend than an employee. With a final bit of reluctance, he turned to move toward his home.

The sound of Lanskard's laugh was still ricocheting off the hills when the bullet struck him in the forehead. Mason drew his Glock, scanned for a target, and knelt beside his employer. With his free hand, he yelled into a radio and then let the quiet return. Wet clumps of snow fell onto, then burned off of, the dead man's face. The frozen clusters seemed to gravitate to Lanskard's skin as if they instinctively knew that certain things aren't meant to survive long in the winter. They knew. They just didn't care.

Pittsburgh, Pennsylvania

Smoke from the thug's cigarette intruded upon the few remaining pockets of clear air in the room. He moved to a section of the attic where the ceiling hung only a few inches above his head, let the cigarette drop on a board, and crushed it under a charcoal boot. The man crossed his arms and smirked enough to where a chipped tooth peeked out from behind a scarred lip. He looked down into the shadowed corner of the room and focused on the silhouette of the man strapped to the chair.

Sounds from a television and two men talking could be heard through the thin floorboards. Nothing special about the tone of the conversation downstairs. Nothing indicated anybody in the house was giving a second thought to the fact that a man was being held against his will directly above their heads. The man with the chipped tooth lit another cigarette and spoke in heavily accented English.

"You are lucky, man. You know this, right?"

The man in the chair strained to raise his head toward the voice.

"I tell them long time ago that you have nothing left to say. I tell them we cut you up in bathtub, toss parts in river, and be done with you."

The prisoner's head dropped, the weight too much for his neck to handle.

"In my home country of Estonia, I once used a saw to make a body disappear. It is hard work, but it—how do you say? It builds character."

Chipped Tooth laughed at his observation, but his broken smile faded when the man in the chair didn't respond. The captor strode across the room and grabbed the prisoner's chin, lifting it so the men were eye to bloodshot eye.

"He is on the way," spat Chipped Tooth. "He is coming and then we will know for sure that you tell us everything."

He let the prisoner's head drop and paced with heavy feet across the thin floor.

"They say he is like a machine, you know?" he continued. "I heard that when he was in Kaunas Prison, a guard liked to hit him in the back with stick right before the lights go out and everyone goes to sleep. One night, he goes in cell and the guard locks the door. In morning, when lights come back on they find the guard's body in the cell, but *he* is gone. They searched all over Lithuania, but he is nowhere to be found."

Chipped Tooth knelt in front of the prisoner and said, "And when they found the guard in that cell, do you know what he was missing?"

The man in the chair made a sound.

"What did you say?" asked Chipped Tooth.

"A ghost story told to fools," the prisoner managed to whisper. "Go to hell."

Chipped Tooth grabbed the prisoner's hair and violently yanked the man's head backward. He punched the restrained man in the face and produced a straight razor.

"I was told to make sure you not die before he gets here. But I do not think you will die if missing part of your face."

Chipped Tooth leaned in with the rusty blade, but drew back when he heard commotion coming from beneath his feet. He rushed to the attic door, closed it behind him, and ran down a set of stairs. The man in the chair clung to consciousness as shouts filled the air. The sound of Chipped Tooth's rapid footsteps descending the stairs stopped and, after all this time in captivity, the prisoner could tell not all the steps had been touched. Chipped Tooth had descended two-thirds of the flight before halting abruptly. The prisoner's heart sank as Chipped Tooth's boots once again ascended into the attic. Other footsteps followed, but now the entire house seemed to be coming alive with chaos.

The prisoner managed to raise his head enough to see Chipped Tooth fly through the door with the blade extended in his right hand. The criminal reached the dark corner where the captive sat helplessly awaiting his fate and placed the razor against the prisoner's neck. The captive waited for, and even welcomed, the decisive slash, but instead of feeling the burn of the cut, the room erupted in gunfire. Chipped Tooth fell hard and the room grew quiet.

In the doorway stood a figure in jacket emblazoned with the word POLICE on one side. The figure swept the room with his eyes and gun before taking cautious steps toward the prisoner whose head had fallen once again.

"Police," said the cop. "Let me see your hands!"

The man in the chair did not move.

The cop shone a light into the corner. Now he could see the

restraints around the man's wrists and ankles. He was still wary, but asked, "Buddy, are you okay?"

The prisoner willed himself to move, but couldn't get his body to comply. He managed to remain conscious and heard more footsteps approaching. From the sounds, he deduced at least two more officers had squeezed through the narrow door.

The cop with the flashlight took cautious steps toward Chipped Tooth, reached down to toss the razor out of reach, and conducted a quick search for additional weapons before checking the man's vital signs. The cop looked back at the other officers and shook his head. He placed two fingers on the prisoner's neck and checked the carotid artery for a pulse.

"I think this guy's alive," said the cop. "Tell the EMTs the house is clear and get them up here fast."

For several seconds, radios crackled and blared. The cop lifted the prisoner's head and checked the neck for any cuts. He shined the flashlight from one side of the neck to the other before allowing his gaze to find the man's battered face.

"Jesus Christ," he said softly, not believing what he was seeing.

The other cops approached, making a semicircle around the chair.

"Is that...Is that Trevor Galloway?" asked an officer wearing a Pittsburgh PD baseball cap.

"Jesus Christ," the cop with the flashlight quietly repeated.

More officers entered the room and the prisoner's name was whispered and mumbled in funeral home tones.

The prisoner's head dropped and the cop with the flashlight once again checked for a pulse. The cop tried two more times, maneuvering his fingers to find the artery. Trying to sound calm, he turned to another officer and said, "Billy, go find the EMTs and get them up here this second."

TARGET 1
NEEDLES, SWORDS, AND BULLETS

CHAPTER 1

One year and three days later

Am I still holding the gun? It should be there, but what difference does it make? If I can't see, I can't shoot, and my eyes are flooding thanks to this weather. I know those were people in front of me, but now they're nothing more than spots that rise and fall with the bleached horizon as I burn through whatever firewood remains in my body. My erratic strides aren't painful anymore, but my shoulder still aches. I can't feel my legs and my steps are muffled by the heartbeat pulsating in my ears. I can barely make out what the people are saying. Why am I even running toward them? For what purpose?

Sergeant Pullman—that was his name, I think. Most of the instructors at the police academy made the recruits run for miles at a time. But not Sergeant Pullman. He shuffled us into that musty weight room and paced from station to station screaming, "You can run all day, but what are you going to do when you get there?"

What are you going to do when you get there?

Jesus, how long has it been since the academy? A career ago. My days on the street have come and gone and I hear Pullman's gravelly voice now, in this place? His voice rings in my ears while I'm in this barren field and nearly blind. An icy anaconda is constricting my lungs and I can't even tell if my fingers are wrapped around the damn pistol. My snow-hindered steps are

9

*making the figures ahead of me float and sink, and I can't dis-
tinguish one face from another.*

*I'm blinking hard and I can tell from the motion in front of
me that I've been spotted. Please don't turn toward me. Don't
you do it! I have too much ground to cover and not enough
time to react. "Action is almost always quicker than reaction."
Pullman used to say that too. I need to raise my arm preemp-
tively and pray the gun is still there in a hand I can't feel. I'm
closing the gap, but the up-and-down motion is disorienting. I
might cover the distance, but to what end?*

What am I going to do when I get there?

Good question, Sergeant Pullman.

Action is almost always quicker than—

Four days earlier

"Are you armed?" the man asked.

"No," I said.

"I'll need to check you," he told me.

"No," I said.

"Then, we have a problem," he concluded.

"No, we don't," I told him as I walked back toward my
SUV.

As the engine came to life, a woman who appeared to be in
her late twenties rushed out of the house and waved for me to
stop.

I unrolled my window as she approached and she said, "Mr.
Galloway?"

I nodded.

"I'm sorry about that. Sometimes they can be a little
overprotective."

We listened to the engine purr and I watched her shiver as a gust of wind whipped through the landscape.

"I'm Susan Lanskard. Will you please come inside?"

"Ms. Lanskard, like I said on the phone, I really don't think I can help you. The police have been all over the case and you obviously have resources, like private security personnel, at your disposal."

"I remember. But please...just a few minutes."

I let the engine hum for several seconds before turning the key back toward my chest. The woman took two steps away as I opened the car door and took a reluctant step in her direction. She forced a smile and led me back to the entrance I had been all too happy to leave moments ago. Retracing my footsteps, I wondered how desperate this woman had to be if she wanted to hire me.

I entered the house and was once again sized up by the bulky security guard. He was dressed in a long-sleeved shirt and khakis and wore a sport coat that didn't make much of an attempt at concealing the firearm on his right hip. I did my best to leave all the snow from my shoes on the doormat before the slim woman led me down a wide hallway. The décor inside wasn't that of your typical Central Pennsylvania home, but then again most homes in this part of the state weren't built by millionaires. Although the owner was obviously in a tax bracket most would never climb into, part of me still expected to see hunting trophies or some sort of fishing memorabilia. Instead, the walls were lined with tasteful paintings and the occasional photos of ski trips and other vacation memories. Somewhere a grandfather clock chimed the quarter hour and I picked up the scent of a fireplace in use.

We walked into the living room where a uniformed police officer was sitting on a sofa. Her shoes were dry. She had been here a while.

Ms. Lanskard made the introductions. "Mr. Galloway, this is Chief Colby. She's with the township. Chief Colby, this is Trevor Galloway."

The chief stood, extended a hand, and said, "Please, call me Sally."

"Trevor," I said. We shook hands while I eyed the unusual olive green uniform and the shoulder patch that read *Washaway Township Police.*

I had never heard of the municipality, but that wasn't a surprise in a commonwealth of countless townships, villages, and boroughs scattered around towns and cities.

Our hostess gestured to the furniture and said, "Please have a seat. I'll get you both some coffee." She moved out of the room and I noticed Colby's eyes watching her every step.

While we took our seats and waited, I appraised the woman in uniform. Sally Colby was in her thirties, but young chiefs weren't unheard of in small municipalities. She was an attractive woman who carried herself with an air of confidence. Her brown hair was in a tight ponytail and her Gore-Tex boots were as clean as possible for the season. Her brown eyes were young, but not naïve.

The faint ticking of the grandfather clock made its way into the room as we waited in near silence. I checked my watch for no reason, as I became aware that every move I made was being watched by the woman sitting across from me.

"I've heard of you," Colby finally said. "When Susan asked me if I knew anybody who might be able to lend a hand, I couldn't think of anyone specific. So I called Chase Vinson with the Pittsburgh Police and he told me he knew just the man for the job. When he said your name, my jaw dropped. You were in the news a lot."

I didn't speak.

"I was surprised you were no longer with the PD. But I guess retirement is appealing when you hit your mid-fifties. You must have had enough of working narcotics cases in Pittsburgh."

I looked at her and said, "I'm forty-three."

She hesitated and stammered, "Oh...I'm...it's not that..."

I'm well aware I look older than my age and I should have smiled to let her know I wasn't offended. But I rarely smile, and when I do, some people interpret it as insincere. I did my best to put her at ease.

"It's okay. I'm high mileage." After an awkward silence, I said, "I retired on disability."

Colby cleared her throat and shook of the last trace of embarrassment and asked, "So now you're an investigator for the district attorney's office down there?"

I shook my head. "Not anymore."

"I suppose you had enough of dealing with lawyers," she said with forced levity.

"They were fine, but I was asked to resign after my very first case."

"Oh," she said. An awkward silence followed. Then, in an attempt to get some footing, she asked, "So are you a private investigator now?"

"Nope."

Colby swallowed hard and started to wonder if she was the butt of a bad joke.

"Well, Chase said if there is trouble to be found then you'll find it," she said.

I tilted my head and gave her a skeptical look.

"Okay, okay. He said the trouble would find you," she admitted.

Colby's attention shifted and she beamed as our hostess returned and placed a tray down on the table. Ms. Lanskard asked me how I took my coffee, but didn't bother to ask the police chief. She took a seat and we all sipped the warm brew. It was my third cup of coffee for the day, but I had to admit it was by far the best.

"Mr. Galloway, were you briefed as to exactly why I want to hire you?"

I gently put my cup down on a coaster and folded my hands in front of me. "Last year your father, Mr. Peter Lanskard, was murdered while standing outside of this very house." I paused for a moment and added, "I'm truly sorry about that."

"Thank you," she said with no small amount of sorrow in her voice. I glanced at Colby whose expression mirrored that of our hostess.

I continued, "My understanding is that your father, who owned a company called MRS, had been receiving numerous threats from all directions. He had been harassed by unemployed coal workers, anti-fracking activists, anti-mountaintop removal protesters, clean water advocates, the list goes on and on. The case was investigated by the local authorities—which I assume means Chief Colby's department."

"And the State Police's Major Case Team," Colby added.

"Okay," I said. "I believe the conclusion was that the scant evidence points to a lone sniper using a weapon that fires a .308 round." I leaned back in my chair and said, "That's all Chase told me and I'm assuming he got that from Chief Colby, so I haven't seen any files. I remember the media reports and the case seems to have gotten a lot of attention from both cops and reporters. That's why I'm not sure I can be of any assistance."

Colby said, "I was the first officer on scene that day and since that time I've gone over the facts a million times. It isn't easy for me to admit that I'm stuck, but I'm not going to be stupidly territorial about this either. The state police did a good job of checking out the environmentalists and disgruntled former employees, but the case drifted away when they couldn't come up with anything. Regardless, I don't think they were looking at the right people."

I leaned forward and spoke to both the women. "I have absolutely no doubt that Chief Colby's department and the state investigators did the best job possible. As law enforcement officers, they have access to a myriad of intelligence databases and can intimidate suspects by threatening to take away their freedom. I want to be perfectly clear about something. I'm a private citizen. I don't have a badge and have no legal authority in *any* jurisdiction. I am terribly sorry about the death of your father, but I don't want to give you any hope that I can achieve a result different from what you have now."

"Trevor," Ms. Lanskard said, "one of the weaknesses that you claim to possess is exactly why I want to hire you."

I gave her a puzzled look.

"You have no authority in *any* jurisdiction," she continued. "You also have no limits as to where you can travel to search for answers and question potential suspects. Thanks to my father, I'm a woman of means and I will fund your investigation and pay your expenses as needed."

"I appreciate that, but I have a life back in Pittsburgh," I lied. "I can't go flying around the country for weeks at a time trying to track down pissed-off coal miners and college-aged protestors. I'm very sorry, but I really don't want to waste your time. I know you said you would pay me five thousand dollars to come up here and listen, but I really don't want your money. I'm only here because a friend asked me to hear you out."

I stood up as if there was an urgent need for me to drive the three and a half hours back to my apartment in Pittsburgh. My good friend Chase Vinson, a grizzled eighteen-year veteran in my former department, would give me hell for bailing out on the favor he was asking of me. However, I also knew that his real motivation in giving my name to Colby was to keep me, and my mind, occupied.

When referring to my previous job as an investigator with the DA's office, Colby had suggested I had had enough of dealing with lawyers. The truth was that I did have a problem with the prosecutor I was working with on my first assignment with the DA's office. He made a critical error during prep for a rape trial and had tried to convince me to perjure myself on the stand. I refused and testified truthfully. Later, outside the courthouse, he accused me of not being a team player and threw out some not-so-nice words that touched on my previous deep undercover work with the police department and my battle with heroin addiction.

In all fairness, I hadn't become a junkie by choice. My cover had been burned by an informant, and as a result, a drug ring mostly consisting of thugs from former Soviet republics held me captive for several weeks. During that time, I was tortured and repeatedly injected with heroin until I was hooked and nearly forgot my own name. Deep down I think people knew my affliction wasn't my fault. However, once you get the "addict" label slapped on you, the context has a way of becoming irrelevant.

To make a long story short, the result of the conversation with the antagonistic prosecutor ended with him having a broken nose and me being unemployed. This led to my having a slight relapse with opiates and a halfway decent romantic relationship getting wrecked on some rocky shores. There were some other issues, but I was doing my best to leave those behind.

Lanskard crossed her legs and used her left hand to push

strands of red hair away from her appealing face. I didn't see a wedding band and she had made no mention of any other family members who were interested in the case.

I said, "I noticed most of the photos around here are of you and your father. Do you have any other family?"

"My mother died years ago and I'm an only child. My father was everything to me, and someone took that everything away. I don't expect you to understand how I feel, but I can't live with the fact that my father's murderer is still out there."

The pain welled up in Susan Lanskard's eyes and Colby leapt up and handed her a tissue.

I told her, "It would be irresponsible for me to not let you know that you may never get the closure you are seeking. I was a cop for a long time, and the conclusions reached at the end of a case are rarely happy ones. Even when a killer is caught, a hollowness remains and will never be completely filled."

She seemed to ignore me and said, "If you agree to take the case, and you work fast, there may not be any travel involved. However, in one week the suspects will be scattering to the four winds and you—or somebody else—will have to head out of state if any more questions need to be asked."

I sat back down and moved my eyes between Lanskard and Colby. Poker faces all around.

"Are you saying you think the killer is still here in Centre County? Right now?" I asked.

"I know he is," Chief Colby replied calmly while sipping her coffee. "In fact, he's right next door."

CHAPTER 2

"You have my attention," I said unnecessarily.

Susan Lanskard wiped her eyes and said, "My father's case is vitally important to me, which makes this a bit awkward. But I'm afraid I have a teleconference I have to attend in the other room. When my father died, ownership of the company fell to me. And honestly, reliving all of this is very difficult for me."

"I have a few questions before you go. Were you here when it happened?" I asked.

"No. I was finishing up my graduate degree at Dartmouth. Obviously, I made my way here as soon as Brady called."

"Brady?"

"Brady Mason is our head of security. He was standing beside my father when...anyway, he called me. He and his team work for me now."

Her face had gone pale and another wave of emotional turmoil washed over her as she dabbed at her eyes.

She explained, "Unfortunately, along with inheriting the company, I inherited the threats that come along with this type of business. Therefore, there is still a need for security personnel."

Colby watched Lanskard for several seconds and shook off a concerned look before standing up and saying, "Let's take a drive, Trevor. I'll explain everything on the way. If you aren't intrigued by the time I'm finished, I'll bring you back here and you can get in your car and head back to Pittsburgh."

"Where are we going?"

"Like I said, the suspects are right next door."

It turned out that *next door* was a relative term. The Lanskard property consisted of an immense expanse of land that placed the closest neighbor several minutes away by vehicle. The Washaway Township cruiser was the typical Ford police package and the chief of the township kept the vehicle immaculate. She drove cautiously down the icy roads and lowered her police radio to a near whisper.

"How many officers do you have reporting to you?" I asked.

"Three at the moment. We had one retire last month, but we haven't replaced him yet."

I said, "I assume from the green uniforms, the department has been around for quite a while."

She shot me a sideways glance and asked, "What makes you say that?"

I pulled a pair of sunglasses out of my jacket pocket as the sun broke through the clouds, illuminating the terrain.

"Well, I've only seen a few departments with green uniforms. The West Virginia State Police, the Chesterfield County Police in Virginia, and the U.S. Border Patrol all chose green long ago because they needed it for sneaking up on moonshiners or hiding in the brush. I've never seen a newer department choose to wear green."

Colby gave a nod and said, "It's the same with us. We were organized during prohibition and the uniforms stuck. From time to time, someone makes a push to change them because they think we look like park rangers, but I'm partial to them."

The road bent around a cluster of trees and Colby slowed to the car to a near crawl before a small straightaway appeared.

"How do you know Chase? Did he work narcotics with you?" she asked.

"Everybody knows Chase."

She laughed. "I suppose that's true. Of course, your name seems to get around, too."

I went silent and let the moment pass.

"You don't talk about yourself much, do you?"

"Not much," I said. "No need. Like you said, I was in the news. I'm sure you guys have Internet access here and I bet you looked up my history."

"I did," she admitted. Her eyes shifted away. "There was some pretty rough stuff online. I'll understand if you don't want to talk about it, but I can't say I'm not curious."

"Maybe later," I lied. "For now, why don't you tell me what I don't know about the case?"

Colby took a breath and seemed to collect thoughts about an investigation that was personal to her.

She began, "Nearly one year ago, Peter Lanskard was returning home from a meeting in Arkansas and he was gunned down near the spot where you parked your car. It was a single shot to the head that came from the eastern tree line. The distance from where the shooter set up to where Peter fell is about five hundred yards."

I arched an admiring eyebrow and she caught the look.

"I know," she said. It was a pretty impressive shot, especially considering it was snowing at the time."

I weighed this and recalled all I knew about snipers. "I suppose it's impressive, but not astounding. The best shots out there can hit a target from about a mile away if the conditions are right."

"Just wait, you'll be more impressed in a minute," she said. "Mr. Lanskard was being driven home from the regional airport by his long-time driver Jason Leonard. His head of security, Brady Mason was riding shotgun and the rest of the detail was already in place on the property. Four minutes before the car entered the property, Mason was notified that one of the electronic perimeter alarms had been tripped. He advised Lanskard that when they arrived at the house, he should remain in the car until someone could check it out, but Lanskard insisted on getting out."

"He wasn't concerned?"

"The alarm being tripped was a common occurrence. Lanskard absolutely refused to put up any fencing around the property, so deer and coyotes were always setting the thing off. It drove his security detail nuts, since they were the ones who had to check it each time, but Lanskard didn't want a tall chain-link fence sullying the environment."

Recalling what I knew about Mountain Resource Solutions, I cocked my head and said, "You do see the irony, right?"

Colby smiled and said, "It is not lost on me one bit. Anyway, Lanskard got out of the car, dallied around for a minute, then fell dead from a .308 round to the head. We found the shell casing later. Mason never saw the shooter and another security man, Mark Letterman—who you had the pleasure of meeting at the house—failed to locate the shooter even though he was already en route on a tracked ATV to see what set off the alarm."

"Letterman doesn't seem like a real people person," I said.

The chief slowed the car around another hairpin turn and observed, "You don't exactly strike me as a social butterfly either. So far, I haven't seen you smile once."

"Point taken," I said. "Do you have any idea how the shooter managed to escape detection?"

"He didn't, exactly. He set off the alarm, took the shot, and alerted the system again on the way out. Letterman said he was right there the entire time and can't figure out how the shooter got by him."

I shrugged and said, "Things like that happen. It's not that hard to miss someone in the woods. Or maybe Letterman isn't very observant."

"Perhaps," she said. "But the questions lay in the timing. That's the most intriguing part of all of this."

"How so?"

"Get this," she began. "The alarm sensor that was set off is nearly one mile from the tree line."

I let that sink in for a moment as the car crested a hill and descended into an open valley. I said, "Are you telling me that someone ran a mile in the snow at a breakneck pace, set up in a shooting position, and managed to get off a perfect headshot before escaping the same way?"

A corner of Colby's mouth curled up as she said, "Nobody ran."

I felt stupid for my initial assumption and said, "Of course not. They used some sort of all-terrain vehicle."

The chief shook her head and said, "Nobody heard a vehicle and we didn't find any foreign track marks. All the ATVs up here have tracks on them so they can get through the snow and it seems Letterman had the only one in the area. So no vehicle was used."

I waited, but Colby was enjoying my confusion. I cleared my throat, prompting her to end the game.

"Skis. The shooter skied onto the property and crossed relatively flat ground in no time at all."

My mind processed this information and I stayed silent as our car approached some sort of complex. Finally, I came to the realization that the facts of the case—if accurate—were extremely telling. Part of me wanted to chastise the young chief for not fully understanding that her baffling case wasn't so baffling after all.

"At first glance, you have two highly possible scenarios," I said. "The first is that Letterman is lying and he's your shooter. It is awfully convenient that he was on an ATV and managed to not see anyone out there."

"Letterman was checked for GSR, passed a polygraph, and has no criminal history whatsoever."

"If he covered himself up appropriately, wore gloves, and disposed of the clothes, he could keep the gunshot residue off of him," I argued. "And lots of people beat the box—polygraphs are only so useful. Also, his lack of a record might just mean that he's smart enough to escape detection by law enforcement."

Even as I stated my argument, I was becoming less convinced of its validity.

"He had no known motive and had been working for Lanskard for three years. What's your second scenario?"

"This one is your game changer," I declared confidently as the complex of buildings and snow mounds grew closer. "The other option is your shooter is someone who can ski cross-country at a ridiculous pace. He has to be in incredible shape, so he won't become totally exhausted and will be able to control his breathing well enough to shoot with pinpoint accuracy." I held my hands up in front of me as if I was presenting a conclusion that anyone should have seen from the onset. "There can only be a handful of people in the country who can pull that off. If your shooter is local, it couldn't possibly be that hard to find him. It would be like finding a sword in a haystack."

The police cruiser came to a stop. "Actually," Chief Colby

said, pointing through the windshield toward a sign, "it would be more like finding a sword in a stack of swords."

Even with my sunglasses, I had to shield my eyes from the glare of the sun. I focused on a painted plywood sign affixed to an old barn. The words *Central Pennsylvania Biathlon Training Camp* were painted in crimson letters that jumped out from the gray background.

My eyes widened as I leaned back in my seat. I said, "Are you telling me that the Lanskard property sits beside a camp full of highly trained athletes who spend much of their lives skiing around with rifles?"

Colby swiveled to her right, patted my arm, and said, "Washaway Township has a lovely little inn where you can stay. I'll tell Earl Maddox you're coming."

CHAPTER 3

The Eagle Valley Inn was more bed and breakfast than hotel. The GPS on my phone had guided me to the two-story Victorian off Chambers Street. The proprietor, Earl Maddox, practically rolled out the red carpet for what must have been one of the elderly man's few guests of the winter. A rapid-fire, whirlwind tour was supplemented by stories of long-dead famous Pennsylvanians who had once stayed there. The tour ended with my room, which was clean and radiator-stuffy.

"You let me know if you need anything. Anything at all," said Maddox. "I live right downstairs and I don't sleep much so I'm always available."

"I'll be fine," I said. "Thank you very much."

"If the radiator acts up, don't hesitate to say something. The building has character, but she's as temperamental as a three-legged tomcat in a tree climbing contest."

I had no idea what that meant, but I said, "I will. Thanks."

He waited for me to say something more, but eventually waved the white flag and left me to get settled. I placed my small suitcase down and the stubby, plastic feet tapped out a quick drum solo. I hadn't been lying to Susan Lanskard when I told her I didn't think I'd be much help, but I'd packed enough clothing for a short trip. The floorboards creaked under my feet as I walked the room and examined the rustic fixtures and hunting prints. I searched for a television that did not exist. Below my feet, the muffled voice from what sounded like an

AM radio station made its way through the floorboards and I heard my host cough. Given the layout of the inn, I surmised that Earl Maddox's bedroom was directly below my accommodations. It became obvious that the Eagle Valley Inn had few amenities and privacy was not among them.

I used my cell phone and called my friend Chase Vinson who answered on the first ring.

"Are you taking the case?" he asked.

"Well, 'Hello' to you too."

"Uh-huh," came through my phone and I could visualize a toothpick sticking out of his mouth.

"I'm going to poke around for a while."

"Take your time," he said. "No need to rush back here."

"Thanks for reminding me. No job, no wife, no kids, no rush."

"But one Lithuanian," he added.

"There is that," I said.

"The chatter is picking up that he's in the area."

"The chatter likes to chatter," I said philosophically.

"You need to take this seriously. You killed the man's cousin. He's going to want revenge."

Keeping my voice down due to the thin floor, I said, "His cousin did help hold me hostage and enjoyed beating on me. I'd say I deserve a pass."

"These organized crime types don't really deal in mitigating circumstances."

He was exaggerating a bit. The city isn't exactly a hub for organized crime. However, Pittsburgh is a city filled with people who have long memories and lots of ammunition.

"You know he's mostly a myth, right?" I said, not believing it myself.

"Just don't rush back. If you stay hidden in the middle of the state for a while, maybe things will play out and he'll catch a bullet from some other Russian gangster."

"Lithuanian," I reminded him.

"Whatever. You've done the smart thing by lying low and moving around since..." his voice trailed off.

"Since the word got out that a sadistic killer with an affinity for blades wants to take my eyes as trophies?"

Chase let the subject drop and made me promise to call him if I was tempted to stick a needle in a vein. I placed my phone on the nightstand, lay back on the bed, and replayed the day's events while the radiator spat out the occasional hiss.

Colby hadn't taken me into the biathlon camp after our drive. She simply turned around and took me back to my SUV parked at the Lanskard property. On the way, she set the scene for me and patiently answered my questions. The story that unfolded was the kind that left ink on your fingers and stuck in your mind.

"The Camp," as it was referred to by the locals, was owned and operated by two brothers, Seth and David Wrangle. Seth, the older of the two, was a former Olympian and in 2002 had finished just off the podium in Salt Lake City, after which he retired from competition. David Wrangle was never close to being Olympic caliber like his brother, but had held his own during his prime, which had passed for the forty-year-old. Seth had never married and David was a divorcee whose ex-wife and son lived in Vermont.

The siblings were business partners with the husband-wife duo of Linda and Jaden Fredrick, who not only helped run The Camp but also co-owned the property with the brothers. The Camp had been in business for seven years, and in the snowy months served as a cross-country skiing and biathlon course. During the warmer portions of the year, the spot was ideal for trail races, bike competitions, and other activities. Colby mentioned the Wrangles and Fredricks had never caused any real trouble in the community. None of them had any criminal history, aside from David Wrangle's DUI the previous summer. According to Colby, David was known to frequent the local bars and would occasionally get a little rowdy.

Colby said, "Peter Lanskard's driver, Jason Leonard, is friends with David. Jason isn't much of a drinker so he drives David home on the bad nights."

"Obviously, you questioned both the Fredricks and the Wrangle brothers," I said to Colby as we weaved our way out of the valley.

"I did, and the state guys did as well. The Fredricks alibied each other, claiming that they were driving up to the university in State College to grab lunch. They said they paid in cash, so the story couldn't be confirmed. David Wrangle said he was at home paying some bills. And his brother Seth, who really runs the operation, said he was setting up targets for the competetion, but nobody could verify if that was true."

I asked about the competition and Colby informed me that The Camp hosted annual biathlon events that drew competitors from all over.

"The really good ones tend to hang out around bigger camps in New York and Maine," she explained. "So the ones who show up here are primarily amateurs and hobbyists."

"How many people are we talking about?" I asked, dreading the answer.

"Forty-two, last year," she said. "They're expecting less for the competition later this week. The Camp hasn't been doing particularly well the past few years due to some warmer winters. People told Seth that putting a camp this far south was a bad idea, but he's from the area and insisted that it would be good for the region."

"Your suspect list is ridiculously long and there is no guarantee the shooter is here. He could have competed last year and skipped this year. Or," I added, "he might not have been a competitor at all."

She shook her head. "It was Seth."

I waited.

"It's all about the timing. You see, the perimeter alarm was broken at three-oh-two p.m. After Brady Mason checked Lanskard's vitals, he placed a call to nine-one-one, which was logged at three-oh-seven p.m."

"So?" I said.

"So that means the shooter traveled a mile on skis in approximately four minutes, got off a perfect shot and retreated at nearly the same pace. Even if you allow an extra minute for Mason to make the nine-one-one call, the timing is extreme. The perimeter alarm was tripped again at three-twelve p.m., presumably when the shooter was leaving the property. This means the shooter was not your average cross-country skier. Only top-level athletes can make a run like that. Although he's retired from international competition, Seth still participates in the occasional recreational race here in the U.S. I looked up his times, did the math, and accounted for the fact that the shooter would basically be sprinting and wouldn't need to conserve energy for a longer race. I also checked the times of his brother and the Fredricks, who also take part in the occasional competition. While their times were good, none of them can hold a candle to Seth. Also, his brother David hurt his knee a while back and hasn't competed for over a year. As far as any of the competitors who were in town for the race, I went online and checked their times from previous races and doubt any of them would have the speed or skill to pull this thing off."

"That's pretty thin," I observed. "Even if your math is right, ability does not equal motive."

"There were all sort of rumors swirling around that Seth and Peter were discussing some sort of land deal and the talks had turned contentious. Peter wanted to buy Seth's land, but Seth refused and it created some bad blood between them. It was the talk of the town."

"Is there any truth to the rumor?"

"Nothing I was ever able to confirm. I asked Seth about it when I interrogated him about the shooting, but by that time he was furious with me. I wasn't very tactful in my approach," she admitted.

"Ms. Lanskard said the suspects would be scattering in a week. If you think it's Seth, and he's local, then why would she say the suspects are leaving?" I asked.

"I'm the one saying it's Seth. Susan isn't completely on board with my theory," she said, with a wounded expression. "She doesn't want to exclude anyone, but I know it had to be Seth. Anyway, Seth, David, and the Fredricks will be leaving at the end of the week. The Fredricks only come down here from their home in Syracuse when there's a race scheduled. The Wrangle brothers head up to Maine as spring approaches to help out at a bigger biathlon camp up there. They return to Pennsylvania later and coordinate the summer events."

I didn't understand something and needed clarification. I reminded Colby, "You originally said the state investigators were more focused on the threats from environmental activists. It seems pretty clear-cut that the shooter could be somehow involved with The Camp."

Colby stopped the car in front of the Lanskard home. She said, "I may be overstating some items as being *facts.*"

"All right," I said. "Where did we cross the line between evidence and theory?"

She sighed and explained, "Peter Lanskard's security team has been known to hop on skis and dart around his property to patrol the area and also to get some exercise. That's why there are trails of packed snow that allow skiers to glide along fairly fast."

I nodded and said, "And that would mean there would be ski marks all over the place until the next decent snow."

"Yes, and some of the security team had been out there the day before. Peter had traveled to Arkansas in the early morning hours of his death and returned just as a heavy snow began to fall. By the time I had responded and my deputies had searched the woods, the ski impressions were disappearing. I took photos and explained to the state guys that the ones leading to and from the tripped perimeter alarm looked fresher, but they had their doubts." Her shoulders sagged as she said, "Over time, some their doubts became my doubts. But in my heart I know I'm right."

"I have two more questions," I said.

She straightened her back and mustered up the confidence that's so crucial to have in law enforcement.

"First question: Why am I here? Susan Lanskard could hire teams of reputable investigators. Besides, I'm sure you questioned the Wrangles and Fredricks at length. I have no doubt you checked The Camp for weapons that can fire a .308 round. It's not likely I'll come up with any new physical evidence, so you're hoping I'll shake something loose by talking to people. Why do you think anyone is going to talk to me?"

This made her visibly uncomfortable, and she seemed to resign herself to answering a question she knew would inevitably come.

"It wasn't my idea. Susan insisted we bring in a fresh pair of eyes and like I said, Chase recommended you. In fact, he told me you *needed* a case. That's what he said—*needed.*"

I grimaced, knowing my friend was throwing my name around because he was afraid my idleness would lead me back to the needle.

"But why contact me and not some high-powered investigative firm? You have to understand that no one has any reason to speak with me. I'm a private citizen and if you're hoping I can build rapport by talking about skiing, you will be sorely disappointed. I've never skied in my life and I'm not learning this week."

"You may have more in common with Seth Wrangle than you know," she said. "In 2005, you were a patrol officer in Pittsburgh and you responded to a hostage situation at an office building downtown."

I recalled the incident, but had no idea where she was going with this.

"You were the first officer on scene and even after the negotiator got there, the guy holding the gun wouldn't speak with anybody else. I think he'd just been laid-off or something."

"I remember," I said cautiously.

"The gunman was threatening to kill an intern who had just started that day and happened to be in the wrong place at the wrong time."

"What's your point?" I asked with some measure of impatience.

"You talked the gunman into surrendering and everyone walked out alive," she said. "The name of that intern was Josh Kalinoski. He's Seth's nephew."

One coincidence can be acceptable. Two are unreasonable. Three are insults to the rational mind.

"And you just happened to call Chase, who happened to refer you to the man who happened to save the nephew of the man who happens to be your best suspect?" I asked rhetorically.

Colby held her hands up in a surrendering pose and said, "I may have asked if he knew you. And like you said, everybody knows Chase."

Internally, I had to applaud the clever approach. I asked, "How did you manage to put all of that together? I didn't even remember the name of that kid."

"The Internet is a beautiful thing," she said. "I remembered hearing about Seth's nephew getting caught up in that mess. When Susan insisted we pull in an outsider, I didn't see any value in it because Seth isn't going to talk to just anybody. So I started wondering what ever happened to the cop who saved Seth's nephew. When it turned out to be the Tin—," she paused and tried to reset. "When it turned out to be the famous Trevor Galloway, the undercover legend, I couldn't believe my luck."

"Go ahead. You can say it," I said.

"What?" she replied hesitantly.

"I've heard the nickname. I'm not ignorant of the fact that I can be very stoic."

"With all you've been through, it's understandable. Chase called it a term of endearment."

"Never believe a man who has fifty-two tattoos and owns a Chihuahua named Cujo," I said, speaking of my friend who was currently assigned to Pittsburgh PD's Robbery Squad.

"You don't seem heartless to me. But the Tin Man has a nice ring to it."

One of the Lanskard security men walked out of the front of the house and began what I assumed would be a long check of the property. I watched him disappear around a corner of the house.

"You said you had two questions," Colby said.

I brought my eyes to meet hers.

"Are you involved with Susan Lanskard or just in love with her?"

Colby froze before turning her gaze to the windshield. Several seconds passed before she spoke.

"It's that obvious?"

"It is."

"We became close over the past year. One thing led to another and…it doesn't mean I'm not objective."

"It *absolutely* means you can't be objective," I said. She opened her mouth to protest, but I held up my hand. "However, it doesn't mean you can't be right."

She nodded, took out a notepad, scribbled on it, and ripped out a piece of paper. She reached into the back seat of the car and grabbed a thick binder, and placed everything in my lap.

"The official reports are in the binder and the address for the inn is on that paper," she said.

"Thanks."

"Do you have GPS so you can find the place?" she asked.

I told her I did.

"I'll pick you up at eight tomorrow morning."

"Make it ten. I need to play some catch-up," I said as I got out of the car.

CHAPTER 4

My arm is tied down and the familiar steel of the needle moves along my skin. Voices—some close and some distant—saturate the air with promises of pain. The threats weren't being delivered to me through screams and insults, although that would have been preferable. When ominous statements reach your ears in calm tones that convey premeditated, calculated malice, the effect on your mind is much worse than hearing the harshest curses bellowed inches from your cheek.

Blurred faces rotate around my chair and I catch the scent of cedar and insulation. The bare light bulbs in the attic sway and shadows expand and contract in all directions. Many of the voices aren't in English, but somehow I know what's being said. There's a debate as to whether I have outlived my usefulness. One man argues that I have been bled of all the information I can provide while others think I am holding back. A few don't care and only want me to continue suffering. One particularly agitated figure suggests that I have been feeding them bad information and that I'm toying with them. However, one cool and decisive voice from across the room silences the rest.

From far away he says, "I know he'll tell us everything."

Suddenly, in an impossibly fast interval of time—faster than a blink of an eye—the man's mouth is pressing against my ear as he whispers, "He is coming for you, Detective. Soon you will understand true suffering."

The needle that has been tracing my arm is burning now.

The steel point presses against my skin and the skin gives way.

The vein goes next and I hear, "He is here. His knife is here. You belong to him now."

I bolted upright in the bed and tried to blink away the terror. My hand shook wildly as it held my Sig Sauer handgun—the very same gun I had lied about to Susan Lanskard's security guard when he had asked if I was carrying. A sliver of light cut between heavy drapes revealing that the room at the Eagle Valley Inn was exactly the same as it had been when I had drifted off. The echo of firepower-on-wood rattled the emptiness as I placed the gun back on the bed stand. Mentally, I pulled the imaginary needle from my skin and tossed it back into the past where it belonged.

The inn's pipes ached and then calmed as the bathroom sink came to life with arctic water. I splashed the water on my face and let it drip down old track marks that sometimes felt like new wounds. Shaking my head, I could still hear Colby referring to me as an "undercover legend." Nothing could be further from the truth, but the media had mangled the truth long ago.

The sad facts were that I was a star in my department who had a knack for being in the right place at the right time. Of course, that was before I was held captive and beaten in the attic of a dilapidated house and turned into a junkie zombie who would say or do anything for the next fix. Over the weeks I had been missing in action, I gave up everything I knew about narcotics operations in Western Pennsylvania. I told my captors the names and aliases of any undercover agent I could think of and dimed-out each informant I had ever used. I failed everyone who trusted me, and I later found out two informants had been killed thanks to my weakness.

My life had been saved when I was discovered by chance on a routine drug raid. Three of the seven men who had been holding on to me were arrested, but the others hadn't been in the house when the battering ram hit the door. I got myself back into shape and spent much of the next year hunting down the four remaining men who had made me bleed. The last of those men, a Lithuanian named Lukas Derela, had been holed up in a fleabag motel and pulled a knife on me as I came through the door of his room. That was the end of him and, although I didn't realize it at the time, my career. Over the next few months, the media loved me and most in the department forgave me. But I never forgave myself and my mind started playing tricks on me. I quit the department and went to work for the DA until I punched my way into a forced resignation

The radiator in my room hissed as I dressed then rattled off some push-ups. I tossed my laptop computer onto the desk and powered it on. As I had expected, my accommodations didn't include a Wi-Fi connection. I didn't see any jacks for an Ethernet cable and I certainly didn't want to deal with a dial-up connection, so I repacked the computer and carried it down the stairs where Earl Maddox greeted me with a firm handshake. I glanced around the dining area where my host had set out a pot of coffee and one solitary pastry.

"Mr. Maddox, I'm starting to get the feeling that I'm your only guest," I said.

He waved an arm sporting a faded anchor tattoo and said, "Aw, all those Ski Zeros stay in the chain hotels up around State College and Bellefonte. This place isn't modern enough for them. And just call me Maddox like everyone else. No *Mister* and no *Earl*."

"Okay," I said. "I'm sorry; did you say something about *Ski Zeros*?"

Maddox pointed out a window and said, "You know, the biathlon folks. Every winter they show up, sit in the local restaurants, and ramble on about ski brands and zeroing their rifles so they can hit little black circle targets. See? Ski Zeros!"

I gave a nod and poured a coffee into a paper cup.

"You don't seem to be a fan of the biathlon crowd," I observed.

He made a dismissive gesture and said, "I don't understand the thing. Skiing is a sport. Even shooting can be a sport. But it seems to me that if someone is going to grab a rifle and hop on a pair of skis, it should be preceded by someone saying, 'Hold my beer and watch this.'"

The old man's laugh was raspy and jagged and for a second I thought I might actually smile.

"You look like you've been around a while," he said. "You're what...in your mid-fifties? So I figure I've got about twenty-five years on you. Do you ever remember seeing any-thing like this biathlon thing when you were growing up?"

Any thoughts I had of smiling faded as I cringed and I said, "I'm only forty-three."

Maddox paused to see if I was kidding. When he saw I was serious, he raised an eyebrow and slowly uttered, "You don't say?"

I answered his original question while eating the pastry that had been offered. "I've only seen some of the biathlon when I've watched the Olympics on television. Honestly, I don't remem-ber much."

"Well, you should read up on it. It's the damnedest thing," said Maddox.

"I was on my way to do that very thing," I said as I finished off my breakfast.

Maddox gave me directions to the local library which was on

the other side of town, so I opted to drive rather than deal with the early morning cold. I pulled up alongside a heavily salted sidewalk and carried my laptop to the main entrance. I opened a heavy door that squeaked with age. An elderly librarian looked up from behind a desk, undoubtedly expecting to greet a long-time patron of this small-town establishment. Her back stiffened in her chair and she forced a smile as she took in my black leather jacket, dark jeans, and darker demeanor.

She half-stood and said, "Hello, there."

I gave a nod and started walking toward an empty table in the corner. After about five steps, I remembered Colby's observation that I wasn't exactly a "social butterfly" and realized I should have actually said something to the woman rather than simply give her the "guy nod." Being an outsider in this rural environment, it would be in my best interest to win over the townspeople by trying to muster up whatever charisma I might possess.

My laptop bag twirled around me as I turned back to say something brilliant like, "Hello," but she was already pecking away on the keyboard in front of her. Not wanting to interrupt her, I decided to turn away. Just as I started the motion, she looked my direction, so I spun back toward her, causing the laptop case to twist and tangle some more. I opened my mouth to speak just as she looked down again and pounded away on her computer. Once again, I spun away and the strap on the bag further constructed around my waist.

By this point, I was standing awkwardly in a library with my mouth gaping open, while wearing a laptop bag that doubled as a straitjacket.

Charisma.

I worked myself free from the restraints of my own making and slinked away to a table even further away from the librarian than the first one I had chosen. I set up my laptop and picked up a Wi-Fi signal in a matter of seconds. Within minutes, I was scrolling through page after page of information about the biathlon. It was wildly popular in parts of Europe, but hadn't become part of the mainstream in the U.S. The more I read, the more admiration I had for those who competed in the physically grueling activity. As a recreational distance runner, I wasn't unfamiliar with how endurance athletes typically train, but Maddox was on to something when he suggested the sport seemed like something one would choose to attempt if they were drunk or wanted to win a bet.

Quickly, I learned that biathlon events varied in distance, but sometimes covered as much as twelve miles of skiing around a cross-country trail system. The trips around the course were broken up by shooting stations on each lap where competitors typically fired at five targets. Five small targets that demanded every single ounce of a competitor's focus. Some of the shooting rounds demanded that the competitors fire from a prone position, while some required that the shooter remain standing. I thought about the marathons I had run before the job had taken its toll on me, and how poorly I would have handled a weapon in the middle of a race. The skill and physical conditioning the biathlon required was incredible.

I became discouraged as I read the information about the specialized rifles biathletes used. Most used a bolt-action rifle made by a company called ANSCHUTZ. The weapons were designed to be easy to carry and fired a .22 caliber long range round, significantly different than the .308 bullet that killed Peter Lanskard. The rifles and the sights were intended to allow the shooter to hit a small target at fifty yards, not the estimated five hundred yards that was covered on the Lanskard property. This, along with the difference in caliber, made it obvious that whatever rifle killed Lanskard, it wasn't a biathlon rifle.

I started to question if Colby was even in the right neighborhood when she made the assumption that a biathlete, and specifically Seth Wrangle, was involved in the shooting. Then I remembered what she had said about the timing of the alarm signals. She was operating on the theory that the shooter covered a mile in approximately four minutes. If that were true, and it really was doubtful anybody at The Camp other than Seth Wrangle could make that kind of run and still shoot with any accuracy, then I certainly understood why Colby had focused on him.

A search of Seth Wrangle's name pulled up no big surprises. He was a former Olympian who had picked up the sport of biathlon while he was in the U.S. Army. From reading an interview he had granted to a magazine, I learned that many biathletes from around the world were active in the military or law enforcement. The Army had paid for Seth to represent his country in competitions around the world and he had thrived. His fourth-place finish during the 2002 Winter Olympics in Salt Lake City was historic for the U.S., although the accomplishment faded quickly from the news. After the Olympics, Seth had retired from competition and convinced his brother and family friends Linda and Jaden Fredrick to join him in purchasing the property where he now ran the Central Pennsylvania Biathlon Training Camp. I mentally filed away the man's military experience, knowing that the Army trained its soldiers in the use of rifles with an effective range much greater than fifty yards.

My online search of Seth's brother, David Wrangle, told a similar tale, but with less fanfare. David had followed his older brother's footsteps and joined the Army. Before long, the brothers had become formidable biathletes, with only Seth reaching the highest levels. From the few articles I could find, David's career seemed to be marred by injury and frustration, while his brother became the star for the United States.

I started to search for information on the Fredricks, but noticed what time it was, so I headed back to the inn. When I pulled up, Colby's patrol car was idling on the street. I parked my car and put my laptop in the back before shuffling over to her car.

"Good morning," she said as I slid into the passenger's seat. "Have you experienced all there is to offer in our fine town?"

"Not yet."

Colby looked at me like she was assessing damage to a house after a storm.

"Did you sleep last night?" she asked.

"A little. I never sleep well in strange beds."

Glancing at my car in her rearview mirror, she said, "Find out anything interesting at the library?"

I started to tell her about me having to go there so I could get a good Internet connection when I stopped cold.

"I didn't say I was at the library," I said. "Did you drive by and spot my car?"

Colby kept her expression blank and said matter-of-factly, "No."

I thought for a moment and said, "The librarian?"

The police chief nodded and said, "Edna."

"She called you?" I asked. "She doesn't even know who I am. I didn't introduce myself."

"You mean delivering a curt nod and performing an escape act with your laptop case isn't a proper introduction in your book?" She teased.

I still didn't understand why Colby had been called, so I stared at the chief and waited.

Colby sighed with a smile and said, "Welcome to Wash-away, Trevor. It's a town where the news gets reported almost before it happens."

I decided to let it drop and said, "I was taking Biathlon 101 over at the library. It's an interesting sport."

"It is," she said. "And the athletes are interesting too. Even at the state and master levels, the competitors in this country know each other very well. They're a very tightknit group since they tend to run in the same circles, so to speak, and there are few notable competitions outside of Europe and Russia."

She put the car in gear and said, "We can run up to Susan's house and you two can work out your fee before we get started."

"That's not necessary. I'll work it out with her later."

Colby looked perplexed and asked, "Are you that trusting?"

"Susan said it herself. She has money and she's obviously willing to spend it. I'm sure whatever she's paying is fair."

"Okay then." She chuckled. "Let's head up to The Camp."

"No, first I want to visit the Lanskard property, but not to talk to Susan. I want to talk to the head of security if he's there."

"Brady Mason? His account of the shooting is solid. I interviewed him and the driver, Jason Leonard, myself."

"I don't doubt that," I said. "But I have to hear things straight from the source to make things click. It's just the way I work."

Colby shrugged and pulled the car into the small-town traffic. We didn't say anything as we watched the town scroll by, transition to scattered houses, then totally fade away in the car's mirrors. After a few minutes, she broke the silence.

"I probably should have told you upfront about my rela-tionship with Susan."

"No problem," I said. "If it's not relevant to the case, then it really isn't my business."

"It's just...I really care about her, and the fact her father was gunned down and his killer is free eats at both of us. She holds it all together by burying herself in her work, but it haunts her every day. Her father was not well-liked because of his business dealings, so it's not like we can't understand how this happened. Having a grasp on the possible motives is one thing, but the lack of closure is crushing."

"We don't know anything about motive."

"I think we can safely deduce it was related to Peter's dealings with Seth, or if I'm wrong, his company's operations," Colby said. "Even if I'm way out in left field about Seth, Peter's business dealings put him at risk."

"Did anything change?"

She furrowed her brow and said, "What do you mean?"

"I mean did anything change when Susan took over the company? Did MRS suddenly adopt environmentally friendly policies? Did they stop participating in mountaintop removal or fracking?"

"No," Colby responded.

"Then, absent revenge for some of his company's past dealings being the motive, killing him doesn't make much sense from a business or environmental perspective. It didn't accomplish anything. It wasn't a means to any noticeable end."

Colby reluctantly nodded and said, "Okay. So you want to concentrate on other angles?"

I shook my head and said, "I don't. I don't want to focus on any angles. Let's simply step back and act as if we are starting from scratch. We'll look at the evidence without making any assumptions and see where it takes us. Nothing will be out of bounds. If the evidence tells us that Lanskard may have been killed by a circus clown operating a hot air balloon, let's check it out. We'll try to keep everything we know from the previous investigation in the background, but not assume any of it to be true."

Her expression was dubious, but she didn't protest. We arrived on the Lanskard property, got out of the car, and were met by the security man who insisted I be searched on the previous day.

I extended a hand and said, "Mark Letterman, right?"

After some hesitation, the harsh-looking man shook my hand and said, "Right."

"I hope we didn't get off to a bad start. My name is Trevor Galloway and I'm looking into what happened here last year. I'd like to talk with you later if you don't mind, but I want to clear it with your boss, Mr. Mason, so that I don't put you in an uncomfortable position."

Letterman seemed to appreciate my respect for following the chain of command because he relaxed visibly.

"Mr. Mason is around back in the command post," he said while jerking a thumb in a general direction. "Chief Colby knows where it is," he added with what sounded like a trace of resentment.

Colby and I left Letterman standing in the snow and I heard the man's radio crackle as we walked around the corner of the house.

"They like to call it a command post," explained Colby. "But it's really a tiny guest house that serves as a communication center where they can monitor the alarms."

"What kind of people are they?" I asked.

"What do you mean?"

"I mean, are these guys real deal professionals or are they rent-a-cops merely collecting a paycheck?"

Colby formulated her response and said, "They strike me as professionals. I'm not saying there isn't a little soldier of fortune in attitude with some of them. I'm sure you picked up on that with Letterman. But overall they seem to be a squared away group."

"Okay," I said. "What about cameras? Are there any on the property?"

"Mr. Lanskard wouldn't allow it, and neither does Susan. This has served as their refuge from scrutiny for quite some time. The fact that all that was shattered hasn't changed Susan's desire to have an escape from being under the microscope."

"Her privacy is that much more important to her than her well-being?" I asked with a trace of disparagement.

Colby smirked and said, "Well, maybe she figures the security detail will be able to use binoculars to spot those killer circus clowns flying around in hot air balloons."

Funny.

We reached the door of the guest house, and it opened as Colby raised her hand to knock. The figure in the doorway was a wiry six-foot-two and looked like he could handle himself. As opposed to Letterman, the man was immediately smiling and appeared to be genuinely pleased to see us.

"Good to see you, Chief," he said taking Colby's hand.

Turning to me, he introduced himself. "I'm Brady Mason, Mr. Galloway. I've heard a great deal about you."

"Please, call me Trevor."

"Nice to meet you, Trevor. Come on in out of the cold."

The guest house was tastefully furnished and looked more like a home than a place where an armed security team took shelter from the elements. We followed Mason into a back room where computer monitors and a radio battery charger sat on long folding tables. A woman sat in front of the table and glanced up from a magazine when we entered. On the monitors, I could see what appeared to be maps of the property with pulsing icons in strategic locations. I surmised the entire alarm system was controlled from this room and any security response was dispatched by radio. In the event something more than handguns was needed, a gun rack holding four shotguns was mounted in a corner.

Mason noticed me studying my surroundings and said, "Ms. Lanskard told me that you might be looking into what happened last year and that I'm to assist you in any way I can. Any of us are happy to answer any questions you may have."

"How many of you are there?" I asked.

"Five of us are full-time. You've met Mark Letterman. Gene Stewart and Tom Banter will be working the night shift, and this is Sandy Linn."

The woman reading the magazine gave a quick wave and then returned to flipping pages.

"You said 'full-time'?"

"Whenever one of us needs some time off, we contract out for some temporary help. It's usually an off-duty police officer from Harrisburg, or we use some other vetted personnel."

"And when Peter Lanskard was shot?"

"Mark and Gene were here for the day shift. I was traveling back from Arkansas with Mr. Lanskard, and Sandy and Tom were scheduled to come in for the midnight shift."

"No contractors that day?"

"No contractors."

"This is a pretty small operation for a family as prominent, and infamous, as the Lanskards," I said.

"That's the way Mr. Lanskard wanted it," Mason said. "He knew my father and when Mr. Lanskard heard I was in the security business, he insisted on hiring my company. I told him I would completely understand if he went with one of the big boys out there, but he always blew-off the suggestion. He liked to say he would rather be surrounded by five people he could trust than twenty he didn't."

I asked Mason if he would sit down with me and recount everything that had happened on the day of the murder. We retreated to the living room and arranged ourselves around a coffee table. Colby took out a notepad and pen and started taking notes while Mason described the events as they had been recorded in the official reports I had read. When the story arrived at the critical juncture, where Lanskard had exited the car and unwittingly placed himself in the sights of a sniper, Mason's face grew sullen and tense. He sat back in a leather chair and involuntarily clinched his jaw as he described how his employer stood out in the open in spite of the perimeter alarm being triggered. By the time Mason had relived the instant the bullet struck Lanskard, he was clutching the arm of the chair as if trying to take hold of Lanskard's last breath.

When he finished, I gave him a moment to collect himself before I said, "My opinion doesn't matter, but it sounds like you did all you could."

"If that were true, Mr. Lanskard wouldn't have died from a gunshot wound to the head."

"He died from exposure," I said. "And to some extent it was self-inflicted."

"I appreciate you saying that," Mason said. "But I'll never see it that way."

He looked out a window, and I was sure the snow he was seeing was a year old.

"Brady," Colby interjected. "I know we've covered it before, but can you give Trevor a rundown of how the alarm system works?"

Mason spent the next several minutes explaining how the system was a network of sensors spread out along the outskirts of the property, with no sensors inside the perimeter. The system used microwave technology and could detect an intrusion from anything larger than a fox or large raccoon. The head of security admitted that the frequent triggering of the alarm by a deer or the occasional black bear was annoying, but in the end it was the setup Peter Lanskard had wanted. Upon his death, Ms. Lanskard had refused to supplement the property's security with cameras, just as her father had done.

"If he was receiving so many threats, then why didn't he take every precaution?" I asked.

Mason shrugged. "He was hated in a lot of circles for a long time. I think he had become immune to it all. In the months before his death, he seemed to have come to accept that the risk was going to be omnipresent as long as he stayed in business. The man...well, I don't know how else to say it, but after a while he seemed to dare trouble to head his way."

Colby looked up abruptly from her notes.

"Brady, you never mentioned that to me before," she said incredulously.

"I know. I don't think I saw it before. It's not like he was a big risk-taker and had decided to take up skydiving or anything. He just became more complacent when it came to his own safety."

Silence filled the room as Colby smoldered at not hearing this information first.

"Were you the one who traveled with him on business trips?" I asked.

"I typically accompanied him everywhere off these grounds," Mason replied. "Most of the time Mr. Lanskard would only allow one security person with him when he was out, and he generally preferred it to be me."

"Did that include local trips? Things like trips to the hardware store, restaurants, and doctor appointments?"

"Yes," answered Mason cautiously.

Silence intruded as I tried to think of any other questions.

Before I could ask any follow-ups, Mason stood and said, "I'm sorry, but it's my turn to relieve Mark outside. I may be in charge, but we all pull our weight around here."

I stood and thanked him for his time.

He was nearly out of the room when I asked, "If Mr. Letterman is coming inside, do you mind if I ask him a few questions?"

Mason shook his head and said, "I'll tell him to come see you."

Once Colby and I were alone in the room, she burst out, "What the hell? I interviewed him twice and he never said a word about Peter acting recklessly!"

I kept my voice low as a signal for her to do the same. "He said 'complacent,'" I corrected. "There's a difference."

"He could have called me anytime," she barked. "Hell, I'm up here several times a week to see Susan!"

"Maybe that's the problem," I said.

"I told you, I can be objective. He should know that."

"I'm not saying otherwise. But there's a chance that—"

I was interrupted when Mark Letterman entered the room while dusting snow off his coat.

"Do you have questions for me?" he asked flatly.

"Yes," I said. "We were hoping you would be willing to sit down and tell us about the day Peter Lanskard was killed."

Letterman gave no indication that he intended to sit. He simply held his ground and recited, "An alarm on the eastern perimeter—sensor twelve to be exact—signaled an intrusion. I called Brady and told him that when he arrived with Mr. Lanskard, they should stay in the car until I made sure we were secure. Then, I ran out back and jumped on the ATV we keep out there. By the time I reached the area, the coast was clear. I never saw anything."

"You saw ski marks, didn't you?" I asked.

"Sure. I saw them behind the house, at the wood line, and pretty much everywhere else. Some of us had been out on skis the day before," he said while waiving an arm toward a window. "Hey, shouldn't you be writing this down?"

"I have a good memory," I said. "How long did it take you to get out there?"

"Maybe a couple of minutes from the time I called Brady." He stopped talking and glanced at Colby.

"I know where you're going with this," he said. "The chief here has this theory that someone managed to ski right past me, even though I was directly in between the location where the shot originated and where the alarm was tripped again when her suspected super-skier escaped. That's bullshit," he raged. "I was right there and nobody got past me. Nobody."

I started to ask another question when he turned on his heels and left the room.

Colby sighed and said, "He's been defensive since the day it happened. He really resented me asking him to take a polygraph. Needless to say, I'm not his favorite chief of police."

Whiteness.

Snow.

Wind.

Goosebumps on my arm.

Hey, are you all right?"

My head jerked up and I refocused my eyes. I have this maddening habit of staring at the floor and letting my eyes go out of focus when I'm deep in thought. Sometimes I go so deep I manage to completely tune-out the world around me. I call these moments my *blur-outs*. They help me mentally reconstruct crimes and have been crucial to my work in the past. Unfortunately, I have to make some sacrifices to achieve that level of concentration. Sacrifices I hoped would have minimal consequences for the time being.

"Yeah, I'm fine. Just thinking."

"I assume you want to talk to the rest of the security team. Do you want to go back in the other room and talk to Sandy Linn? Then, we can talk to Gene Stewart and Tom Banter when they come in for the night shift."

"Let's come back to these guys," I said. "I think we've created enough waves with the security team for the day. What do you say we head over to The Camp and see if they'll talk to us?"

I started toward the door and Colby touched my arm.

"You learned something here, didn't you?"

"I always learn something," I said. "But then again, I always have a lot to learn."

TARGET 2
COFFEE, BEER, AND OTHER BODILY FLUIDS

CHAPTER 5

We didn't make it to The Camp. As soon as we pulled away from the Lanskard property, Colby was called to a traffic accident with a fatality on one of the roads in her jurisdiction. The path to the scene ran through town, so she stopped her vehicle just long enough for me to jump out a block from the Eagle Valley Inn. I stopped by my vehicle and grabbed my laptop that I'd tossed in the back before heading inside the inn.

"Welcome back," said Maddox as I moved through the inn's entrance.

Looking at my watch and seeing it wasn't yet noon, I said, "Good morning, Mr. Maddox."

"Would you like me to brew some more coffee?" he asked.

I said, "No, thank you," as I began my ascent up the unreasonably noisy staircase.

"Are you sure? A big-time celebrity like you needs to keep his strength up."

I froze then retraced my steps back into the lobby.

"Excuse me. What did you say?"

"Well, I know it's only the *Washaway Tribune*—not exactly the *New York Times*—but everyone around here reads the articles."

I approached the front desk and looked down at the proprietor who was seated with a newspaper spread out in front of him.

With one finger, Maddox tapped on a page and said, "I

thought you were pulling my leg when you said you were only forty-three years old, but here it is in black and white."

My stomach turned and I asked if I could see the article. Maddox seemed surprised that I didn't know about it and even more surprised that I didn't appear to be pleased. He slowly spun the paper my way. The headline read *Cold Case Expert Investigating Lanskard Murder.* I skimmed the ten-paragraph story and saw it essentially spelled out my involvement in the case. The fact that I was not a "cold case expert" by any means was apparently unimportant. I did have to admit it was better than if the headline read, *Recovering Junkie Ex-Cop Targeted by Lithuanian Killer Bumbles around Central Pennsylvania.* Thank goodness for small favors.

"Mr. Maddox, I've been here one night and I'm quite certain I haven't talked to any reporters. I have to ask, did you call this in to the paper?"

He looked offended and said, "No, sir, I did not. But there aren't many secrets around here. People are too nosey if you ask me. Of course, nobody asked me anything." Pointing to the article he said, "They didn't even call me to confirm you were staying here."

My stomach took another tumble and I re-read the story. Sure enough, it mentioned the Eagle Valley Inn.

"From your expression, I'm guessing you don't like being noticed," Maddox observed.

"Is this online? I mean the paper. Is the newspaper available online?" I asked while trying my best not to sound concerned.

"Sure it is," answered Maddox. "In fact, they tried to get me to advertise in both the hard copy and online editions. I told them it wouldn't do me any good. The only people who read that paper already live here and certainly aren't going to need a room at my place."

His reasoning was rock solid and so was the feeling in my gut. I wondered if the Lithuanian used Google Alerts. Probably not. Certainly not. I had absolutely nothing to worry about. However, I was starting to think it might be best if I moved out of my room. My internal deliberation was interrupted when another thought crossed my mind.

"I bet you know everyone in town," I said.

"I suppose I do."

"So you would know if any strangers showed up. Especially a stranger with an accent and possibly a lot of tattoos."

"I suppose I would," he answered while growing more wary.

"I'm sure it's nothing," I said. "But back in Pittsburgh, there's a man who is a little upset with me."

"How upset?"

"Mortally."

Maddox raised his eyebrows and contemplated this for several seconds. "It sounds like this guy would stick out like a sore thumb around here. What else can you tell me about him?"

I mentally filed through everything that was known about the mysterious Lithuanian. His first name was possibly Jonas or Joseph. Nobody knew his last name. He was a "problem solver" for his friends in the drug trade and he worked the Rust Belt pipeline from Pittsburgh to Cleveland to Detroit and all points in between. Some thought him to be a myth, but during my ordeal I had heard my captors speak of him. Even my tormentors, despite some of them being from Lithuania, simply called him The Lithuanian. He was thought to be a big fan of knives, but didn't mind using a gun. The tattoo thing was a guess on my part, but an educated one. Every member of the crew I had been investigating had ink from the neck to the hands. There were all sorts of stories about the killer, but the most disturbing one had to do with him taking the eyes out of a prison guard in his home country. It was likely a fabrication perpetuated by a ragtag group of drug dealers who wanted to build the legend of a small-time enforcer. But still.

"I said, what else can you tell me about him?"

Damn. I'd faded away for a moment. It was starting to happen more often.

"He's serious," was the only response I had for Maddox.

"As serious as you?"

I didn't respond and slid the paper back over the desk.

"I keep a rifle in the back," said the old man. "Do you want it?"

I shook my head and looked the chiseled man up and down. He wasn't frail, but he was old. His face was all triangles and his arms were socket wrenches fixed onto a screwdriver body.

"You keep it," I told him. "In fact, I should probably check out of here so you don't have to worry about anything. I don't want you to get caught up in anything."

He waved a hand through the air and said, "Don't be ridiculous. I'm safer with you here!"

"How so?"

"Well the way I see it, it's already in the paper that you're staying here. If this guy comes looking for you, then this will be his first stop whether you're here or at the Super 8. At least if you're here, he's more likely to kill you than me. If you aren't here, he might just kill me because he thinks I'm holding out on him. So I'm actually safer with you around."

"Once again, Maddox, your logic is infallible."

"Yeah, well let's just hope that rifle I have in the back is just as infallible. I haven't fired the thing in a year. I'm going to bring it up here."

I said, "Thank you," but he was already off to wherever he had his antiquated hunting rifle stored. Watching Maddox limp away, part of me wondered whether the rifle was designed to fire bullets at a deer or musket balls at a Redcoat.

In my room, I set my laptop bag on a table and withdrew the computer out of habit. I chastised myself when I remembered it was useless to me in this room. Hoping to let in some natural light, I walked over to the window and pulled back the curtains. The view allowed me to look out onto Washaway Township's main drag and not much else. The sidewalks were shoveled and pedestrians floated back and forth in front of businesses that had probably kept the same names since the attack on Pearl Harbor. It seemed a world away from the knotted mass of steel and bridges where I lived. For a moment, I lost myself in thoughts of having a life in a town like this one. Had I even seen a bridge since I arrived here? In Pittsburgh, bridges were busy arteries providing rhythm for the heartbeat of the city. How strange that a town like Washaway could feel more like an island to me than a city surrounded by rivers.

I lay back on my bed and dreamt about a small-town life I would never have, and probably didn't really want. I could hear footsteps belonging to Earl Maddox invading through the floorboards. The sounds reminded me of horrors and captivity. I recalled hearing footfalls and the sickening feeling I had when I heard them approach. In my mind, I tried hard to pretend the sounds weren't Maddox's footsteps, but something more peaceful. A heartbeat. My brain transformed the sounds into the beating of a heart. One beat. Then another. Then another.

The knock on the door caused me to jerk awake. The light from the window was fading and I glanced at my watch. I hadn't felt tired, but my body had apparently disagreed. The knocking grew louder and I made my way to the door. I had started to blindly open it then remembered that now I was anything-but-anonymous thanks to the local newspaper.

"Who is it?" I asked and shifted to the side of the door.

"It's Colby," said a tired voice from behind the thick wood.

I opened the door and saw that the chief had a look in her eyes that was all too familiar to me. It was the look of one who had seen too much in one day. People forget about the so-called "routine" duties of a police officer, including those surrounding traffic accidents. Colby's expression betrayed an overloaded mind. That's the thing about seeing so much blood on the job— the eyes can only absorb so much at one time.

"Bad one?" I asked.

"One dead, one survivor. Teenagers. Texting," was all she said.

She stood in the doorway and I fought the urge to say something lame like, *I'm sorry you had to see that.* Or, *That's one of the toughest things about the job.* Or God forbid, tell a war story of my own.

"I have to go notify some family members here in town," she said. "I just stopped by to tell you we can't head over to The Camp today."

"Of course."

Colby lowered her eyes and shuffled her feet, but didn't make any motion to leave. After a few seconds, I felt compelled to say something. To say anything.

"Have you worked a lot of fatalities?" I asked.

She shrugged. "A few. We've had our share of crashes, farm accidents, overdoses, and a couple of suicides."

"But this one..." I prompted.

She slid her hands in her coat pockets and said, "When I was in the eighth grade, my brother was killed in a car accident. He was seventeen at the time and was riding around with some friends after a high school football game. He was in the front passenger's seat, wasn't wearing a seatbelt, and was ejected

60

from the vehicle. He's the only one who didn't make it.'"

Her face turned expressionless and I knew she was remembering some scene from her youth. Whatever she was seeing was probably something that had once caused her pain to become evident and readable to those around her, but now she appeared to have trained her facial muscles to give an appearance of numbness.

"He was my hero," she said. "He looked out for me, let me tag along with him and his friends, and never teased me the way some older brothers do." Her lips hinted at a smile as she said, "He always used to say that someday the two of us were going to burn rubber getting out of here and burn money once we got where we were going." Her mouth straightened as that memory slid away.

"Maybe you should have one of your deputies make the notification to the family," I suggested.

She shook her head and something even darker than sorrow appeared in her eyes.

"Do you want to know how my family was notified? A call. We got a phone call from Washaway Township Police Chief Monty Caskins." Colby's voice had taken on a mocking masculine tone when she'd said the man's name. "Monty fancied himself some sort of Western lawman although I doubt he had ever traveled outside of Pennsylvania. He was tall, tough, and carried a pearl handled six-shooter. He had the reputation for being tough on crime, but he was tough on everything. So when it came to the more delicate parts of the job, he stampeded through, picked up the phone, and said things like, 'Mr. and Mrs. Colby. I'm afraid your boy's dead. Yep, no seatbelt. It's a damn shame about kids these days. You'll want to get out to Wilson's Branch Road and see for yourself.'"

Colby looked disgusted as she said, "Caskins died a few years later and was revered like he was a pistol-carrying saint. But that's not how I remembered him. Not from that night, anyway."

I doubted that at Colby's age she had actually been on the phone when the notification call had been made, but I imagined there had to be an element of truth to her recalling the tale. In a profession like law enforcement in which some level of disassociation has always been vital, callous interactions with the public are not uncommon. Even more so back when Colby was a kid and initiatives like community policing were rarely taken seriously.

"When I took this job," Colby continued, "I promised myself I'd never be like that. There's nothing I can do to ease the pain of the families, but I sure as hell won't make it worse."

Part of me wondered if Colby's experience with the old chief of police had not only influenced her decision to personally make death notification, but perhaps drove her to take the job in the first place. It wasn't the time to ask, so I held my tongue.

She seemed to shake off layers of emotions and said, "I'll call you in the morning."

"Sure."

She started to walk away, turned back, and said, "Trevor?"

"Yeah."

"You look like hell. Get some sleep tonight."

"I will," I said.

I closed the door and listened to her police boots retreat down the stairs, thankful that I'd never have to make a death notification again. I turned back to my empty room and realized I had absolutely nothing to do for the next several hours and I wasn't going to fall back asleep anytime soon. I walked over to the window and surveyed the street. The snow was coming down hard again. All of the sidewalk shoveling being done by the townspeople would have been for nothing.

I rubbed more sleep out of my eyes and let my gaze go from one end of the street to the other. At the end of the block, under a streetlight, I thought I saw someone already starting the futile task of snow removal. Then I realized the figure wasn't moving, but was standing next to a post and looking toward the inn. I rubbed my eyes again and thought I perceived a trace of movement through the gust of windblown snow. The sheet of snow dissipated and left me staring at nothing more than a town slipping into hibernation.

CHAPTER 6

A police psychologist once told me that addicts should avoid any substances that can weaken one's ability to resist temptation. Then again, that shrink had never been stuck twiddling her thumbs in Washaway Township in the dead of winter. The Red Barn Tavern was a short walk from the Eagle Valley Inn and seemed a nice enough place. I was on the receiving end of stranger-in-town stares from the moment I took a seat at the bar. Or perhaps the looks were more of the guy-who-was-in-the-local-newspaper variety but it didn't really matter. Most of the customers appeared to be kind, but rugged town folk and none appeared to be particularly angry or Lithuanian.

I pretended to be interested in a news broadcast on a television above the bar while downing a dark beer. A second beer made my head start to swim and I realized I hadn't eaten since breakfast. I grabbed a menu and placed an order for a cheeseburger with fries and ordered a third beer. Staring into the drink, I found myself back in that thirty-dollar- per-night hotel room where I had cornered Lukas Derela and he had pulled a knife, forcing me to shoot him three times in the chest. I mean, he was in the act of pulling the knife. Rather, his right hand had gone behind his back and I found the knife on the floor beside him after he fell. I had followed procedure, identified myself, and told him not to move before I fired. Or was it during? Or...

A hand fell on my shoulder and I turned to see a man with a smooth face and long blond hair. He placed himself on the stool beside me and said, "You are the police detective, right?"

The tavern was noisy, but I was certain he spoke with a European accent. Or was it Russian? Or was it something I'd heard before while tied to a chair in Pittsburgh?

"No," I said. "I'm not a cop."

The man gave a watered-down-whisky smile and winked at the bartender who apparently knew what drink to bring the man.

"Sure you are," he said. "You are big news around here. You are looking into Peter Lanskard's murder."

I looked at the man's neck and hands. I couldn't see any ink, but there was no way to know what designs might lay under his ski jacket.

"I'm just doing a favor for a friend," I said. "I didn't catch your name."

He didn't extend a hand and kept a smile pasted on his face. We must have looked like quite the pair—the man with short black hair who never smiles and the long-haired pretty boy who never seemed to stop smiling.

"My name is Markus," he said. "Markus Faust."

"That's an interesting accent," I said. "I can't quite place it."

"I am German."

"I didn't figure Washaway Township would have a big German population. It doesn't seem like the type of place people flock to."

"And yet you are here too. The news article said you are not from here either. I guess we are both outsiders."

The bartender brought Faust the drink he had never verbally asked for and moved on to other customers.

I nodded in the direction the bartender had walked. "You seem to be a regular."

Ignoring the comment, Faust sat on a stool next to me. "I am very interested in things like criminal investigations. I watch all of those shows on television. Shows like *CSI* and *NCIS*...I find them very curious."

"Is that so?" I said flatly.

"Yes, yes. It seems the people in those shows are always running around shooting people and getting into car chases. It is not really like that, right?"

"Right."

He sipped his drink and continued, "Why do you think the people who make those shows do that?"

"Do what?"

"Why do they make the shows so unrealistic?"

The bartender brought my food and again moved on.

I said, "Nobody wants to watch a cop sit in a courtroom for three hours or spend forty-five minutes logging evidence into a vault. Not to mention, conducting surveillance or listening to wiretaps for hours at a time is as fun as watching paint dry on a rainy day."

"Yes, yes," agreed Faust. He acted as if I had said something deep and philosophical and pondered my words as he took another drink.

Then he said, "There is also another thing that always happens in those shows. It seems like every few episodes the main characters come across a police officer or FBI agent who is corrupt or very puzzled. The police officer either takes money or tries to arrest the wrong person for a crime."

"That's mostly Hollywood stuff too," I said.

Faust nodded and the smile melted off his face. He said, "I do not know. I have heard stories of police officers who become confused and go after good people. I suppose it could happen anywhere, even a small town like this."

"Anything is possible," I said.

The man turned slightly and checked his hair in a mirror behind the bar. I thought he might be finished and ready to walk away, but he stayed right beside me.

I said, "Mr. Faust, can I ask you a question?"

The smile returned and he turned back toward me. "Of course."

"You wouldn't happen to be affiliated with the biathlon camp, would you?"

"Yes, yes. I visit here every year and compete. I also help teach some of the newer athletes."

I took a bite of my cheeseburger and took a sip of beer.

"They are good people," said Faust.

"Who are good people?"

"The Wrangle brothers," he said. "They are very good people and I was here last year when the woman...the police supervisor..."

"Chief Colby."

"Yes. Chief Colby. I was here when she questioned them. The woman was certain that Seth had done something criminal, but I assure you that he did not."

"How can you be so sure?"

"I have known both Seth and David for years. They would never kill anyone."

"They were both in the military, right?"

"Yes."

"Isn't being willing and able to kill someone kind of a prerequisite for being a soldier?"

Faust didn't answer. He scanned the room and I got the feeling he wanted people to look at him. To look at us.

"Why are you here, Mr. Faust?"

"I told you—"

"No," I interrupted. "Why are you here in this bar? I heard

that most of the athletes stay in the chain hotels down the road. And wherever you find chain hotels, you find chain restaurants and bars. Why are you here in this particular bar on this particular night?"

He smiled again, but for the first time the smile seemed sincere.

"As you noted, I am sort of a regular. Every year, I come into this bar a few times. But tonight I am here to see you of course. This town only has one place to eat other than this one. I figured I might find you near the place where you are staying."

"And since the newspaper said where I was staying, you had no problem finding me."

He nodded.

My patience was wearing thin and I felt something familiar stirring deep inside of me. I turned in my seat and squared up to him. He mirrored the motion, which is precisely what I wanted him to do.

"What exactly do you want to say to me, Mr. Faust?"

The smile was gone again and his eyes turned dark. Suddenly, I could see it had taken effort on his part to keep pleasant expressions plastered on his face. He was no longer putting out any effort.

"I wanted to tell you that you should be very careful in who you trust, Mr. Galloway. You should be careful in your investigation. You may not be a police officer any longer and this is not a television show, but what you are doing is still dangerous work."

I leaned in close. "I was really okay with the first thing you said. I really was. But the second part—"

I slammed my hand into his groin and squeezed. He doubled over and his ear was next to my lips.

I whispered, "The second part sounded a bit like a threat. I am not a fan of threats, Mr. Faust. They make me uncomfortable and when I'm uncomfortable I tend to make others uncomfortable." I squeezed tighter.

Faust whimpered and was starting to slide off his stool when the bartender noticed the commotion and approached. The sizable barkeep was in his forties and was sporting a gray handlebar mustache.

He calmly put both his hands beneath the bar and said, "You are going to be on the receiving end of whatever I have under here if you don't take your hands off him right now."

I released my grip, but the bartender kept his hands out of my sight. Where was Maddox with his Revolutionary War musket when I needed him?

Seeing I was no longer welcome, I asked the bartender if I could have a box for my dinner. He unenthusiastically slid down the bar and returned with a container. I packed up my food and threw some cash down. As I reached the exit, I glanced over my shoulder long enough to see Faust and the bartender were shooting daggers from their eyes. I lifted my jacket collar when I hit the street. The snow was tapering off and I looked around in every direction, wondering if I was being watched. Some people say they have a sixth sense when it comes to being watched. While I couldn't tell if eyes were on me, I did know one thing for sure. Tiny Washaway Township, Pennsylvania, was getting smaller by the second.

CHAPTER 7

A hint of daylight had clawed its way into a defiant sky by the time Colby picked me up. We sipped Eagle Valley Inn coffee in paper cups as her patrol car eased through the hills. The chief had tired eyes, and I knew I didn't look much better.

After a few miles, she asked, "Get much sleep?"

"Some."

"What did you do last night? Our little town isn't exactly a hotbed for nighttime activities," she said.

"I went to a bar and felt up some guy."

She was nodding, but stopped as the words soaked in. "Has anyone ever told you that you're a bit odd?"

I didn't respond and watched heavy clumps of snow fall from evergreens. We rounded a bend and I recognized the surroundings. The front gate of The Camp was buzzing with activity. Colby slid the car off to the side of the road and wished me luck.

I did a double-take and asked, "You're not coming?"

"If you want to build any kind of rapport with Seth, it would be best if I'm not present. I went after him pretty hard over the past year and he made it clear that he's finished cooperating with me."

"And if I walk in there and he tells me to piss-off?"

"You have my cell number. Shoot me a call and I'll turn back around to pick you up."

"You don't want to wait here?"

Colby shook her head. "I need to go check on something. I think I know what you were getting at when you were questioning Brady Mason yesterday and I want to dig a little."

The frosty wind slapped my face as I opened the door and told Colby I wouldn't be more than an hour. Groups of people in snowsuits peered around skis, which were hoisted over shoulders as they noticed me get out of the marked car. In the distance, I could hear the pop of gunfire. I wasn't sure how far I was from the shooting range, but I could still tell the small-caliber pops were more subdued than those of a typical police academy firing line. I strode in through the main gate and found a sign directing me to the main office. Chilled hinges groaned and a bell clinked dully on top of the door as I pushed it open.

A woman in her thirties looked up from behind a desk and asked, "May I help you?"

I introduced myself and told her I was hoping to speak with Seth Wrangle.

"He's out on the course right now." She seemed to size me up and determine I wasn't at The Camp for a simple chat. "We're pretty busy finalizing the course for tomorrow's competition." She picked up a portable radio, but didn't press the button to speak. She managed a smile and asked me, "Does he know you?"

"I'm kind of a friend of the family," I said.

"You said your name is Trevor?"

"Right. Trevor Galloway."

She pressed a button on the radio and put it up to her mouth as she swiveled back and forth in her chair.

"Seth?"

After a beat came the reply, "I'm here."

She swiveled away and lowered her voice, but I could still hear every word.

"There's a serious-looking man in the office to see you. A Trevor Galloway. He says he's a friend of the family."

Another pause.

"Don't know the name. Is he selling something?"

"Are you selling anything?" the woman asked while swiveling back my way.

"Look at me," I said, while keeping my usual expression. "Can you imagine anybody buying anything from me?"

She keyed the radio again and spoke into it. "Not a chance."

"Give me five," came the response.

I passed the time dodging questions from the woman who told me her name was Gracie. She was nice enough, but in the minutes that passed she informed me she had three kids, two cats, and loved Jesus. After hitting me with a half dozen questions, she discovered I wasn't going to discuss kids, pets, or religion. My non-responsiveness must have worn her down, because the stream of questions dwindled to a trickle and eventually froze completely.

We listened to the wind compress snow against the side of the building until the door opened and a lean man with a weathered face appeared.

To no one in particular he said, "That wind needs to die down before tomorrow or we're going to set a record for penalties."

From my online research, I recalled that depending on what rules were applied, the competitors were required to either ski a penalty lap for each of the five targets they missed or they would have time added at the end of the race. In most cases, competitors would take five shots at five targets each time they stopped at the shooting area. Misses would be extremely costly. Not much room for error in this sport. I assumed that high winds could wreak havoc in a sport where precision is vital.

Seth Wrangle removed his gloves and looked me over.

"No, you don't look like you're selling ski wax."

"People put wax on skis?" I asked, not joking.

The man smiled and walked toward me, still not knowing if I was being factitious.

He seemed to come to a conclusion and said, "If I didn't know any better, I'd say you were a cop."

"I'm not."

"Were you?"

"I was," I said.

With no small amount of sarcasm, he said, "And I suppose it's a complete coincidence that you are here around the one-year anniversary of the murder of my neighbor—a murder for which I was relentlessly questioned."

"It's not."

"Get the hell out," he instructed as he began moving toward a back office.

"I met your nephew," I said quickly.

He turned back around, annoyed.

"I have two nephews, not that it matters. You need to leave now," he commanded as he disappeared through a doorway.

"I mean Josh. We met briefly in Pittsburgh when I was an officer there," I said loudly.

For a second I thought he might not have heard me, but then heavy booted footsteps rolled my direction and Seth Wrangle reappeared and stared at me with gunmetal eyes.

He seemed to sift through his mind for information that had been filed away for over a decade before he said, "Galloway. Officer Trevor Galloway. Now I remember the name. You were the one who talked the psycho into surrendering."

I nodded and he walked back into the reception area.

"It's funny," he said. "Back then, I pictured you as some

73

young baby-faced patrol officer. But, I see now that you must have been in your forties back then."

"Actually, I'm only..." I began, before surrendering in a losing battle. "I'm only here to take another look at things," I said. "I have no preconceived notions and I'm skeptical of anything I hear. In fact, I'm generally terrible at listening to other people's advice or opinions."

He glanced down at my left hand, grinned, and said, "Well, that would explain the lack of a wedding ring."

I noticed he wasn't wearing one either.

I shrugged and said, "It probably explains a lot of things."

His grin widened and he seemed to relax.

"I suppose it's a complete coincidence that Chief Colby asked you of all people to come see me."

"You don't strike me as being dim," I said. "I was hand-picked because of my connection to your family. Chief Colby thought you might open up to me and admit to murdering Peter Lanskard in cold blood." I peeked out the window as another powerful gust tossed snow against the glass, causing it to vibrate. "Look, I'm staying at the Eagle Valley Inn, my room doesn't have a television, and I think I ate Mr. Maddox's only pastry yesterday. So it would be great if you would break down and give me a tearful confession. If you can lend me a pen and some paper, I'll even take careful notes while you do it so you won't have to repeat yourself later."

Gracie's head popped up, but her jaw nearly hit the floor.

"I'd love to," he said, not missing a beat. "But I have competitions to coordinate over the next two days and I wouldn't want to miss out." He jerked his head toward his office, prompting me to follow. "Oh and I didn't kill anyone, so maybe I shouldn't confess."

"I guess not," I said as we took seats on each side of a metal desk.

"So now you aren't with the police?"

"I'm retired on disability."

He rubbed his chin and seemed to be searching his memory. "My sister still lives in Pittsburgh. I didn't make the connection when Gracie said your name, but my sister emailed me some stories about you a while back." His tone became tentative and he disclosed, "I read that you went through a real rough time."

I didn't speak.

He continued, "I also read that you got the bastards who did that to you. Good for you."

Sensing his sincerity, I swallowed and said, "Thank you."

"You didn't want to stay with the police department any longer?"

"No. They let me retire early," I repeated.

I think he wanted me to add more, but he decided to move on when I dropped the conversational ball.

"You don't seem like a man who likes to waste time with chitchat, so let's get to it," he said. "What's your first question?"

I looked around the room and noticed that there was no sign of the former Olympian's ego around his office. Other than a couple of posters that promised that Fischer skis would dramatically improve an athlete's performance, the walls were bare. A black equipment bag slouched in one corner and a file cabinet stood its ground in another.

"What's the distance of tomorrow's race?" I asked.

"I thought you would want to talk about Pete's murder?"

"I do," I said. "But I know very little about the biathlon and so far I'm fascinated."

"We're holding two events this week. Tomorrow is the ten-kilometer sprint. Ten kilometers is—"

"Six point two miles," I said. "I'm a distance runner, or at least I was. I've run my share of ten-Ks."

He continued, "We always have a relay the day after the ten-K. In tomorrow's race, the competitors complete three laps and shoot twice. The first time they shoot, they do it from the prone position and the next time they'll be standing. They shoot five shots each time and if a shooter misses any of the five targets, he has to complete a penalty loop of one-hundred fifty meters before continuing."

I asked, "How long does it take someone to finish the penalty loop?"

"It depends on the athlete. The best in the world can knock it off in about twenty seconds. But the ones we have here aren't world class. Some of them will take much longer to get through it."

"How long would it take you to complete the loop?"

Seth Wrangle's eyes narrowed. "Damn. Are you buying into Chief Colby's theory that I'm the only person who could have skied onto Pete's property and escaped simply because I'm fast?"

"I told you, I'm not buying into anything."

I waited and for a moment I was certain he was going to ask me to leave. But then he said, "Yeah, I could have done it."

"You seem pretty sure."

"Mr. Galloway, I finished fourth in the sprint in Salt Lake City. Do you know how many Americans have ever finished that high in any biathlon event?"

"One, according to Wikipedia."

"That's right, I'm the only one. Now I'm retired, but I could still make the run Colby described if the conditions were right."

"You aren't exactly eliminating yourself as a suspect," I said.

"That's because you aren't asking the right questions, Mr. Galloway. The biathlon is an amazingly complex sport where the smallest details mean everything. A competitor has to think about what skis to use, what kind of ski wax to apply and how much, the stone grinding of the skis, and multiple other variables. But more importantly, there's one thing that can mean the difference between gaining and losing huge chunks of time during a race."

I thought for a second before saying, "The rifle."

He explained, "The rifles we use are highly specialized and usually customized, to include unique cheek pieces and pistol grips. They're designed to hit targets as small as golf balls at fifty meters. Do you know what all that means?"

Knowing something about how easy it is to become accustomed to using a specific weapon at a specific distance, I said, "You can't hit crap from five hundred yards, can you?"

"I bet I could," he said with a sharp nod. "But certainly not after skiing on flat ground at a blistering pace. My guess is that whatever rifle was used would feel bulky and awkward compared to what I typically use. Besides, the scope alone would have thrown me off. Shooting a biathlon rifle is a very specific skill. I won't go so far as to say that I would have accidentally shot myself with a heavier rifle, but I doubt I could have hit much at that distance with my heart pounding away."

The man had a point. I let my eyes drift down and lose focus.

"Mr. Galloway?"

Damn. How long had that one been?

"Yes," I said.

"I asked if you had ever handled a biathlon rifle?"

"No," I replied. Then something I'd realized during my minor blur-out came back to me.

"You called him Pete."

"Yes, I did," he said.

"I haven't heard anyone call him Pete. Up until now, everyone except for his daughter has referred to him as Mr. Lanskard or Peter."

It was Seth's turn to go silent. I waited.

"I knew him. I didn't agree with his business or his politics, but I knew him and liked him," he said. "How is Susan doing?"

"She misses her father," I replied.

His face drooped as he said, "I've kept my distance out of respect. I assumed Colby put it in her head that I may have had something to do with her father's death. She listens to Colby way too much." He shook his head and added, "The fact that Chief Colby and Susan are an item is the worst-kept secret in the county," he mumbled. "I haven't seen Susan since the funeral. When you talk to her, please give her my best."

I could tell his mind was wandering back in time and we sat in silence.

He drifted back to the present and said, "I know there's been some gossip that Pete and I had problems, but we got along fine. I'm not sure where the rumors about existing animosity came from, but they aren't true. Every time I saw him he gave me a hard time about the land, but it was all good-natured."

"The land?" I said innocently.

Seth smiled. "Pete's interest in my land is the second-worst-kept secret in the county." He stomped a foot on the floorboards and said, "This land right here is an anomaly, Mr. Galloway. Pete wanted to buy it from me and offered me a ton of money for it too."

"Why?" I asked too quickly. "I mean—not to be rude—it's a beautiful piece of land, but it's not much more than hills and trees."

"And rock," Seth corrected.

"Okay."

"Have you ever heard of Goshen stone?"

I told him I hadn't.

"It's a tremendously valuable type of stone typically found in New England. It turns out that this little piece of land is a Pennsylvania rarity and Goshen can be found right here under our feet. It sells for about one hundred dollars per ton."

"How many tons could you get out of this land?"

"The land has to be properly surveyed, so I'm not sure exactly. But it will be enough that the four of us who own this land will be multimillionaires someday."

"The other three people being your brother and the Fredricks," I said.

"Right. You've done your homework. Good," he said. "In a few years, we'll close this place down and sell it to a company that can mine the stone, but Pete understood that I wasn't ready."

I noticed Seth didn't mention how ready the other three stakeholders might be to rake in a monster payday.

"Do all of you have to agree to sell?"

He nodded.

"Aren't the others ready to strike it rich?"

"All good things in time," was all he said.

"Why don't you want to sell now?"

"This is a special place, Mr. Galloway. There are just a handful of biathlon camps in this country and most of them only hold events for serious competitors. I *love* biathlon and I *love* cross-country skiing. I want kids to learn about it, and their weekend warrior parents to come out here and have fun. The biathlon is wildly popular in Russia and in various European countries. It could be like that here if people have a chance to get exposed to it without feeling too much competetive pressure. I know I should sell this place and buy another piece of land up north or overseas, but I grew up not far from here and this is still my home. Maybe I'm holding on to a senseless dream, but I'm not ready to sell out." Seth's passion hung in the air and he said, "Now, what else would you like to ask me?"

"When the police talked to you before, I assume they asked you about guns?"

"The chief asked me if I owned a rifle that fires a .308 round. I don't, nor have I ever. I gave the police consent to search the entire camp and they didn't come up with anything."

"You were in the military," I said. "I would assume you fired all kinds of rifles back then."

"Nothing that used a .308," he said. "I'm not going to lie, I was pretty decent with a M16 back in the day, but that was a long time ago. Now, I'm so used to firing .22 rounds out of the ANSCHUTZ that shooting a rifle with a sizable scope on it would feel like I'm handling an elephant trunk."

"Where were you when Mr. Lanskard was killed?"

"I'm sure you read or heard that I was out on the course, making sure the targets and wind flags were set up."

"I did. I also heard nobody could confirm your whereabouts. It seems pretty busy around here so it seems odd that nobody remembered seeing you at that moment."

Seth Wrangle leaned forward and said, "The competitors were still starting to arrive that day. Look, I was where I said I was. That Colby woman has tunnel vision. She sees me as a target and she's focusing on me so hard that she's blocked out everything else. I didn't kill Pete. I had no reason to. On the contrary, someday he was going to make me rich."

"But now someone else will," I said.

"I suppose."

He looked at his watch, "I don't mean to be rude, Mr. Galloway, but I really don't think I can help you."

I knew the meter was about to expire so I asked, "Did you see Mr. Lanskard much in the weeks preceding his death?"

"Sure. We'd run into each other in town and, like everyone else, I'd get the evil eye from his security goon. About a week before he died, we had a drink together and he made another hard push to buy this place."

I said, "From what I can tell, Mr. Lanskard's company had plenty of other projects and I assume you would have given him first crack at buying your land, so why the push?"

This made him tense and he gazed at his desk. He was slow in responding. "I have no idea. He was an aggressive businessman, I guess."

I fixed my eyes on his face until he looked over to me. "I'm not an insurance investigator. I'm not looking to hurt anyone."

Seth Wrangle wilted into his chair. He started to speak but stopped.

"How sick was he?" I asked.

Several seconds passed before he spoke.

"He had less than a year. Cancer."

The air seemed to thicken around us and Seth tapped a finger on his desk.

"Susan shouldn't lose the life insurance if this was what I think it was," he said. "If the police declare it a suicide, I assume the insurance company would go after the money."

"I don't report to the police," I said.

He perked up at hearing this and said, "Aren't you working with Chief Colby?"

"I was hired by Susan Lanskard. I'll report my findings to her. What she does after that is her decision."

Seth seemed relieved at learning this, which happened to be true.

"What made you guess he was sick?" he asked.

"There were indications he was coming to terms with some things and may have become complacent about life in general. Aside from that, he stayed out in the open in spite of knowing of a possible threat. The shooter could only have known to be in position if he knew exactly when Lanskard was arriving. The timing was too precise. It was clockwork."

"So that's it?" he asked. "You're going to tell Pete's daughter that he set up his own killing and she'll decide if she wants to tell Colby?"

I shook my head and said, "Not yet. This is just a theory. Unless you have any information that can point me to the shooter, I don't have any evidence one way or the other."

"I have no idea who shot him," said Seth. "That's the absolute truth. The chief's theory sounds good if you don't understand the intricacies of biathlon shooting and weaponry, but in the end it doesn't hold water. It would be nearly impossible for a person—any person—to pull that off."

"The week it happened, did you notice any new competitors who were particularly talented?"

With growing frustration, Seth said, "No, and I'm telling you that sprint and shot would be damn near impossible. When I was in the Army, I saw some of the Special Forces guys do some amazing stuff, but this is beyond amazing. Last year, the camp had pretty much the same pool of people as the year before and nobody unusual stuck out."

"What about a guy named Markus Faust?"

"What about him?"

"I met him last night. He...makes an impression."

Seth allowed himself a little smile and said, "He's an arrogant prick. But he's not a bad guy at heart and means well. He's fiercely defensive of David and me. I assume he strongly suggested you leave us alone?"

"He did."

Seth laughed and said, "He's never been good at reading people. You don't seem like you're any kind of shrinking violet. How did you respond?"

I cocked my head and gave an *about like you would expect* expression.

"Yeah," said Seth. "Anyway, he's harmless."

"Is he good?"

"At the sport?" asked Seth. "Yes, he's very good. But like I said before, I can't imagine anybody being able to pull off the job Chief Colby envisioned. Not Faust, not me, not anybody."

I decided to temporarily abandon the topic of the smiling German. "Did anything out of the ordinary happen during the week of the murder?"

"Nothing," he said, but I saw his growing discomfort as he debated telling me something.

"What is it?"

I got the impression he'd accidentally let me read something he'd wanted hidden. Whatever he was thinking about was something he'd intended to keep to himself.

"I'll wager you're better than Faust at reading people," I said. "I'm not going to let go."

He stretched his back and then settled back into his chair. "The night after the shooting, I thought I heard something outside my house. I was still a little edgy because Pete had just been killed and the cops had been questioning me all day. There's a shed in my backyard and I thought I heard something trying to get in there. I assumed it was a raccoon and I opened the back door and clapped. The next thing I heard was something racing through the woods. I guess I scared it off."

"It could have been a person," I said unnecessarily. "Did you check the shed? Was there any damage?"

He crossed his arms and quickly said, "I checked and nothing was missing."

I wasn't sure why, but he was starting to sound evasive.

"Did you mention the incident to the police?"

"Hell, no," he snapped. "They had been running me through the wringer all day and freaked out some of our athletes. I was done with all of them."

"Okay," I said as I stood. "I really appreciate you talking to me. If I have any follow up questions, I'd like to call you if that's all right. Do you have a card?"

He handed me a business card and I added, "Since you have the ten-K tomorrow and the…"

"Relay," he said.

"And the relay the next day—would it be possible for me to talk to your brother and the Fredricks today?"

Seth pondered this and eventually gave me directions to the shooting range where he suspected the three of them were.

I took a step away, but turned back and asked, "What about Susan?"

"What about her?"

"Well she runs MRS now. Has she made you an offer for the land?"

"No, but I'm sure she figured that if I wasn't interested in selling to her father that I wouldn't be interested in selling to her either."

"Right," I said.

As I made my way out into the cold, I tried to tell myself that the suicide theory was solid and I was simply performing mop-up duty for a rich guy who didn't want to waste away in a hospital. But as I walked closer to the sound of gunfire, I was troubled by the feeling that a blizzard of trouble lay ahead.

CHAPTER 8

A man in a white snowsuit and vest stood watch over six shooters lined up in a row, all lying prone. The yellow reflective vest made him stand out from the shooters and passing skiers. On the opposite end of the firing line, a woman wearing clothing identical to her counterpart kept one eye on the shooters and another downrange where red wind flags fluttered. The flags led up to circular targets barely visible from my position. I did my best to stay off what I assumed was the race course as athletes intermittently zipped past me, propelled by ski poles and sheer will. To my untrained eye, it appeared the course was filled with biathletes learning the course and preparing their rifles for a bloodless battle. A momentary wave of envy washed over me as I found myself wishing I had the endurance and skill to take part in the sport. I was deep in a daydream where I could ski and shoot like few others as I stepped toward the shooting range.

"Watch it!" I heard a voice say a split second before I felt the impact.

I didn't see my life flash before my eyes. Instead I saw a shoulder, then a ski, then a glove, and then a whole lot of snow. Instantly, I knew what I had done and my embarrassment significantly outweighed the pain in my ribs. Reflexively, I reached toward the holster concealed on my back and confirmed my Sig Sauer P250 was firmly in place. The 9mm version of the compact handgun was a new purchase and I had yet to

86

fire more than ten rounds out of the semiautomatic. The model was somewhat unusual for the manufacturer as it was hammerless and always fired in double-action, meaning it consistently maintained a fairly heavy trigger pull. A heavier trigger pull can decrease the accuracy of a shot, but I couldn't foresee a circumstance where I'd be shooting at someone from any distance. Actually, I was hoping I wouldn't be shooting at anyone period. Now that I had been firmly planted in the snow, I would have to make sure to disassemble and dry the gun once I got back to the Eagle Valley Inn.

"Idiot!" yelled the man whose path I had clumsily obstructed.

I apologized and helped the skier to his feet. He looked me over, noted my blue jeans and black leather jacket.

"Are you lost?" he asked sarcastically. "The *Happy Days* reunion isn't for another month."

I started to stick my thumbs up and give the man the trademark Fonzie, "Heyyyy," but I remembered I look very stoic and I'm almost never funny.

"I really am sorry," I said again. "I hope you aren't hurt."

The man huffed, mumbled a profanity, and sped away as I rubbed my ribcage.

I flinched as I noticed motion coming at me from the periphery. I was sure I was about to get pancaked again, but the two people rushing my direction were not on skis and had no trouble stopping a few feet away.

"You need to get off the course," commanded the man as he pointed to a spot a few feet to my rear.

Not being one to challenge Darwinism, I concurred. The three of us moved off the path and into deeper snow and I said, "I'm looking for Jaden and Linda Fredrick, and David Wrangle if he's around."

The couple glanced at each other before the woman spoke. "I'm Linda and this is Jaden," she told me. "David is around the bend. We're busy out here. What do you want?"

Linda's directness was anything but charming, however I'm not exactly someone who should pass judgment on such things. Getting to the point, I introduced myself and told the couple why I was there.

"It doesn't matter who the police send out here, nothing has changed," Linda said.

"We went through all of this a year ago," Jaden said. "I don't think we have anything else we can add."

I tried to ignore the pain in my side, but I was starting to wonder if I had cracked something.

"Well, like I said, I'm not with the police. I'm...independent," I clarified vaguely.

"It makes no difference," Linda said. "A dozen private eyes can ask a thousand questions and we won't have anything else to add. You can tell that to that Colby...*woman* the next time you see her."

Linda seemed pleased with herself for showing some restraint and referring to Colby as a woman rather than whatever unpleasant name had been on the tip of her tongue.

"I don't want to take up much of your time," I told them. "If you could answer a couple of questions for me, I'll get out of your hair."

For the next two minutes, I asked the couple about their whereabouts on the day Peter Lanskard was murdered and they recited the same facts I had been told previously. The couple had headed up to the town of State College to have lunch. Yes, they had paid in cash. No, they didn't know of anyone who could corroborate their story.

Linda's responses were factual and staccato and gave me the

bare minimum. The one exception was when Mrs. Fredrick volunteered to lend me her insight by letting me know I was being a pain in the ass and that I had one more minute before they walked away, but even that was stated in an efficient manner.

"I know all these inquiries must be frustrating for you," I said, realizing that I had better move on to questions that may have never been asked before. I did my best to look disarming, which usually comes across as phony, and said, "I'm sure all of you are very tired of all the questions since the shooting. You're probably ready to cash-in on the land and retire in style, right?"

Jaden spat, "What the hell is that supposed to mean?"

I remained silent and gave a shrug. An awkward silence ensued.

More charisma.

Linda Fredrick's mouth twitched and she pulled up a sleeve and read the digital display on her watch. The readout was upside down to me, but I noted the time as well.

"We aren't ready to retire yet," she said. "Now we have events scheduled for the week and we have a small staff. Excuse us."

As she stormed away, her husband said sardonically, "I'm sorry we couldn't be any help."

"Maybe David Wrangle can help me out," I said. "Your wife mentioned he was around the bend?"

Jaden pointed and let out an exasperated breath. "David is up there around that curve. If you're going to walk to him, then you should cut through those trees and stay off the course. We wouldn't want you to get hurt," he sneered.

I'm not saying there was ominous organ music playing in my head when he said that last sentence, but I was pretty certain he didn't really have much concern for my well-being. I thought again about lightening the mood by doing the Fonzie thing, but reminded myself that I'm not funny and that fewer and fewer people would get the reference these days anyway. I thought I might try it on old man Maddox back at the inn, but I wasn't sure he'd appreciate the impersonation either. He struck me more of an Andy Griffith fan and I wasn't even sure he had a television in his own room. By the time I reached David Wrangle, I'd decided to give up the whole *Happy Days* thing and to remain unfunny.

David wasn't doing much of anything when I found him. He had brushed off a seat on a boulder and was snacking on a protein bar when I approached him and made my introduction. As opposed to his energetic brother and the abrupt and alert Fredricks, he looked tired and disinterested. I extended my hand and he tentatively removed a glove before we shook.

"Your name's familiar. Have we met?"

I told him of my temporary, but apparently useful, connection to his nephew.

"Oh, that's right. Thanks for all that. Josh was always a good kid," he said in a weary voice as his bloodshot eyes followed a skier around a curve. "He's got a good job and kids of his own now, you know. He doesn't talk about that day much, but I know he's grateful for what you did."

The realization struck me that the hostage situation I seldom thought about had a significant impact on someone's life. I looked away and thought about the beautiful absurdity of being a police officer. As an officer, often you meet a person on the absolute worst day of his life. The day's events are permanently etched into the mind of the individual who may have been a victim, a witness, or even a suspect. However, to the officer, it's just another day in which any momentary sense of heroism is dashed away by the sound of the next call coming across the radio.

Brining myself back to the job at hand, I said, "Susan Lanskard has asked me to revisit her father's murder."

"It was suicide," he said while keeping eyes down the path.

Even after dealing with Linda Fredrick, his directness gave me pause. I waited for more, but the man's gaze stayed distant and he didn't appear to be interested in clarifying on his own.

"Why do you say that?" I asked.

"Did you talk to my brother yet?"

"I did."

"I bet he didn't tell you that Peter was sick, did he? He thinks he's protecting Susan's life insurance money, the reputation of her father, or some nonsense. It's ridiculous. The family is loaded. The insurance money is probably a drop in the bucket. I don't know why he doesn't just tell people that Peter was dying. I suppose he wants to protect the man's legacy or something."

David seemed to become more aware and turned to look at me. "Do you have any idea who pulled the trigger for him?"

"Not yet, but some new information has been uncovered that may shed some light on things," I lied. "Sometimes investigations are like archeology. Things get dug up and they don't make much sense until a few other pieces are found. The next thing you know, you're looking at a lost city."

I was starting to sound like I was making some sort of Indiana Jones reference and I thought I might mention it to David. But I thought about the disastrous fourth film of that franchise and abandoned the notion purely on principle.

David shifted on the boulder and checked his watch. I was starting to become offended by all the timepiece checking. Instinctively, I glanced at his Garmin GPS watch but had difficulty reading the numbers as his hand trembled. His gaze rose as another skier passed by, causing the snow to whisper with speed. His expression was something between jealousy and resentment.

I asked, "Are you in a program?"

He looked up at me and I expected him to act like he didn't know what I was talking about, or to issue a grand denial. He didn't.

"AA, on and off," he replied.

"I've been down a similar road," I said. "I'm five months clean since my last relapse. It sucks," I added truthfully.

"It sure does," he agreed.

"How long have you been in AA?"

He brushed snow off his forehead and said, "For the better part of a year."

I remembered Colby had told me that David had suffered a knee injury not too long ago. I wondered if the knee injury was a story concocted to camouflage his illness or if the drinking started after the injury. Ultimately, I decided it didn't much matter.

"If you don't mind me asking, what's the longest you've been sober?" I asked.

He tapped a gloved finger on the boulder beneath him and said, "I did pretty well for the first four months of the program. Since then, it's been hit or miss."

"Have you thought about checking yourself into a rehab program? You know—one of those thirty-day places?"

Now he was focusing on me completely. "Of course I have. I thought about it, looked up a couple facilities on the Internet, made a few calls, and do you know what I found out?"

"They are expensive as hell," I answered from experience.

"I'm sure the cost of admission to hell is a lot cheaper," he mumbled as I noticed a beautiful hawk land on a branch across the path. I thought David was going to mention the bird, but he didn't seem to notice its arrival. He asked, "Are you going to write up the shooting as a suicide?"

"I don't know," I said. "I need to exclude any other possibilities before I can make that claim. I'm sure you know there's a theory that an incredibly skilled skier and marksman was the shooter. Some people think your brother fits the bill."

The hawk in the tree slowly expanded its wings then drew them back in close. It was an amazing specimen and although I was sure David was used to seeing such things, I was surprised he didn't comment.

David shook his head and said, "Seth wouldn't be involved. He liked Peter and, even if Peter asked him to take the shot, I can't imagine my brother would."

"His alibi is pretty weak," I mentioned.

He shrugged and said, "I guess it was a bad day for alibis. I was home alone and nobody could verify my whereabouts either. That Colby bitch and her state police friends interviewed us for days and made us feel like criminals because we couldn't find twenty people to say they saw us somewhere else at the time of the shooting." He turned on the boulder as anger started to build. "Have you ever thought about how many times in a day you don't have an alibi, Mr. Galloway?"

"I guess it's good I've rarely needed one."

"I guess so," he muttered.

The wind strengthened and blew snow sideways into our faces. The temporary distraction calmed the man who was obviously waging a physical and emotional battle with an affliction I knew all too well.

"I heard this land is worth a lot of money to all of you. I guess you'll be able to afford any rehab center you want when your brother decides to sell this place."

David slid off the boulder and adjusted his coat. "It was

probably his own security people, you know."

"What?"

"It had to have been an inside job," he said while turning to walk away. "It was an inside job and deep down his daughter knows it."

"What makes you say that?" I asked to his back.

He turned his head and I could barely hear his reply over another gust of wind as he moved away. He said, "Because if your father was gunned down on his own property, would you trust the same people to protect you?"

Now standing alone, I turned toward the branch where the hawk had been perched, but it was gone. Odd. I hadn't noticed it fly away. How in the world had I not seen it take off?

"I know...some Tin Man," I told the empty branch, thinking of David's point about the Susan Lanskard retaining the security detail. "More like the Scarecrow searching for a brain."

CHAPTER 9

As warm as Colby's car was, it still took me fifteen minutes to heat up after the wait. I'm sure I could have found a seat inside the main office, but I had gotten the sense that Gracie the receptionist would either want to have a long conversation or subject me to an uncomfortable silence after I asked her boss to confess to a murder. I opted to risk frostbite.

"How did it go?" asked Colby as we started our ascent out of the valley.

I blew into my hands and tried to put feeling back into the fingertips. "They don't like you much."

Colby smiled, "How many times did they call me a bitch?"

"Once," I told her. "But it was implied several times. I think Linda Fredrick was aiming even higher, but discretion got the best of her."

"Did you get to talk to all four of them?"

I nodded and flexed my fingers.

"You should buy some gloves," she said. "And a heavier coat. And definitely some boots."

"I know."

The car temporarily lost traction on some ice, but Colby expertly regained control. I focused my eyes through the windshield. This heavy snowfall couldn't possibly keep up.

I could feel Colby's stare before she said, "Would you care to tell me what they said?"

"Not yet," I said hoping the subject would drop, but suspecting it wouldn't.

The car came to a punitive stop and Colby slammed the car into park.

"Excuse me?" she said indignantly. "Is that some kind of joke?"

"I'm not good at telling jokes," I said. "In fact, I scrapped an entire Fonzie impression twice because I was overthinking the whole thing."

She glared at me disbelievingly.

"You don't know who Fonzie is?"

She gritted her teeth and her lips barely moved as she said, "Of course, I know who Fonzie is."

"Sorry," I said. "You're younger than me so I wasn't sure if you'd remember. Even at my age, I only remember *Happy Days* being shown in reruns. I'm never sure when references like that become obsolete. Sometimes old television shows get remade or end up being movies, so occasionally the references make sense. I think there might have been an A-Team movie a few years ago. So I assume a lot of young people who never saw the show would have seen the movie."

Colby blinked.

I continued, "I never understood how the police and the military could never track down the A-Team, but anyone and everyone seemed to be able to hire them by doing things like calling numbers posted in classified ads. Maybe the military police should have just read the classifieds and offered to hire them. Then, catching them would have been a piece of cake. Do you know about the A-Team?" I asked, being sincerely curious.

"Yes, I know about the A-Team," she replied in an unhappy, drawn-out sentence. "And yes, it was also a movie starring—"

She closed her eyes and shook her head. "Why are we talking

about old television shows?" she shouted. "What did you find out in The Camp?"

"Oh, I don't want to go into it right now."

"Are you trying to be funny?" she snapped.

"I told you, I'm not good at being funny. I can't even tell a joke or pull off a decent impression."

"It was a rhetorical question! Are we working this case as partners or what?"

I could see she was angry. It's an unfortunate and completely unintentional effect of my personality. I'd have to keep working on that.

"Sort of," I said.

"What the hell does *that* mean?"

"It means I believed you could be objective, but some things have changed. Your relationship with Susan Lanskard is more problematic than I first thought."

Colby put her hands on the steering wheel and tapped her fingers.

"Okay," she said in a calmer tone. "How about I tell you what I was doing while you were in The Camp, and let's see if it puts your mind at ease."

"Fire away," I urged.

She glared at me, then reached between the seats and produced a notepad and flipped to the appropriate page. "Back when you were talking to Brady Mason, you were bothered by Peter's behavior before his death and by the fact that he had no qualms about staying out in the open even when there was a report of a possible threat."

"Of course," I said. "I'm sure it bothers you too."

"Right. But then you asked Brady if he accompanied Peter on normal errands like going to the store or the doctor. That question struck me as odd. You could have listed a dozen everyday errands, but you specifically mentioned going to the doctor. Brady got a bit edgy and ended the interview."

"So…" I prompted.

"So I happen to know that Peter ran most of his local errands in Washaway Township. It stands to reason he might use one of our two general practitioners if he needed a doctor. It turned out he was a patient of the first one I visited—Dr. Larry Ward. I asked him about Peter's medical history."

I raised my eyebrows and said, "Just like that? He didn't pull the doctor-patient confidentiality card?"

"He started to, but I got Susan on the phone and she gave him permission as next of kin. Dr. Stanton walked me through the records and informed me that Peter had cancer and only had a few months to live. He was seeing an oncologist in Philadelphia too, but the outcome was inevitable. Your suspicions were right. The whole thing might be an elaborate suicide."

I didn't say anything.

"That doesn't mean that Seth is in the clear," she said. "If Seth pulled the trigger, he still needs to be brought up on charges for assisting the suicide."

"*If*," I emphasized.

We processed the new information for a minute before Colby resumed the conversation.

"Now, why are you holding out on me?" she asked.

A slow-moving car drove past us and I watched it disappear behind some evergreens.

"If it's determined that Peter's death was a suicide, it would nullify any life insurance claim. Even now, the insurer would come after any payments already received."

Colby leaned back slightly and considered my words. I had been trying to avoid offending her and was failing miserably.

"You think I might not want this to be a suicide because of Susan!"

I took a deep breath and tried to walk a conversational high wire. I explained, "An objective observer might question if you would want your lover to miss out on what I assume is a substantial life insurance payment. Your knowledge that Peter Lanskard may have had a reason to stage his suicide puts you in a bad position. It may be why Brady Mason never told you about Peter's behavior in the weeks before the attack. He probably didn't want to have to hurt Susan financially or put you in a bad spot personally. If I'm holding back, it's with the best of intentions."

She looked away and I relaxed while giving myself a mental pat on the back for diffusing an extraordinarily bad situation.

"Bullshit!" she screamed as she whipped back around.

I decided I better stop mentally patting myself on the back in case I needed to physically ward off some blows.

"I asked you to come out here to help me discover the truth, not to withhold information!"

"You asked me to come out here because Susan Lanskard wanted to hire someone to take a fresh look at things," I corrected. "I'm willing to share information, but I have to be sure the integrity of the investigation remains intact."

She spoke slowly through gritted teeth. "The integrity of the investigation will remain intact. I'm the chief of police, not some love-struck teenager. My job comes first—period! Got that?"

"Got it," I said, because I could hardly say anything else under the circumstances.

"Now, I would really appreciate it if you would tell me what you learned down there at The Camp. Do you think you could possibly take a few minutes to brief the local *Chief of Police* on the progress of her own investigation?" she asked sardonically.

Since Colby had already discovered the most critical piece of information I had come across, I spent the next several minutes filling her in on what the Wrangles and Fredricks had told me, including Seth hearing something near his shed the night of the murder and the information about the land being worth millions. I also made mention of David Wrangle's struggles with the bottle.

"Well, that would explain the DUI on his record and his reputation for getting out of hand from time to time," she said. "Has he tried to check himself into a place to dry out?"

"Those places are extremely expensive. I got the impression he'd be willing if he had the money."

"Well if Seth would agree to sell the land, money wouldn't be an issue. I'm sure David believes the money would solve a lot of problems."

"Addicts always believe *something* they don't have will solve their problems, but that's rarely the case."

Colby looked at my face and must have seen something in it even more solemn than usual.

"Voice of experience?"

"Voice of experience," I confirmed.

She put the car in drive and we continued up the hill. The snow relented and the surrounding trees stopped swaying with the wind.

Colby said, "If a shooter was hired, I have no idea how we'll find him. I would imagine Peter was smart enough to cover his financial tracks if he paid someone to take the shot."

"If he had to hire someone at all," I said. "It's always possible someone owed him a favor and didn't want Peter to suffer. Peter could have confided in someone about his cancer and asked a friend to deliver a remedy in the form of a bullet."

"Geez. What a weird way to repay a debt."

"There's also the possibility that we are way off-track and this wasn't a suicide at all," I said. "We have four of Peter's neighbors who will be sitting on a pile of money once Seth agrees to sell the land, and then there's the issue of the security detail."

"What issue?" Colby asked. "By all accounts, Peter did everything he could to make it difficult to protect him."

"Not that issue," I said. "It concerns me that Susan Lanskard kept them on after the murder. She has enough money to hire anyone. Why would she keep using the same people who let her father get killed? If nothing else, they're a terrible reminder of what happened. When a person experiences a tragedy, they tend to sweep away anything that would cause those memories to surface."

"That's not always true," Colby said. "Sometimes people want to hold on to things to keep memories alive. Especially memories of loved ones."

"I doubt Susan is keeping the security detail around as a keepsake," I said.

"No," Colby agreed. "But her father trusted them and she valued his opinion in all matters. She's never come out and said it, but I think she would consider it a betrayal to fire the security team."

"I still think it's interesting."

"Are you thinking Susan suspects a suicide?" Colby asked. "You may not believe me, but she's never even mentioned that as a possibility. I agree there's some logic to what you are saying, but I'm sure she would have told me if she had any doubts that his death was anything but murder. Besides, Susan would have told me if she had known her father was sick and she wouldn't have given Dr. Stanton permission to speak to me if she wanted to cover-up that fact."

"I don't want to totally discount that she may at least sub-consciously suspect her father set the whole thing up. But it begs another question: Why would she hire someone to dig around?"

"Exactly."

"Out of curiosity, how much life insurance money did Susan get?"

Colby tilted her head and was obviously uncomfortable disclosing her lover's personal financial information. Eventually she said, "Three million. I know that sounds like a lot, but the company is worth much more. Besides, I know for a fact that Susan would give up everything to have a little more time with her father. Money isn't of any concern to her."

I didn't believe that for a second, but I kept my mouth shut.

Colby continued, "No matter how we look at this thing, we're looking for an exceptionally athletic shooter who knew when Peter was going to be arriving home and knew how to get in and out of the woods like a ghost."

Something in Colby's words resonated with me, but I couldn't put my finger on why that was. I felt my thoughts were scattered and I knew the cause. My conversation with David Wrangle had rattled him, but it had affected me as well. Seeing him in pain that familiar to me was a reminder of what I had gone through on more than one occasion. It was as if I could smell his need. Part of me ached for the needle simply because David Wrangle longed for a drink. The sensation is difficult to explain and I've only found one solution that keeps the barbar-ians at the gates.

"Can you take me back to the inn?" I asked.

"I suppose," Colby replied curiously. "I figured you would want to go back to the house and talk to Brady Mason to press him and see if he knew about Peter's cancer."

I shook my head and said, "I'm sure you don't need me to tag along."

"What will *you* be doing?"

"I need to make some phone calls," I said truthfully. I had to check on a few things that were still haunting me, but more importantly, I had to get my head straight. I felt some demons creeping up behind me, and I needed to outrun them.

TARGET 3
BLUFFS, CALLS, AND A SKULL

CHAPTER 10

Even under ideal conditions, the first mile of a run is always the most difficult. Your lungs don't want to expand and your muscles are reluctant to respond. Particularly in the dead of winter, those first labored strides feel unnatural and your mind tells your body to stop being insubordinate and head toward the nearest fireplace.

Being unfamiliar with the area, I stuck to the main roads but soon realized there was no such thing as a main thoroughfare once you left the township. Shoveled sidewalks vanished quickly and I found myself dodging patches of ice along the edge of rural Pennsylvania roads. The quiet rhythm of my footsteps served as a metronome and steadied my mind. Although I was still shaken by my conversation with David Wrangle, I was able to put some distance between his pain and my past. With distance came perspective. With perspective came an ability to focus.

I was climbing a fairly steep hill, when my concentration was shattered by an approaching car. It's a habit of mine to run on the left side of the road, so I can see oncoming traffic. I had no problem seeing the emblem on the hood of the Chevy as I heard the engine rev and watched the sedan veer my direction. Diving over a steep embankment, I tumbled an eternity and bounced off a couple of small trees.

Coming to an abrupt stop by a creek, I tried to catch my breath and comprehend what had just occurred. Out of habit, my hand reached for a gun that was nowhere to be found. I had left the Sig disassembled and drying out in my room, so I knew it hadn't tumbled away during my fall. Pain radiated from everywhere and I made an effort to move every body part I could think of. I wasn't sure how, but I didn't seem to have any broken bones. I reached up to my nose and wiped away a trickle of blood mixed with flecks of tree bark and other debris.

Digging some pine needles out of my hair, I looked back up the hill. Standing on the edge where I had gone over was a tall, slender man in a denim jacket. His long black hair blew across his face and he brushed it back with a tattooed hand. The man who had to be The Lithuanian stared at me, then his eyes moved from side to side, seeking out a way down the hill that wouldn't cause him to take a tumble. I looked around as well and realizing he had no way of safely getting to me, I called on all my maturity, education, and experience, and presented him my middle finger. I second-guessed this questionable life choice when the assassin's hand became a blur, disappeared behind his back, and reappeared a split second before a bullet zipped past my head. Having introduced him to my charismatic nature, I darted deeper into the woods and zigzagged between trees that splintered as bullets cracked against frozen wood. So much for outrunning my demons. As it turns out, some demons carry handguns and have incredible fucking aim.

The shooting subsided as I vanished into the forest and spent the next few minutes doing my best to keep track of which direction would take me back to town. Once my pulse lowered to something less than that of a mouse being batted around by a cat, I realized I was freezing and that getting lost in the Pennsylvania wilderness was tantamount to a death sentence. Long ago, my father had taken me camping somewhere in West Virginia and I think he said something about moss growing on the north side of a tree. However, my father also told me that women could get pregnant simply from laying down in the backseat of a car, so I learned early on to take his advice with a grain of salt and a shot of tequila.

Making my way to the bottom of a valley, I located some sort of deer path—or what I assumed was a deer path—that seemed to lead in the direction of the town. I hoped I hadn't gotten so turned around that I was about to head deeper into the forest, but staying put with no phone and inadequate clothing wasn't a good option. Ducking under a branch, I stumbled onto the path and started following the hoofmarks and animal droppings along the way. I had almost convinced myself to feel encouraged that the town was ahead of me when a twig snapped behind me.

Son of a bitch.

How in the hell had he tracked me in these woods? Did Lithuanian assassins head off to some survivalist camp in their spare time? Then I realized that as easily as I was following the deer tracks, he had been following mine. Even allowing for the fact that I'm a city boy, I felt incredibly stupid. Still, I had been moving the entire time and somehow he had closed the distance between us. I turned my head slowly, all the time waiting for a bullet to strike me in the head. When I completed the near one-hundred-eighty-degree turn, I spotted my adversary who most certainly did not come from a former Soviet republic.

I'd never been this close to a bear, nor had I ever wanted to. If the bear felt the same way I did, it didn't show it since it was only twenty yards away, was looking right at me, and was edging my direction. The animal let out something between a snort and growl while never taking its eyes off me. Thinking back to my vast experience of a two-day camping trip, I remembered my dad saying that it was impossible to outrun a bear and that they would sometimes bluff a charge to get the opponent to back down. Of course, I also recalled my father telling me that bears hibernated in the winter, but apparently this one didn't get the goddamn memo. Less than an hour ago, I had been coaxing my legs to run so I could get some exercise and clear my head. Now here I was begging my legs not to run when that's all they wanted to do.

As slowly as I could, I took a step away from the black bear. My back was still to the threat, and my head was craned around so I could see what might be coming. Suddenly the bear charged two strides, which covered most of the distance between us. It stopped as quickly as it had pounced, and I knew then it was bluffing a charge. Miraculously, I didn't run and instead took another molasses stride while turning my head slightly in what I hoped was a look of submission. The beast breathed heavily as I let my feet glide over the snow as fast as I dared to move. The sizable animal, which with my expert eye I had gauged to be somewhere between big and damn big, finally turned its head away while occasionally glancing back at me. When I crested a hill and was out of the bear's sight, I let my legs fulfill their wish by running a good half-mile. The entire time I ran, I thanked my father—may he rest in peace—for imparting to me his irrefutable wisdom. How Laura Nightly had not ended up pregnant in the back of my parent's Buick would have to remain a mystery to me for the rest of my life.

The deer path I had been following took me to another creek, or maybe it was the same one saw earlier. Following it, I eventually reached a few houses at the edge of town. Relief and apprehension took turns filling me as got closer to civilization. Knowing that the Lithuanian would be expecting me to return to Washaway, I ran back and forth between houses and buildings as I made my way into the heart of the municipality.

Covered in mud, bark, needles, and blood I caught a few odd looks from townspeople as I sprinted to the front of the police station. In a hurry to get off the street, I pulled the door hard. Locked. That's the thing about small town departments. There's no guarantee that all the officers won't be attending to other duties, rather than manning a desk in the station.

Keeping a close eye for any hostile movement on the street, I ran back to the inn and rushed up the stairs. The door to my room was still locked. I dug into a small pocket in my running pants and was relieved to find that I still had the key. I pressed the key into the lock and turned it slowly, remembering that everyone, including my Lithuanian friend, knew where I was staying. The door creaked as I pushed it open and moved to the side. The room was empty and nothing appeared to have been touched. I closed and locked the door behind me, rushed over to the bed stand and reassembled and loaded my pistol before grabbing my phone. My call to Colby went straight to voice mail and I tried to sound as calm as possible as I left a message asking her to call me ASAP.

Taking the gun into the bathroom with me, I jumped in a shower that was nowhere near warm enough, and did my best to clean my new assortment of cuts and scrapes. As I toweled off, both sides of my ribcage ached and I discovered new injuries as I redressed in my outfit from earlier in the day. I sat on the edge of the bed and thought about the attack. Since nobody—including me—had known where I was going to go for a run, I had to assume the Lithuanian had simply stumbled upon me while driving one of the few roads leading into town. Good luck for him, bad luck for me. I also had to assume he found out I was in Washaway Township thanks to the newspaper article and would have no difficulty finding the inn. His problem would be staying out of sight. He had to know he would stand out in this area and once Colby got the word out that he was a person of interest, the locals would be quick to report any sightings. He would have to lay low, then hit me quick before anyone laid eyes on him. Given how close the guy's first shot came to my head, he had some real talent. Given how close my head had come to being pierced by that bullet, I had a real problem.

I took the steps down to the lobby and Maddox stood up from behind the front desk and smiled.

"I heard you run through the lobby, but you were up the stairs before I could walk out here," he said. "Do you need anything in your room?"

I told him I didn't, but warned him that the man who wanted me dead was in town. I gave him a description and Maddox gave me a mysterious grin.

Pointing somewhere under the desk, the old man said, "I'm locked and loaded. Let him come." He squinted and moved his head to see one side of my face. "Did he do that to you? You look like your face has been in a demolition derby."

"Do they still have those?"

"Demolition derbies? They sure do!" he said proudly. "The county fair has a big one every year. In fact, they have a derby where they use old school buses. You should see those things slam into each other."

With one hand, I felt the new cuts on my face and said, "Well, some of these scrapes are from running through bushes and trees. I had a run-in with a bear."

Maddox's eyebrows raised and he asked, "Was it a boar?"

I hadn't noticed before that he was hard of hearing, but I raised my voice and said, "It was a bear."

"But was it a boar?" he asked again.

I had no idea if those pig-looking animals with tusks could

be dangerous, but I felt it was totally irrelevant to this conversation.

More loudly and slowly I said, "It...was...a...bear!"

Maddox appeared frustrated, but then a smile stretched across his face.

"Trevor," he said in a calm, kindly tone. "A male bear is called a boar."

I don't blush, but if I did, this would have been the time. My ignorance of everything rural was becoming a problem on so many levels. Maddox was watching me and seemed to be enjoying my growing embarrassment.

I was about to concede my incredible naiveté, but realized the absurdity of the question he'd asked.

"I didn't reach between his legs to check, Maddox."

"Are you sure?" He grinned. "I hear you like to do that type of thing when you meet others."

I felt my jaw clench. "God, does everybody in this town find out about every little thing?"

Maddox sat back down in his chair, picked up a newspaper, and acted as if he was reading. As innocently as he could, he said, "I guess if you know the German fella's U-Boat is a *little thing* then your hand must have really spent some time down there."

I heard him try to stifle a cackle as I headed out on foot in search of a place to get some food. Nick's Diner appeared to be the closest option so I seated myself in a lonesome corner. A waitress showed up and I noticed she didn't even bother to wear a name tag. *No need in this town.* She noticed my injuries, but didn't say anything. With a mixture of politeness and briskness, she took my order for a sandwich and brought me some coffee. The drink warmed me as I pressed buttons on my phone.

"Detective Vinson," said the voice on the other end of the phone.

I took another sip of coffee before I said, "I think you can simply say 'Vinson.' Your legend knows no bounds."

"How are things going out there in the sticks?"

"Still snowy."

"Have you solved the case yet?" he asked.

I rolled my eyes. "I've only been here a day and a half and the case is a year old."

"But the legend of Trevor Galloway knows no bounds," he mocked.

I glanced up and noticed the other patrons in the diner were keeping an eye on the grim stranger talking into his phone. Apparently, they didn't get a lot of outsiders in this place. I ignored the stares and lowered my voice.

"Hey, do you know anyone with the Department of Defense?"

"What part? DCIS, NCIS, Army CID, Air Force OSI? DOD is a monster."

"I'd start with someone in the Army, but I'm not sure."

He asked, "What are you looking for?"

"I'd like to get as much info as possible on a few people. Two of them, Seth and David Wrangle, were definitely in the Army."

I heard him flip papers and rattle a cup in search of a pen.

"And the other ones?"

"Linda and Jaden Fredrick. I'm not certain if they were in any branch at all, but Linda certainly came across as military. Her wristwatch was in military time and there was something about the way she talked."

"What do you mean?"

I thought back to the way Linda Fredrick fired off quick

sentences and kept the verbiage to a minimum. It sounded like...radio traffic.

"She sounded like a cop," I said.

"Interesting," he said in his baritone voice. "I'll check with Army CID and the Military Police. What's the deal up there? Any leads?"

I ran through the facts of the case as I knew them and asked his opinion. Contrary to what I told Seth Wrangle, I really do listen to the opinions of my friends—if I agree with them.

I waited for him to say something wise and prophetic, but all he spouted out was, "Biathlon? People do that in this country?"

"They do."

Silence stretched over the connection before he asked, "Is it as difficult as it looks?"

I searched for a comparison that would make sense to my friend who looked like he could be either a MMA fighter or a terror in the NFL.

"Imagine running for two miles at a breakneck pace then stopping to thread a needle perfectly five times in a row. Five targets. And if you miss, there is a substantial penalty. Then, you have to repeat the entire exercise."

My friend contemplated this and decided, "I'd need a lot of bandages for my fingers."

"I appreciate the help," I said.

I went silent, uncertain how to say the next part.

Chase picked up on this and asked, "What is it?"

"The Lithuanian is here."

It was his turn to be silent.

"I'm going to alert the locals and I'm sure they will notify the surrounding jurisdictions, so he'll probably get picked up quickly."

"How do you know he's out there?"

"I saw him driving."

"Where was he heading?"

"My knees."

"That's not good," Chase said.

"Thanks, Captain Obvious."

"It's Detective Obvious to you."

I downed some more coffee then asked, "Hey, did you know that a male bear is called a boar?"

"Of course. Why?"

"One chased me," I told him.

There was a period of dead air and I knew what my friend was thinking.

"Trevor," he said. "Are you still on solid ground?"

Not this. Not now.

"Yes," I said as confidently as I could.

He asked, "How many witnesses were there?"

"To the bear chasing me?" I asked, but I knew what he meant.

"To any of it. To the Lithuanian trying to run you down. To the bear. You know…"

"He's here," I said solemnly. The waitress approached to refill my coffee. I spoke into the phone. "Just call me if you get something from your Army or DOD contacts, okay?"

I clicked off the phone and swallowed hard. Vinson had good intentions, but I didn't have time for self-doubt. Doubt creates hesitation and hesitation gets you killed. I was making enough enemies in this place and I wasn't about to make my own mind one of them.

CHAPTER 11

I did my best to appear congenial and nonthreatening to the waitress when she brought my lunch, but she wasn't having it and retreated behind the counter. As I ate, I thought about my next steps. Colby was talking to Brady Mason and I knew she would speak to Susan Lanskard about Peter's illness as well. I had to trust she would be able to navigate the treacherous waters between her status as Susan's lover and her position as a cop. I wondered how hard she would push Brady Mason. I had little doubt he knew something about his employer's cancer.

Strangely, the excitement from the past couple of hours had calmed some of the background noise in my head. My thoughts were still swirling, but none of them involved putting a needle in my arm. Sitting at the wobbly table in a Washaway Township diner, I let my eyes blur and tried to imagine the scene on the day Lanskard was shot.

My breathing deepened and the tables around me faded into an amorphous cloud. The gray tile floor went powdery white and my skin chilled. Before long, I was standing beside Brady Mason as he tried to prod his employer inside. The clean country air had to have been a nice change from what was recycled through the ventilation system on Lanskard's plane. He'd been down south and was returning to tranquil fields layered with fresh snow. Who wouldn't pause to savoir the scent of the season? Why wouldn't a man who was dying of cancer stop to listen to the sounds of winter? It's that special sense of stillness that gives a man the feeling that his life is shrouded in cotton. Mason had to know it was likely Lanskard's last winter. Is that why he didn't push harder to get the man inside?

As I stood on a remembered landscape made present by my mind, I examined the tycoon while he pleasantly toyed around with his guard. His face went to the sky and he let the flakes fall and melt the way men live and die. I saw his line of vision return to the horizon while he smiled. Then I saw his head explode with pink and red. His eyes went blank and his deceased form became dead weight that dropped to the earth like a sandbag. Mason, a professional, drew his weapon and pointed it in the direction of the shot. The rest of the security detail, hearing the shot and subsequent radio traffic, went into response mode and scoured the grounds for a killer who left little trace other than tripping the alarm twice. Then...nothing. Not one clue, other than a lone shell casing.

But that wasn't right.

My eyes came back into focus and the noises of the diner returned to my consciousness. *Mason's team is a protection detail, not a police force*, I told myself. I'd had enough conversations with Secret Service agents to know that the first rule of protection is *Maximum to the protectee, minimum to the problem.* Unless the news that Lanskard was dead was the very first thing Mason had transmitted on the radio, there would have been a delay while the rest of the detail rushed *toward* Lanskard—not away from him. How long was that delay? Thirty seconds? One minute? Could Letterman have misremembered his response time to the area of the alarm activation? In a panicked situation like that, he may not even remember turning the ATV back toward the house before hearing Lanskard was dead.

If anyone associated with the biathlon camp was involved, I only had a couple more days to sniff around before the events wrapped up. Seth Wrangle had told me there were only two events being held during the week—a 10K competition tomorrow and a relay the next day. Again, I got the feeling I was on the verge of a breakthrough but the feeling faded as my phone rang. The number on the caller ID told me it was Colby.

"Have you talked to Brady Mason yet?" I asked.

"I did and he knew about Peter's cancer. He says he kept his mouth shut because he didn't want to tarnish Peter's reputation, such as it was, and he didn't want Susan to know her father might have killed himself."

"Susan confirmed she didn't know?"

"She had no idea," said Colby.

"Are you still at the house?" I asked.

"I just pulled away."

"Can you come back into town? Something's happened and I need to get you up to speed."

"Something with the case?"

"Not this case," I said. "Something that followed me here."

"I'm on the way. I'll pick you up at the inn."

"Okay. In the meantime, be on the lookout for a tan Chevy sedan. I didn't get the plates. It's being driven by a white male with long black hair."

"Who is he?"

"I'll fill you in when you get here."

I ended the call, finished my lunch, and became cognizant of all eyes being on my scratched up face as I headed to the door. Staying aware of my surroundings, I made my way back to the inn and went into the lobby to stay warm. Glancing over to the front desk, I didn't see Maddox. His newspaper was still on his desk and it occurred to me I should take a look at it to make sure I wasn't mentioned again. As I approached the desk and picked up the paper, I saw a crumpled body lying in a heap. Blood was covering the man's face and hands.

"Damn it!" I yelled as I rushed around the desk.

Maddox wheezed as I turned him over and he managed to say, "I'm sorry. I had my back to the room and he must have hit me from behind. I wanted to grab my rifle, but he was too fast. I think he went up to your room searching for you, but I heard him leave a few minutes ago."

"Don't worry about that now," I said while snatching my phone and dialing Colby.

Colby answered and I told her Maddox was hurt seriously. She advised me she was two minutes away and that she would get an ambulance dispatched.

Maddox tried to spit blood between swollen lips and said, "He liked it."

"What?" I asked.

"He liked it. I never got a look at him, but I could tell. Don't ask me how I know, but I know. He really liked hurting me. You have evil on your trail, son."

"Don't worry about that now," I said again.

"His voice was raspy," Maddox added. "But I could understand him. He said he could have killed me, but he wanted me to tell you something."

"It's okay," I said softly.

"Your eyes," said Maddox. "He's coming for your eyes."

"Don't try to talk."

"I never saw him. He was so fast," he whispered. "Like a phantom."

I propped Maddox's head up on my leg and heard Colby's car slide to a stop out front. Rage boiled up in my chest. Rage I hadn't felt in a long time. Rage I had never wanted to feel again.

What had I said to Vinson yesterday? *No job, no wife, no kids, no rush?* That's right.

No badge either.

No rules.

I repeated Maddox's words in my head. *Like a phantom.*

Another fucking ghost.

Well, I knew one specter I was going to exorcise personally.

CHAPTER 12

"You killed this guy's cousin?" Colby asked as we sat in the waiting room. The ride to the hospital had taken way too long and I was wondering how Maddox had faired during the ambulance ride.

"I did," I said, answering Colby's question.

"If this guy is such a cold-blooded killer, why leave Maddox alive?"

"He wanted Maddox to give me a message."

"Which was?" asked Colby.

"He wants something from me."

"Does he want money? Information? Anything you can give him to leave you alone?"

"He wants my eyes."

Colby sat back in her impossibly uncomfortable waiting room chair and said, "I see."

I gave her a look.

She reddened and said, "I didn't mean it that way. It's not funny."

"I guess not."

"Why your eyes?"

I tried leaning back in the chair and my ribs screamed. "Would you prefer he take some other parts? My heart perhaps?"

Colby smiled and said, "You don't have a heart, remember? No, I mean the eyes...that's pretty specific."

I shrugged and realized my shoulders were conspiring with my ribs to make me miserable. "It's his thing. I've been told he has a reputation for taking the eyes of those who he really dislikes. He simply kills the others."

Colby shifted the metal armrest out of her back and rubbed her eyes. "I've put out a BOLO based on your description of him. It went out all over this part of the state, so every trooper passing a rest area and every sheriff's deputy making a traffic stop within a hundred miles of here will be looking for this guy."

I shook my head and discovered my neck was a co-conspirator in inducing pain. I was starting to feel ganged up on.

"He's still close," I said. "He walked into an inn in the middle of town and didn't hesitate to beat a man nearly to death. Then, he took the time to search the building to see if I was there. I don't think he's wandered off too far. He's motivated."

"Come on, Trevor," the chief said. "It's a long-haired Lithuanian guy in a tan Chevy. This isn't the most diverse area in the state. He'll turn up."

"I'm sure he ditched the car by now."

"We're monitoring reports of stolen cars. He'll grab one from a public lot or dealership and we'll have a bead on him."

I thought about that for a second and I felt sick as I realized The Lithuanian's next move.

"He's going to take a car from someone and kill the owner."

"How could you possibly know that?"

"Dead people don't report their cars stolen. And people who live alone and don't go out much won't be missed for a day or two. You should probably do your best to keep tabs on any elderly citizens who stay inside a lot and wouldn't be missed for a while."

"Please tell me you're joking," she said in a muted voice.

"He's probably already done it. You may have a body or two waiting to be discovered in some isolated farm house."

Colby turned white. "Jesus, Trevor. Our departments aren't prepared for someone like this guy, are we?"

I didn't answer. I didn't have to.

A doctor approached and we stood as she began speaking. Maddox was in bad shape, but he'd live. Apparently, the old man was awake and already badgering the medical staff about going home. Colby talked to the doctor some more as I walked away and found the nearest restroom. After I finished vomiting, I emerged and the physician seemed to appraise the damage to my face.

"You look like you've taken a beating too," she said, looking the scratches and bruises my face had gathered during my earlier adventure. "What happened to you?"

A sociopath whose cousin I killed in Pittsburgh tried to run me over and shot at me right before I got chased through the woods by a boar—which, by the way—is what you call a bear that has testicles.

"I fell during a run," I said.

"Have you been checked out?" the doctor asked.

"I'm fine," I said, noticing her name tag said R. Westerly, M.D. "But thank you."

"Are you sure you aren't overdosing?" asked Dr. Westerly who was attractive and appeared to be ten years younger than me, which is to say we were probably the same age.

What the hell? Did I have *addict* stenciled across my forehead?

I managed to stutter, "Excuse me?"

She smiled and said, "Are you overdosing on testosterone? It's a common diagnosis around here. A man gets his hand caught in a tractor engine and he says, 'It's just a scratch.' Another man falls off a cell phone tower and determines his concussion is no more than 'getting his bell rung.' Of course, we see most of you guys later after you pass out driving or piss blood."

"I didn't fall off a cell phone tower," I promised her. "And I've never touched a tractor."

She looked me up and down and said, "Yeah, you don't look local. But testosterone overdoses can happen anywhere."

"I'll be careful to watch out for the signs," I said.

"Uh-huh," she said skeptically. "Did I see you grimace in pain when you stood up a minute ago?"

"I was just stretching my face."

"You're funny."

"I'm not," I said. "Just ask around."

The doctor turned to Colby who confirmed my claim by stating, "He's really not."

"Well if your pain gets any worse or if you experience any dizziness or nausea, come back in and we'll check you out."

"I will," I said, knowing I wouldn't.

Colby and I watched the doctor walk away. When I turned to Colby, she was starting at me and seemed to be beaming.

"Ready to go, Casanova?" she said playfully. It was the first time I had heard her use anything close to that tone.

"What are you talking about?"

"She was obviously flirting with you and, although I don't know you well, I think you may have enjoyed it."

I opened my mouth, closed it, and drew upon my years of experience in talking myself out of uncomfortable situations by carefully choosing my next words.

"Shut up," I said.

"Sure thing, heartbreaker."

We walked out of the hospital, which wasn't actually in Washaway, but rather some other unmemorable township, borough, or whatever. The sunlight bouncing off the snow was blinding and I shielded my eyes. I suddenly felt exposed by walking through the middle of the parking lot with my vision impaired.

When we reached her car and got in, Colby asked, "What now? We can't just sit around and wait for this guy to attack again."

"We work the case," I said somewhat absently. Part of my mind was wondering about the "R" on Dr. Westerly's name tag. Rachael? Rene? Rebecca?

"I've got a deputy at the inn checking for prints," she said. "But if he doesn't find anything there isn't much of a case."

"Not that case. The Lanskard case."

"Are you serious?"

I found it fascinating how everybody kept commenting on my serious expression, yet kept asking me if I was serious.

"We only have a couple of days and then the Wrangles, the Fredricks, and most of the competitors hit the road."

I suddenly realized I needed to ask Colby about another biathlete.

"Do you know a guy named Markus Faust?"

Colby's expression told me she did and that her opinion was not a favorable one.

"What's his deal?" I asked.

"He's the stereotypical hotshot athlete who thinks he's God's gift to women. He's even hit on me a couple of time when we've run into each other in town."

"He's not aware that he's not your...type?" I asked.

"It's not a huge secret that I'm a lesbian, so he knows. In fact, once he told me that my problem was that I've been surrounded by American men for too long and if I gave a German man a chance, I'd never want to be with a woman again."

"Subtle."

"Why are you asking about him? His race times are good, but not quite as good as Seth's."

"You mean you didn't hear what happened?" I asked. Apparently the chief of police didn't get all of the town gossip after all.

"No, I've been a bit busy," she replied. "What don't I know?"

"We met at the Red Barn Tavern. He introduced himself and it went downhill from there."

"That sounds like him. He's a pain in the ass, but probably harmless."

"He said he was around last year when the murder occurred."

Colby nodded and said, "He was questioned like everyone else. I didn't personally talk to him, but one of the state guys did. His alibi was nearly as weak as the others. He claimed he was testing his skis on the course at the time of the shooting. A couple of people thought they might have seen him, but they couldn't swear it was Faust. Are you thinking he might be involved?"

I said, "I don't know. He certainly doesn't want me looking around. He played it off like he was concerned I was going to target Seth, but I think he might have just been trying to deter me."

"Do you want to go talk to him?" asked Colby as she started the car.

"Why not? I would imagine he's out at The Camp right now. If nothing else, it will give him another chance to convince you to change teams."

She gave me a playful glare, but then it turned serious. "You have worked with a homosexual before, right? I mean, you know being gay isn't actually a choice?"

"Nope," I said. "I distinctly remember sitting in my fourth-grade classroom when I was ten years old. The teacher was droning on about the pilgrims or something but I was contemplating deeper life issues. I weighed the potential consequences of being gay or straight. Right then and there I said, 'You know what...I'm going to be straight.' From that point on, I made sure that I was only attracted to women."

I looked at Colby who had her mouth open in shock and I added, "You mean it didn't happen that way for you? You don't remember when you chose to be gay?"

It took her a few beats before she laughed and said, "You're a jerk."

"I'm just getting you warmed up for Faust."

As we left the hospital grounds, I did something I hadn't done in a while. I said a silent prayer. I prayed that Earl Maddox wasn't going to pay the ultimate price for me killing a Pittsburgh drug dealer who, I was starting to admit deep down, didn't have to die.

CHAPTER 13

"Everyone is at the starting area. The event is scheduled to begin in a few minutes," informed Gracie the talkative receptionist. "Markus Faust is always a favorite to win the ten-K. I'm sure he's already out there."

Gracie gave us directions to the starting line and Colby and I walked a path of snow that had been crushed under dozens of boots. We followed both the receptionist's directions and the sound of a voice booming over a speaker until we found a clearing filled with biathletes. The competitors, both men and women, appeared to be lining up in waves for the start and were swaying and gyrating with adrenaline. Seth Wrangle was standing on a wooden platform, giving last minute instructions over the bullhorn. Near the front of the first wave of biathletes, I spotted Faust adjusting his headband and goggles. His face turned grim when he saw us approach.

Colby said, "Mr. Faust, when you finish up with the race, we'd like to talk to you."

The cockiness I had witnessed in the tavern was gone as he said, "If it is about the other night, I apologize. I can be... difficult at times. I do not blame Mr. Galloway for grabbing my balls."

Colby gave me a stunned look which I tried to ignore when I said, "It's not about that. We just have some questions about the Lanskard murder. Find us after you finish the race. We'll be hanging out around the finish line."

Faust removed his goggles and made a show of adjusting the strap, but I noticed him glance to his left. Linda and Jaden Fredrick stood side-by-side not more than twenty feet away from us. They were both geared up for the race and were taking positions in the first wave of the start. However, as opposed to the rest of the athletes who were fixated on their gear and Seth's verbal instructions, there was no doubt the Fredricks were entirely focused on us.

Faust became aware of the attention from his colleagues and did his best to rediscover his arrogant smile. In a loud voice, he said, "I will be easy to find. I will be the first one crossing the finish line. Then, I will have plenty of time to tell you to go to hell. Now, you should clear out of here. I heard you had an accident on this course on a previous visit. We would not want you to get run over again."

Again, Colby gave me the *what the hell have you not been telling me* look, but I simply jerked my head toward an area off the course and we walked away from Faust.

"Did someone try to run you over with a car out here too?" asked Colby as we made our way down a path running parallel to the course.

"Not yet," I answered. I looked up at a nearby hill and said, "They won't be finishing up for a while. Let's go up there to get a vantage point. I'd like to see some of the race."

"Are you sure? It's freezing out here and that leather coat doesn't look like the warmest thing in the world."

"I'll be fine," I said. "If I start to freeze we'll just cut open a tauntaun."

"What?"

"A tauntaun. Star Wars. *The Empire Strikes Back.* The frozen planet Hoth."

Colby's eyes registered nothing.

"Damn, I miss the eighties," I said under my breath as we began to climb. "I was just a kid, but I still miss those days."

"Are you sure you aren't still there?" she asked.

"Things were simpler back then," I said. "Our enemies belonged to specific countries; our police forces weren't presumed to be racist; and our rock stars simply wanted to get laid and do cocaine. Somehow it all made sense."

Colby snickered, "Are you about to lean back in a rocking chair and yell at some kids to get off your lawn?"

Touché.

Colby said, "But I get what you're saying about the racism part."

I looked at her questioningly and said, "Really? This isn't the most multicultural area in the country. Do you run into those accusations a lot?"

"Sure," she said. "I can't tell you how many times I've pulled a car over at two o'clock in the morning, walked up to the driver's side window, and been told by the driver that I pulled him over because he's black, Asian, Hispanic, or whatever."

"And how do you respond?"

She said, "I always ask the driver if he knew what I looked like before I walked up to the window and of course they don't. Then, I point out that I couldn't have seen him until he saw me. Usually, that does the trick."

"I did something similar when I was on patrol."

"It does get old," Colby admitted. "It's tough to not get mad about being called a racist for simply doing your job."

I thought about that for a minute and then said, "You know, I don't think that was the part that made me mad."

"What was?"

"What made me angry were the times I could tell the accusation was based on some questionable interaction the person had had with another officer. It didn't happen too often, but every once in while a driver would tell me a story about being profiled or targeted by the police because of race and I would think there really was something to it. Those were the times I wanted to find that other cop and punch him in the face. All it takes is one bad cop out of a hundred to tarnish the reputation of the entire profession."

Colby nodded and we searched the hillside for someplace where we could see a good portion of the course. The two of us dusted snow off some fallen trees and sat.

"Did you notice Faust's demeanor change when he saw the Fredricks watching us?" asked Colby."

"I did."

"Why do you think that happened?"

I took in a breath and said, "Either he's posturing because he's defending friends who he thinks have been unduly placed under suspicion or he knows something. I'm still bothered by the fact he approached me in the tavern. The reason I thought we should talk to him is there was no real benefit for him to approach me at all. He had to know a former narcotics detective wasn't going to scurry away because of a veiled threat. In fact, he had to know that by discouraging me from looking into Seth, he was only going to drive me in that direction. No, it was almost like he was proving himself to somebody. It was like he wanted to tell me something, but make a public demonstration that he wasn't going to help out with any investigation."

"Who would he be proving himself to?" Colby asked. "Did you see the Fredricks or Wrangles in the tavern?"

I shook my head. "No, but I'm sure several people observed our conversation. The bartender certainly noticed. Given the story about me that was in the newspaper the day after I arrived, I get the impression that both words and bullets travel about the same speed around here."

We sat quietly and watched as the race began. The first wave of competitors began moving out and picked up speed as they headed down a straightaway. From our position on the hill, Colby and I could see about a quarter of the course, but segments were hidden by the rolling hills and towering evergreens. I tried to focus on Faust and the Fredricks, but soon had difficulty tracking them in the gaggle of snowsuits and skis.

Two more waves of biathletes surged forward over the next few minutes and Colby and I talked about the amazing amount of endurance even the amateurs must possess. A few moments later, we heard the crack of gunfire as the first wave arrived at the shooting range. We turned to our right and in the distance we could see some of the competitors filing into shooting stations. Eventually, I picked out Faust and the Fredricks who appeared to have arrived at the range at nearly the same time. Each of them fired five shots and since all three skied past the penalty area, I assumed none had missed any targets. Colby and I marveled at the marksmanship as the lead competitors vanished into a portion of the course invisible to us.

We watched the second and third waves enter and leave the shooting range and it became evident that the better competitors had been placed in the first wave. The penalty loop became a popular location and the speed of the skiers was noticeably slower. When the last person from the final wave left the range, we decided to make our way toward the finish line near the entrance to The Camp.

We were taking our time plodding through a patch of trees and rocks when Colby said, "It's Raylene, by the way."

"Excuse me?"

"Dr. Westerly's first name. I'm sure you were wondering what the 'R' stood for. It's Raylene."

I rolled my eyes and said, "The thought hadn't crossed my mind."

Colby continued, "She has a good reputation as a doctor. She's divorced, has no kids, and I think she went to medical school at Johns Hopkins.

"Okay."

"Did you go to college?"

"Yes," I replied before looking off into the hills.

"Since you like to share so much, would you care to expound?" she asked in a tone of friendly frustration.

I turned toward her and said, "I started at VMI, but ended up getting a degree in sociology from the University of Dayton."

"VMI? Virginia Military Institute? You don't seem like the military type."

"They would agree with you."

"You leaving there wouldn't have anything to do with your temper, would it?"

I looked at her inquisitively. "What temper?"

Colby grinned and said, "Oh, you play it stoic and analytical, but you have a hell of a temper."

"How do you figure?" I asked, really wanting to know.

"Well, forgetting the fact that I'm pretty sure you tried to castrate Faust in a bar and you flipped off a man who was trying to run you over, you have a quiet rage about you. You're the type of man who can yell without raising his voice and can threaten with nothing more than a hard blink."

I thought about that before saying, "I have no idea what that means."

"It's behind your eyes. I saw it flash at the inn when we were waiting on the ambulance for Maddox. Wherever your mind went, it was an extremely dark place. Then, I saw it again when you recounted The Lithuanian trying to kill you. Not to mention you've killed before, although I know you had no choice since the guy was coming at you with a knife."

"Right," I said.

Enough, I thought.

"Do you have any hobbies?" she asked. "Something that helps you work out your anger?"

"Yeah, I run," I said more abruptly than I intended.

Colby hesitated and I thought she was going to change the subject, but she said, "Do you have any hobbies where people don't try to turn you into a speed bump?"

I inhaled deeply and said, "I'll look into getting one."

"How did you end up as a cop in Pittsburgh? Are you from there?"

Jesus. It appeared my naturally off-putting demeanor wasn't deterring questions anymore.

"No. I grew up in Atlanta," I said. "I had a cousin who lived in Pittsburgh and he couldn't say enough nice things about the city. By the time I finished college, I had decided to go into law enforcement and Pittsburgh PD was hiring."

"I don't hear a Southern accent," she said.

"It faded away over the years."

Hoping to get off the topic of me, I asked, "What about you?"

"I grew up here, went to school at Lock Haven University, and joined the department immediately after graduation. I never wanted to do anything else but this. Of course, I never intended to be the chief of police, but things just worked out that way."

"Well, it turned out good for everyone involved," I said, realizing I was coming dangerously close to giving a compliment while having an actual conversation, neither of which is really my thing. "And you certainly aren't like Chief Caskins."

"I hope not."

"Do you think seeing how badly the former chief handled your brother's death influenced your decision to become a cop?"

"I don't know," she said. "But I knew I couldn't turn down the promotion."

I nodded my understanding.

"So are you going to call her?" she asked.

Oh good, this again.

"I assume you mean Dr. Westerly," I said. "She lives here. I live in Pittsburgh. That doesn't seem very practical."

"I think you should at least take her to dinner before you leave town. You never know how those things will work out."

"Maybe I should resolve some things first. I'm no expert, but it seems eye-plucking Lithuanian assassins can be kind of a third wheel on first dates."

"That's a valid point."

Colby estimated that the first wave would be finishing soon, so we stood and made our way down the hill. We emerged from evergreens and approached the finish line where tables were lined with bottles of water, sports drinks, coffee, and bagels. Several onlookers were gathered around the finish and I assumed most of them were friends and family of the competitors. Colby and I helped ourselves to bagels and coffee and waited for the first athletes to finish the race. Colby called the hospital to check on Maddox. She was told he was improving steadily and the tough bastard was bouncing back like a man thirty years his junior.

"It looks the first finisher is coming around the curve," Colby said.

I looked up and saw someone madly sticking ski poles into the frozen ground. I squinted and determined it wasn't Faust or either of the Fredricks. The bearded man powered through the

finish and collapsed in exhaustion. He was immediately surrounded by some of the onlookers who offered congratulations
while helping him remove his skis and get upright. Another
skier, a man in an orange ski suit then three more I didn't recognize came across the line. The next finisher was a woman, but it
wasn't Linda Fredrick.

Several minutes went by before Jaden Fredrick appeared on
the final stretch. He crossed the line wearing a disappointed
expression. Three more weary athletes finished and then Linda
Fredrick completed the course with an expression similar to her
husband's. Time passed and still no sign of Markus Faust.

"I guess he's not as good as he thought," said Colby with no
small measure of satisfaction. "I suppose I'll have to remain a
lesbian for one more day."

I watched Jaden Fredrick who was lingering behind the
tables. Then my gaze found his wife who, while only a few
yards away, didn't look at or speak to Jaden.

"Something's wrong," I said. "They aren't talking."

"Probably a marital spat," Colby suggested. "Maybe one of
them cutoff the other on the course or something."

Two more competitors came in and neither was the smiling
German. I spotted Seth and David Wrangle side by side. They
had made their way to our location and were milling around
and shaking hands with various people.

"Come on," I said to Colby and made a beeline for Seth.

I came up behind the former Olympian and touched him on
the shoulder. He turned and smiled until he saw Colby beside
me.

"Mr. Galloway, I don't mind you being here, but I don't
have anything to say to the chief and I'd like her to leave."

"Have you seen Faust?" I asked.

"I told you," Seth said while waiving a hand in the air. "He doesn't mean any trouble. I talked to him about him giving you a hard time and I don't think he'll be bothering you anymore."

"Have you seen him since the start of the race?" I asked.

Seth looked around. "I'm sure he's here somewhere. He would have finished a while ago."

"He didn't," Colby said. "We've watched everyone who crossed the line."

Seth's smile morphed into an expression of real concern and he grabbed his radio and asked if any of the volunteers around the course had seen Faust. The response was nothing but dead air.

"He must have gotten injured," said Seth while trying to appear less worried. "We're already sweeping the course. He was probably talking trash to someone before the race and now he's limped off somewhere feeling embarrassed."

"Has he done that before?" I asked.

Seth didn't answer. He walked away and rounded up several event volunteers. I couldn't hear the conversation, but I knew he was explaining the situation and sending them out on the course. In less than a minute, the volunteers were organizing a search party that would comb the course and the surrounding wooded area.

I turned to David Wrangle who was still standing beside us and said, "Has anything like this happened before during a competition? Have you lost track of a competitor?"

David wasn't looking any better than the first time we met. His face was pale and he had bags under his eyes.

"Not on this course," he said. "Since everyone is competing in multiple waves over a nothing more than a deformed oval, there aren't many moments at the beginning of a race where a skier will be out of sight of everyone. By the end, everything thins out quite a bit, but nobody goes off the radar for too long.

It's possible Markus simply flew off the course on one of the turns and is banged up a bit. The volunteers will find him."

David was right. Eight minutes later, Markus Faust was found over the edge of an elevated turn in the course. Danielle D. Trimble, a seventeen-year-old junior at West Haven High School, noticed what she thought was the barrel of a biathlon rifle sticking out from behind a snowdrift. She walked down off the course and found Markus Faust non-responsive with his head resting on the ground. When the kid tried to wake Faust by turning him over, she saw that his head wasn't lying comfortably on snow as she had first thought. Instead, Faust's head appeared to have smashed against a jagged rock. From nearly a half-mile away over hills draped with insulating snow, the teenager's screams had no trouble reaching my ears.

CHAPTER 14

The motto "no man left behind" is possibly the most recognizable of any phrase used by the U.S. military. An odd reversal of that philosophy was evident at The Camp on the day Markus Faust's body was strapped onto a gurney and taken by the medical examiner. Even an hour after the dead man had departed, it seemed no member of the shocked crowd wished to leave the grounds. I had little doubt many of his fellow competitors disliked Faust, but that made no difference. He was a biathlete. He was one of them. Now he was gone and dozens remained, absorbing an absence laced with empathy. Each athlete, new and experienced alike, mourned while silently repeating the same phrase: "It could have been me."

The downhill turn where Faust lost traction and sailed off the course had the reputation for being the fastest part of the track. This wasn't the first time someone had taken a misstep and gone over that edge, but it was the first time the result was more than minor bumps and bruises.

"Bad luck," a man in his thirties was saying.

"Freak accident," mumbled a redheaded woman with an even redder nose.

"Murder," Colby said after finishing a discussion with one of her deputies and a state police investigator. She leaned against the external wall of the main office building where I had been taking shelter from the wind. "There's no way this was an accident. It's too coincidental."

I didn't say anything.

"There isn't anything at the scene to indicate it was a homicide, but I'm not buying this. Are you?"

I shook my head and watched the zombie crowd march about, not knowing what to do with itself. Each member of the swarm seemed to ache with the need for connection. People from all walks of life, with little else other than biathlon in common, were consoling each other like they were close relatives. The camaraderie was something to behold. It made me wonder if they were predisposed to bonding like this in the face of tragedy, how difficult would it be to pry secrets from their lips?

My eyes blurred and my surroundings were muted. I breathed slowly and let myself fall out of the present and into a different setting. I can submerge myself into my blur-outs fairly quickly, but this time I plunged deep into the waters as if an anchor was tied to my neck. In no time at all, my mind had placed me on that curve, watching Faust approach. He tucked the poles under his arms and bent at the waist to reduce the air resistance. But he wasn't alone. Another competitor was right beside him and then...

The boundaries of my imagination swiftly changed and trees and hills became walls. The walls were close on each side. The sudden transformation felt disorienting and constricting. A tunnel? No. A hallway. A gold number on a hotel room door. A knife. None of it in Centre County. Someplace else. Somewhere I'd seen before. Somewhere—

"Trevor?" Colby said.

I brought my eyes up and looked at the crowd before turning to her. I felt nauseated, confused, and unfocused. This isn't how these moments work for me. My mind takes me to one place at a time and never waivers. Never. Until now.

Colby spoke my name again and followed it up with something I didn't catch.

"What?" I asked.

"You aren't thinking Faust happened to fly off the course and hit his head on the one rock within twenty yards, are you?"

"No," I said. "The Fredricks killed him." I pulled up the collar of my coat to shield against a frigid gust of wind and explained what I had been thinking while Colby and the other cops examined the area around Faust's body. "They teamed up to knock him off the course and then they went over the edge and slammed his head on that rock. One of them probably helped restrain Faust while the other grabbed his head and smashed his skull."

I had said all of this with some measure of confidence, but something seemed off when I heard the words aloud.

"That's not right," I said, shaking my head. My disrupted blur-out was throwing me off my game. But the hallway in my vision...I knew exactly where room that was. I knew exactly what was waiting behind that door.

"Well?" Colby prompted.

I took a breath and gathered my thoughts. I tried to formulate a theory again. "Faust saw the way the Fredricks were eyeballing him when he was talking to us. He would have had his guard up if both of them closed in on him during the race."

Colby nodded and said, "I was thinking Jaden Fredrick kept up with Faust and knocked him over the edge when nobody was in sight. Then, Linda Fredrick comes from behind and heads down to where Faust has crashed. Maybe Faust thinks Linda is there to help him, or maybe just threaten him, but somehow she gets him in a position where she can kill him. Jaden finished slower than normal and Linda completed the race long after her husband. The timing would fit, although it's anything but conclusive."

Colby's theory made much more sense than my original thought and I told her so.

"Are you okay? You don't look well," she asked.

"Yes," I replied as I thought about the area where Faust's body had been found.

Remembering the rock found under Faust's skull was not huge, I asked, "Is it possible Linda picked up the rock and hit him with it?"

"No," Colby said. "After all the photos were taken and the evidence guys were finished looking through the area—which the volunteers had trampled through, by the way—I had the forensic tech collect the rock for evidence. He had a hell of a time pulling it out of the frozen ground."

"Okay."

"Yeah," she said as she scanned the crowd, which was reluctantly starting to drift toward the camp exit. She seemed to hesitate, but finally said, "There is another variable involved."

"What's that?"

Colby took a breath and said, "Since Seth hates me, I kept my distance and had a deputy talk to him. After the start of the race, Seth made his way along the course in a way similar to us. He was out of sight and alone for part of the race. It's possible—"

"Sally," I interrupted, realizing I had never addressed her by her first name.

"I know," she said. "People think I'm fixated on Seth, but I'm simply saying he may have had an opportunity. It's even possible he colluded with the Fredricks and all three of them killed Faust."

"Why?" I said to myself as much as Colby. "Why Faust?"

We didn't say anything for a full minute, each of us rolling multiple hypotheses around in our heads.

"Let's go see his hotel room," I suggested.

"Sure," Colby said. "But it's highly unlikely we'll find anything connecting Faust to Peter Lanskard?"

I shrugged and said, "We need to figure out if Faust was really a player in all of this or if we're simply going snow blind. I don't know if he was involved in the Lanskard murder, but for some reason he chose to put himself on the radar when he approached me at the tavern. He was obviously uncomfortable when Linda and Jaden saw him talking to us and then he overcompensated to show he wasn't happy that we wanted to talk to him today. I assume he has a car here somewhere. We'll need to search it, but his hotel room is the main thing. If I learned anything from years of working narcotics, it's that people inevitably hide things where they sleep."

"I'll have my deputy check on the car situation. I'll have it searched here, towed, and then fully inventoried. Let's go in the office and ask Gracie where Faust was staying."

"I'll wait here," I said, which drew a look from Colby who could see I was freezing. "Gracie is...chatty," I explained.

Colby sighed and walked inside to get the info we needed. I leaned back against the wall and watched the procession go past. It was a sluggish river of somber faces that hours ago were electric with excitement. The column snaked along in front of me. Each person was different. Each person was the same. In my periphery, I noticed one point on the far side of the column. One pixel on the sorrowful screen was stationary. I blinked against the wind and a face came into focus. The man's mouth was turned down, his jaw set in anger. His eyes, directed at me, were unbreakable stones. Seth Wrangle stood his ground for several seconds and showed no indication of wanting to go anywhere at all. The wind crossed my face and I blinked hard. In that split second, he inexplicably melted into the masses.

The hotel was your typical cookie-cutter, continental breakfast serving, interstate pit stop. After a brief conversation with the desk clerk, Colby walked away from the counter with a key to Faust's room. A slow hydraulic elevator took us to the third floor and I needlessly knocked on the door of room 316 before Colby inserted the card key and watched a light beside the handle go from red to green.

On the bed lay clothing that Faust presumably tossed around when deciding how to dress for the competition. I looked down at an assortment of magazines spread out on a chair and glanced at the covers. Pictures filled with skis, motorcycles, fast cars, guns, and other high-adrenaline interests. I picked up an issue of *Speed Bike Monthly* and four subscription cards fell out onto the floor, which worsened my mood. I hate those things.

"How do you want to go about searching the room?" Colby asked as she handed me a pair of latex gloves.

"Let's start along the walls. I'll go clockwise high and you go counterclockwise low, then we'll switch. After that, let's check the bed, closet, and bathroom."

Colby grinned and said, "This isn't a narcotics case. I don't think we need to be that systematic."

I nodded and said, "Force of habit. I've seen people stash drugs in places you wouldn't believe. I'm still used to checking every square inch of a room and then some."

She shrugged, put on her own gloves, and started the search process the way I had suggested. I joined in by moving along the walls and removing the bad hotel artwork and checking each print by carefully removing the backing. Colby took her time going through each drawer while I inspected a television that for me was chest high. In the old days, people loved to hide contraband inside televisions, but flatscreen models like they had in this hotel had changed the game. Still, I checked all the screws and panels and didn't see any evidence of tampering.

Colby had made her way to the desk and was examining the furniture's backing as I balanced on a chair and used a pocket knife to turn tiny screws that secured the air vents near the ceiling. I put the covers back on the vents and scooted it to another spot so I could pull apart the smoke detector. Finding nothing but a generic 9-volt battery, I reassembled the detector and climbed back down. Colby finished her search and we switched roles and I re-searched the lower portions of the wall, including electrical outlets, the dresser, and a mini-fridge that held nothing but two bottles of a reddish sports drink. Colby stayed busy repeating my work in the higher areas.

The bed was next and it took little time to strip it down and discover there was nothing of interest to find. The closet was equally as useless. Faust's suitcase was olive green and well-used. I unzipped each compartment and felt along the lining until I found a seam. Knowing the owner would not be using the suitcase again, I ripped out the lining and searched for any additional areas where items could be concealed. I tossed the case aside with some frustration after I probed the last corner. If Faust had been keeping anything incriminating in his room, he'd taken steps to hide it well.

Colby took another look in the closet and shifted the ironing board enough so the legs started to drop with a shrill squeaking noise. Colby and I both flinched at the unpleasant sound, and I moved into the bathroom, which would be easy to search. In less than a minute, I had searched the toilet tank, the tiles around the sink, and the shower and tub. The lighting was supplied by bare bulbs surrounding a mirror, so there were no fixtures to check. The air vent was near the floor and I could see it was empty. Feeling defeated, I sat on the side of the tub and shook my head.

Out of the corner of my eye I saw something on the edge of the white tub. It was barely visible, but it was there. From a certain angle, I could see the faintest trace of a smudge, but not a randomly shaped one. This smudge had distinct lines and dimensions and as I leaned in closer, I knew what it was. The triangle was from the tread of a shoe and I knew exactly why it was there. I looked at the ceiling above the tub for the hiding place that had to be there. I'd seen this a hundred times before—cocaine hidden in a drop ceiling; meth squirreled away in a bathroom fan; weed in the shower curtain rod. But none of that applied here. The ceiling was hard, smooth, and absent of any lights, fans, or ledges. The curtain rod was solidly bolted into the walls and traces of rust around the edges told me it hadn't been removed in years. The bathroom seemed to be a brick wall at the end of a short tunnel of hope. I stood balancing on the edge of the tub and steadied myself by gently pulling on the thick shower curtain.

"It looks like this is a dead end," I observed while beginning to step down to the floor. "Maybe your deputy found—"

Another piercing squeal came from the other room as Colby replaced the ironing board.

She said, "For as long as I live, I'll never understand why ironing board legs have to make that sound. Whoever designs these things has to be completely deaf. I'd rather my clothes be wrinkled than unfurl one of these damn contraptions.

I cut short my descent and left one foot hanging in mid-air. I've stayed in my share of hotels over the years and many times I chose not to use the ironing board. Instead, I would steam my clothes in the bathroom by sending scalding hot water through the shower. Sometimes I hung my clothes as best I could on the back of the door or off the shower curtain rod, but occasionally there was a better option.

Slowly, I put both feet back on the tub and moved the shower curtain to the side. There it was. Several inches under where the curtain was attached to the wall was a steel disk that had been obscured by the cumbersome curtain. There was a small hole in the center of the disk where there was supposed to be a cord, which one could pull out across the length of the tub to use as a clothes line. Supposed to be.

The center of the hole was empty and there were slight traces of damage around the disk. Two screws held the device in place and I easily removed those with my knife. The disk popped off and revealed a hole six inches across but twice as deep. I squeezed my hand through and reached around to see what I could find. The tips of my fingers found something plastic and the object swung back and forth. I allowed my digits to climb the object until I found the clothes line I knew had been re-appropriated for other purposes. I carefully unwound the cord from a pipe and pulled the clear plastic storage bag out of the wall as Colby entered the room.

"Unbelievable," she said.

I opened the bag and withdrew the black leather case. I set the case on the edge of the tub, pulled the zipper, and let each side fall open.

"I don't think he's a closet diabetic," Colby said, staring at the syringe, spare needles, and alcohol swabs.

"I'm sure he wasn't," I said.

"I don't understand," Colby said. "Faust was a junkie? Then, where are the drugs?"

I thought about Faust and his ego—his confidence; his pride.

"He wasn't a junkie," I decided.

"Then what the hell is this all about?"

"Performance," I said. "Faust was all about performance and I think he was enhancing his."

Colby leaned back on the counter surrounding the sink. "He was using steroids?"

"Maybe," I said. "But if he was involved in any serious competitions, then I'm guessing the athletes are tested for steroids."

"But there are ways to beat the test, right? I mean football players do it all the time. Can't the test be beaten by switching urine or something?"

I didn't answer her. In my mind I was still searching the room. I was retracing every step where drugs could be hidden. Performance enhancing drugs were different than cocaine and meth. Sometimes they were stored in vials. They could be legally prescribed and given out to patients. They were often…liquid.

"Idiot," I said.

Colby furrowed her brow. "Excuse me?"

I walked out of the bathroom and to the mini-fridge. I grabbed the two sports drink bottles and returned to the sink where Colby was looking rather unhappy.

"Not you. I mean me. I'm the idiot," I said as I poured out the contents of one bottle, using my fingers as a sieve.

As the last of the fluid from one of the bottles bled into the drain, a small glass vial fell into my hand. I repeated the process with the other bottle and another unlabeled vial materialized. I set the vials beside the sink and shook my head at my own stupidity.

"Steroids are easy to test for and have gone out of style. My guess is this is HGH—human growth hormone—which is more difficult to detect without a blood test. I'm not expert when it comes to HGH, but I bet it needs to be refrigerated. At first I didn't notice the sports drink bottles had been opened before and I didn't have the right mindset for what we might be looking for. Sorry about that."

Colby picked up one of the vials. "Faust went through a lot of trouble to hide this stuff. Even if housekeeping found a syringe and vials in his room, they probably would have assumed he was injecting insulin.

"I'm sure Faust didn't want to take any risks. I think he really does respect Seth and doesn't want to disappoint him. I've only had one real conversation with Seth, but I don't think he would have any tolerance for a cheater in his sport. In fact, I think Seth would cut all ties with Faust, ban him from The Camp, and probably spread the word that Faust was doping."

"Are you ruling Seth out as a murder suspect?" Colby asked.

I gave her a questioning look. "Of course not. Why would you say that?"

"So you think Seth may be capable of murdering his neighbor, but would never condone a cheater?"

"Sounds about right."

"You aren't quite right in the head," Colby observed.

"Yeah, it's hard to believe I'm single," I muttered. "I'm quite a catch."

CHAPTER 15

A waitress took our orders, left, returned with plates and bread, then pranced away to a table surrounded by a family of four. We had bagged Faust's drugs and accompanying paraphernalia and transported them to Colby's station where she packed everything to be shipped to the state lab for analysis. Colby's deputy had not found anything of value in Faust's car and there were no other developments from The Camp, which was still being treated as a potential crime scene. It was getting late by the time Colby finished the lab paperwork, so Colby insisted she drive me to an "authentic" Italian restaurant, which turned out to be an Olive Garden near I-80.

"Have you ever been married?" Colby asked while chewing on a breadstick.

I hesitated and took a sip of water, once again feeling uncomfortable with what I assumed would be the topic of this conversation, namely me.

"Why? Are you thinking about switching teams?"

"In your dreams," she said. "Even if I were straight, you have more baggage than an airport conveyor belt."

I nodded, looked down, and stroked the table. When I glanced up, I could see Colby was concerned she had crossed a line and somehow hurt my feelings. She hadn't meant the jab to be mean-spirited, but as is the case with most cops, the words had come out with an unintended edge. I knew the comment wasn't malicious, but as is my standard operating procedure, I had failed to give the appropriate smile that would have let her know that I hadn't taken any offense. To put her mind at ease, I decided to answer her original question.

"I'm divorced. It was finished a lifetime ago."

Her face relaxed and she asked, "What happened?"

"The job," I replied reflexively.

She snorted, "That's crap. That's what everyone in this line of work says when they get divorced. It's such a copout, if you'll excuse the pun."

I gnawed on my breadstick and avoided eye contact.

"Come on, Trevor."

I put the bread down and took a drink. On one hand, I liked the way Colby didn't mind calling me out on a weak answer to a complex question. On the other hand, I'm not exactly extroverted, and I dislike talking about myself, much less my rocky relationships.

"It was my fault," I said. "I wasn't very considerate to her needs and my stubbornness eventually pushed her away. Meredith grew up a quiet, reserved girl in a small town in Michigan and had only come to Pittsburgh to finish her doctorate at Carnegie Mellon. She always thought we'd leave Pittsburgh and she'd teach at some small college in the middle of nowhere, and we would live out our days on fifty acres of rural land under a canopy of stars.

"You didn't want that?"

"I guess not. When it was clear I was happy in the city, liked the people around me, and enjoyed the convenience of having our—well, my friends within a few miles reach, the dream started to come apart. I reacted in the worst way possible, by trying to change her and make her be more sociable. I constantly made plans for us to have dinner with friends; I dragged her to parties; I pressed her to go to sporting events with my social group. I was pushy."

The family of four at the table nearest to us was deep into their meal. A man and his wife were talking to a boy who looked to be about four years old while his younger sister sat in a high chair, tapping a plastic spoon against a tray. They looked to be completely in their element, each playing the role for which they were intended. It looked...right.

"So, she left you?" Colby said, bringing my attention back to our own table.

I nodded.

We sat quietly for several seconds and I watched condensation slide down my glass of ice water. The toddler's tapping stopped and I looked up to see she had found some item of food interesting enough to distract her from her musical pursuit. I was forty-three years old. Forty-three and single. Forty-three with no prospects of ever having a family. My heart sank as I thought of mistakes made and time wasted. Now, here I was a former cop, former junkie, and not really a *current* anything. I watched the parents at the next table dote on their children who doubtlessly filled their hearts with joy. Something deep inside of me ached. I was forty-three, alone, and—

The piercing noise from across the table drew a few brief glances from the scattering of customers in near proximity. Colby was holding a napkin up to her mouth and her eyes were watering. I started to rise, hoping I remembered how to administer the Heimlich maneuver, but I realized my dinner partner wasn't choking. She was laughing. She was laughing hysterically to the point of crying.

Confused, I sat back down.

"Wait..." she said, trying to catch her breath. "Wait...you're telling me that your ex-wife divorced you because—Trevor 'Tin Man' Galloway—was too outgoing and social?" With that, she broke into another bought of laughter.

"Okay, okay—"

She held up a hand and struggled to take in more oxygen. "That's classic!" More laughter. "What was the listed reason for the divorce?" More laughter. "Mr. Galloway was too damn perky? Was it...*irreconcilable bubbliness?*"

Now, she was laughing so hard I thought she might pass out. Truth be told, I was kind of hoping she would.

"Very funny." The family of four were now looking at us and smiling, for no other reason than the joviality was contagious.

"Jesus, Trevor. If *you* were too outgoing for her, are you sure she wanted a little house on the prairie? Maybe a morgue was more her speed!" With that, a new round of laughter burst out of my dinner partner wearing the conspicuous police uniform who wasn't even trying to be subtle.

I glanced over to the family intending to give an apologetic nod, but found the girl in the highchair was now pointing directly at me and laughing so hard spaghetti was falling out of her sauce-covered mouth.

Ridicule by toddler. Awesome.

"Are you enjoying this?"

Still laughing, she managed to say, "I am. I really, really am."

I rubbed my forehead and smiled, inwardly of course.

"I'm glad I can be a source of entertainment for you."

She was calming down and said, "I'm sorry. It's a bit hard to imagine you as Mr. Personality."

While I wouldn't say I was *that* personable before my abduction and subsequent addiction, I had to admit I had changed a great deal. These days, nobody was inviting me to join any social circles. There's a sad truth you recognize after you fall.

When you start hating yourself, others tend to follow your lead.

Blessedly, our food arrived and the rest of the meal was filled with conversation that was meaningful only insofar as it distracted us from the investigation that we would resume working in the morning. Working a case is like distance running. You can't go all-out, all the time. You have to pace yourself, know your limitations, and focus on your strengths.

The answers won't come to you if you are constantly reaching for them. It's like trying to remember a forgotten song title. If you push it aside and move on with your life, even if it's only for a few minutes, the answer will come to you. We didn't have any brilliant revelations by the end of the meal, but we felt more like regular people and less like cops. The fact I wasn't a cop anymore but had never stopped feeling like one, was another issue altogether.

"You should stay in a hotel up here tonight," Colby suggested, while we split the check.

"I'm going back to the inn."

With frustration, Colby asked, "Are you suicidal? Every cop in the Central Pennsylvania is looking for your Lithuanian friend, but if he's a good as you say then there is no reason for you to make it easy for him."

"Actually, there is. First, I'm sure whoever you have working midnight shift will come by whenever possible. With the police roaming the town and me being on my guard, maybe we'll get lucky and trap this guy before he hurts anyone else."

"Or," Colby said, "You check into a hotel up here and this guy gets frustrated when he's not able to find you and he leaves town."

I shook my head. "He's not leaving until he's sure I'm gone."

"Or dead," she added, helpfully.

The debate continued on the way to Colby's car and most of

the drive back to Washaway. Colby eventually relented and called ahead to have a deputy enter and search the inn before we got there. As we entered the town, it somehow looked darker, colder, and more desolate than the previous evening. A flurry turned into a genuine snowfall and I wondered how high the snowbanks along the street could get.

The gruff-looking deputy, whose silver name plate read "G. Lemons," was waiting out front when we arrived. He gave me a hard glare as we got out of the car and I had to assume he viewed me as a disruptive force in what was typically a predictable town.

"All clear?" Colby asked Deputy Lemons.

"Yep," he murmured while sinking his hands deeper into his pockets.

"Everything was still locked up?"

Lemons handed Colby a key and replied, "Front and back. The locks are shit and could be picked by any twelve-year-old with a paper clip, but there's no sign of tampering and there's nobody in there."

It hadn't occurred to me that with Maddox in the hospital, and I being his only guest, the building had been left open and unattended when Colby and I followed the ambulance to the hospital. Apparently, Lemons or one of the other deputies had come by, found a key, and locked up. Colby turned and put the key in my hand.

"Since you're competing for 'Dumbass of the Year' and insisting on staying here, you'll need this."

"Thanks, I think."

"Give me a call if you see or hear anything unusual," she said.

"I will. Don't worry, the floors are so thin in this place, nobody is going to get the drop on me."

She nodded to Lemons and said, "Gene will be roaming around town until morning and then I'll be back out on the road. Gene, why don't you give Trevor your cell number in case he needs to contact you directly?"

The deputy's hands somehow descended further and the corners of his mouth did the same. Reluctantly, he rattled off seven digits.

"Eight-one-four area code?" I asked.

The man glared at me as if I were insane for even thinking someone would move here and keep a cell number that had an old area code. His expression couldn't have been any more condescending if I would have asked him if he wanted tickets to a Lady Gaga concert.

"Yes. Eight-one-four," he sniffed before dipping his head and shuffling to his patrol car.

When he pulled away, I said, "I guess you just need to get to know him."

Colby smirked, shook her head. "That would only make it worse."

I locked the door behind me and made it halfway to the stairs before I remembered something. My footfalls echoed through the lobby as I circled behind the front desk and knelt to see if Maddox's old rifle was still there. Sure enough, there was a soft rifle case lying on a shelf under the desk. I wrapped my hand around the handle, set the case on top of the desk, and worked the zipper. Inside was something I hadn't expected.

"Jesus, Maddox," I uttered.

Knowing I would have my pistol with me in my room and not knowing when Maddox would be back and looking for the rifle case, I decided to toss it onto the bed in his room rather than leave it out in the lobby. I closed the case and navigated the hallway that led to three doors that were all standing open, presumably from Deputy Lemons searching the inn.

Maddox's bedroom was every bit as plain as my guest room. Other than a few family photos and some Navy memorabilia, his accommodations were simple and clean. His neatly-made bed squeaked when I placed the rifle case on top of the brown comforter. I felt a tinge of the rage Colby had referred to bubble up inside of me as I thought of Maddox becoming a victim in a battle that started in an urban maze far from this place. I closed the bedroom door and did my best to leave my fury in Maddox's humble quarters.

When I reached the top of the stairs, I saw the door to my room had been left open as well. Since I had the key to my room, I wondered how the deputy had opened the door. I dug into my pockets and pulled out both my room key and the key to the front—and presumably the back—doors of the inn. I held them together and examined the contours. Identical. Maddox obviously believed in simplicity.

As I walked through the room, I tried to take note if Deputy Lemons had snooped around through any of my belongings, but nothing seemed to have been touched. Even though I had the entire inn to myself, I opted to close and lock the door to my room. For now, it seemed better to have as many barriers between me and a crazy Lithuanian assassin as possible.

After a quick shower, I lay in bed staring at the darkened ceiling and tried to regain my focus on the Lanskard murder. The possible drug angle added new dimensions to the case. What if Faust wasn't the only one involved with performance enhancing drugs? What if HGH was a dirty little secret in a very tight-knit biathlon community? How difficult could it be to set up a far-reaching distribution network when you have a core group of athletes traveling the world to attend various competitions? Perhaps Faust was the tip of the iceberg and the entire camp is really nothing more than a hub for dealers and customers. Was I wrong about Seth's morals? Maybe that's why Seth delayed selling the property. Did Peter Lanskard stumble across some damning evidence and try to blackmail Seth into selling at a low price? Was a professional hitter brought in to protect a drug operation? What if...

Damn it, Galloway. Stop that. I turned on my side and slid my hand underneath my pillow. One of the hardest things to do after you work in a particular part of law enforcement is to stop seeing everything in terms of your experiences. If you worked property crimes, you see everything in terms of street value. If you investigated fraud, you try to figure out the con. If you're like me and spent years neck-deep in narcotics, then everything becomes drug-related. I tried to steer my thoughts elsewhere, but wasn't entirely successful.

With my left hand I pulled the covers up a little higher and let the warmth open the door to sleep. I adjusted my other hand further under the pillow and kept whittling away at the drug angle. My eyes got heavy as the facts sorted and slowed in my head.

Faust didn't have enough HGH to be a dealer. But the fact he was a user could still be important. He could owe someone money. Could be blackmailed into...into killing? Into silence? Why did he approach me in the tavern? He had to know I couldn't be scared off. His warning would only serve to feed the fire and send me...

I tucked my right hand further under the pillow for one final adjustment before the day faded to black. Underneath the bulky feather pillow, the tip of one of my fingers grazed a hard edge of my gun.

What if Faust wasn't trying to redirect me? What if he was trying to direct me? Faust wanted to drive me toward...

My tired eyes crept open as I realized I was onto something. In the dim light coming from the window I caught the silhouetted shape of my watch and my gun on the bed stand. My train of thought continued.

Faust acted as if there to protect Seth and David, but what if—

My gun?

If my gun was on the bed stand, then what the hell was under my pillow? I jerked up, withdrew my hand from underneath the pillow and clicked on the lamp next to the bed. The tips of the fingers on my right hand were a shade of red I had seen too many times. With my left hand I lifted the pillow into the air and tossed it to the foot of the bed.

"Christ!" I yelled as I saw a pair of icy blue eyes staring back at me. Between the eyeballs lay four fingers in near-perfect alignment, with the tips pointing toward the headboard. Jagged pieces of bone protruded from the areas where the digits had been cut off. Blood was busy soaking into the sheets, creating a hue of pink, crimson, and sienna. Irrationally, I snatched my gun from the bed stand and swept the room. After a few minutes, I slowed my breaths and retrieved my phone from the dresser. Colby answered and I could tell she had been asleep.

"You need to get over here right now," I said.

"Oh, my God. Did the Lithuanian show up? Are you okay? Is he still there?"

"He's not here," I said. "But he left me another message."

TARGET 4
UNSTABLE

CHAPTER 16

The once-empty lobby was filling up with officers and investigators from most of the neighboring jurisdictions as well as state troopers who could double as skyscrapers. I have never been able to figure out where state police departments find their troopers. They must send recruiters to college basketball and football games to pick out the players who will look the most intimidating in a hat.

Colby and I sat on a couch and she took notes as I recounted discovering the body parts in my bed. The inn's front door opened and a humbled Deputy Lemons squeezed past the troopers. He moved toward the couch and handed Colby and I cups of coffee.

"I don't know what to say," the deputy muttered. "I'm sorry. The place was locked up tight when I got here and I checked to make sure there weren't any people in the building. It never occurred to me to check for...parts of people."

"It's not your fault," Colby said. "You said it yourself—the locks are worthless and can be easily picked. I'm sure they can be locked back as easily as they're unlocked. There was no way of knowing he'd been here."

There was a silence and I pulled out of my thoughts and realized Lemons was looking at me for some sort of reassurance. I couldn't think of anything else to say, so I echoed Colby.

"It's not your fault."

This seemed to comfort him and he told his chief that he

would head upstairs to see if any of the cops up there needed his assistance.

Lemons started to leave, but turned back and said, "I don't get it."

"You don't get what?" Colby asked.

Lemons hesitated and seemed to be uncomfortable asking someone else for answers.

"I mean, you told me about the sick thing with the eyes. You told us he wants to take Mr. Galloway's eyes on account of him killing the man's cousin. But I don't understand the fingers. Why lay fingers between the eyeballs? And why four fingers, but not the thumb?"

I rotated my hand in a circle and watched the coffee in my cup swirl around.

I didn't look up as I spoke. "It means he wants an eye *for* an eye. An eye, four fingers, and another eye. It's a game to him."

Lemons mumbled, "Damnedest thing I've ever heard of. Damnedest," before he once again excused himself.

I sipped the coffee and my stomach churned. The lack of sleep and stress was having a negative impact on my ability to think clearly and, to make matters worse I was starting to feel the itch of the needle again. I drank more bad coffee as much to punish myself as to stay alert. After a minute, I realized Colby was looking at me. Seeing I was checked out, she got to her feet, moved to center of the room and asked for everyone's attention.

"Since you are all here, it's a good time to update everyone as to the situation. I know how word spreads through this area, as evidenced by all of you being here right now, and I don't want any crazy rumors making their way into the newspapers. We're looking at a situation unlike anything we've experienced in this part of the state."

I surveyed some of the older faces in the room, wondering if there would disagreement—some recalling of a "war story" from long ago. Nothing of the sort. The expressions were granite.

Colby gestured to me and continued, "By now, all of you know of Mr. Galloway over there. I had requested his assistance with the Lanskard homicide investigation. What happened here tonight has *nothing* to do with that case. I want to emphasize that point. This is a completely separate issue that originated from one of his old cases.

"We had already put out a BOLO on the man referred to as The Lithuanian. He was last seen driving a tan Chevy Impala, but likely has changed vehicles by now. In fact, unless he swiped another car from someplace and took a chance it would be reported stolen, it's possible the body parts left upstairs belong to the actual owner of whatever he's driving at this moment."

Since Colby was inexperienced with major violent crimes, I wondered how she would handle the flow of information. No matter what Colby said, the rumor mill would be working around the clock. I had no reason to believe the public would be calling in to the police with anything useful, but some information would need to be held back to filter out false leads from legitimate facts. To Colby's credit, she seemed to understand the situation and did all she could to keep a lid on things.

"I'm sure you all heard that some body parts were found in Mr. Galloway's room and I'm not naïve enough to think that information won't get out on the streets. However, I am asking...I'm demanding no other information about the crime scene be released. Do not discuss which body parts were found and do not discuss exactly where they were found."

I held my breath, afraid she was about to mention the specific arrangement and intended meaning of the fingers and eyes. While some of the cops would certainly have heard by now, there was no reason to get the room buzzing with questions and speculation. I knew that if the arrangement became a major subject of discussion, there was potential for gossip to get out of control. The whole thing would become a kids' game of "telephone" where one kid whispers a sentence into another kid's ear and the process is repeated down a line of children. By the end of this telephone line, the words "eyes on each side of four fingers, warning of revenge" would turn into "eyes and thighs and fingers, on the morning of the tenth." I needn't worry, because Colby breezed over the topic and didn't discuss the gruesome message that had been delivered.

"Needless to say, your supervisors will agree with me that this is the top priority for each or our departments right now. A sociopath like this doesn't care about jurisdictional lines and he has already demonstrated that collateral damage is none of his concern. We have to find this guy and find him fast."

She looked around the room with a finger raised and appeared to be counting.

"I see at least five local jurisdictions and the State Police represented here. With the wide net we can cast, there's no reason we can't have this bastard in custody by tomorrow evening. Right now we need to start pulling over every car we see on the roads, assuming we have cause to do so. If a car has a headlight out, pull it over. If you see an expired sticker on the windshield, pull it over. If you notice a vehicle has bald tires, pull it over. Try to get consent to search trunks as well. We aren't going to violate anybody's rights, but let's do our best to lock this place down and smoke him out."

She stopped talking and in all my years the only time I've seen a collection of cops that quiet was at a funeral. These guys were not Pittsburgh or Philly cops who dealt with violence on a daily basis and had learned to dissociate. These cops were different. These cops had their front door kicked in and an intruder spilled blood in their own living room. They weren't disassociating one bit. They were ready and they were pissed. And if they were pissed, their coworkers who were spread out all over Central Pennsylvania were pissed. My weariness lifted a bit and although I no longer carried a badge, I was feeling a sense of pride. I thought, *Okay, you Lithuanian prick. So you're in a gang and you carry weapons. Guess what—our gang is bigger and we've got more weapons.*

Colby never told anyone they were officially dismissed, not that she had really invited most of them in the first place. Pairs of heavy boots trampled out of the crime scene which had already been trampled upon. It didn't matter. This killer wasn't going to be caught with forensics. He was going to be caught with nothing less than a bullet.

When Colby and I were alone, the only sounds remaining were footsteps and muted conversations originating from my room above. The room was being photographed from all angles and dusted for prints. I could imagine an embarrassed Deputy Lemons up there trying to pry up every floorboard and scratching his chin while he contemplated what else he could have missed. I knew it wasn't his fault. What he said was true. He had been looking for a human being, not portions of one. If I had been feeling better, I might have made the effort to console the man. But at the moment, I was exhausted and feeling the itch in my veins. At this rate, there was no way I was going to stay clean much longer. If I could make it until the morning, I might be able to run the curse out of me. However, having nearly been killed on my last run was making me think twice about my fitness routine. A bad situation all around. A runner who can't run is hard to deal with. An ex-junkie runner who can't run is a time bomb. Something in my eyes betrayed my

state of mind, because Colby moved onto the couch beside me
and put her hand on my knee.

"I thought you weren't switching teams," I said, hearing a
tremor in my voice.

"How bad are you hurting?"

"Bad."

"What were you hooked on?"

"Heroin. But right now I'd settle for some Oxy."

She nodded. "That's why you wouldn't let the doctor ex-
amine you at the hospital? You thought you might accept painkillers and that would open the floodgates?"

For some reason, I could no longer meet her eyes.

"Yes," I said. "But I'm also prone to testosterone overdoses,
like Dr. Westerly suggested."

"Raylene," Colby reminded.

"Right."

Colby stood and rolled her head around to stretch her neck
and shoulders. We listened to the sounds of boots on wood and
unintelligible conversations that certainly revolved around spec-
ulating the level of madness needed to commit such an atrocity.
I had no answers. All I had now were the competing desires to
close my eyes and to keep them open. I needed sleep, but I knew
that the moment I closed my eyes, I would see the pair that had
been inches from my face staring up at me. God, I needed a fix.
One evening of the warmth coursing through my veins and I
would be right again. I kicked it before and I could kick it
again.

As if Colby could hear my thoughts, she said, "I'm going to
go see if they finished bagging...everything. Then, you need to
come upstairs and grab whatever clothes you need. You're staying at my place tonight and you aren't getting out of my sight."

Part of me wanted to protest, but then I realized I had

nowhere else to go. If I checked into some hotel off the interstate, I'd be on the road to Harrisburg within the hour. I had no idea where to buy heroin in that city, but I'd sniff it out. For better or worse, I always could.

"Thank you," I said.

Ten minutes later, I had gathered a few items of clothing and my toothbrush and headed out the door with Colby. I'd come back for all my belongings, including my laptop, later. I had a long night ahead of me and, regardless of what The Lithuanian had in store, I still had a case to solve. I was tiptoeing around the edge of an abyss and solving a riddle might help me keep my balance. Well, that or killing the maniac who wanted my eyes.

CHAPTER 17

I was surprised to see a black Audi in Colby's driveway when we pulled up to the house. I had no idea what the township could afford to pay their top cop, but I had a hunch her salary wasn't in the pricey foreign car range. As we walked up to the front door, it opened and Susan Lanskard appeared wearing dark jeans and maroon cardigan. She looked like something out of an L.L. Bean catalogue and the type to drive a new Audi.

"Is it true?" she asked Colby.

"How did you hear about it?"

"Cecil told Stephanie who you know is friends with Brady's wife. She told Brady who filled me in."

Colby nodded as if this made perfect sense. I assumed Brady was her security man Brady Mason, but I had no clue about the rest of the passengers on the Washaway Gossip Express.

"What did you hear?" Colby said as we made our way inside and removed our coats.

Susan recounted the scene from the inn, which was surprisingly close to accurate. Other than the fact she'd heard I'd been left a written note telling me to "Get out of town or lose a finger," the story that had traveled faster than Colby could drive was spot on. However, I knew this was only one of several versions that would be told and mistold over the next few days.

Colby listened to the story Susan had heard and said, "Not all of that is right, but that's the gist of it."

Susan turned to me and said, "Trevor, I'm so sorry we got you involved in this."

For a second I was puzzled, but then I realized she thought the bloody scene in my room was somehow related to the investigation into her father's murder. Colby obviously hadn't had a chance to fill her in on the attempt The Lithuanian had already made on my life.

"It's the other way around," I said while taking a seat on a couch. Susan and Colby sat on a couch opposite from me.

"I brought this psycho into this town—into your lives. For that I'm sorry."

I went on to explain to Susan in general terms how The Lithuanian held a grudge against me and had tracked me to the middle of the state. I was afraid she would ask a lot of questions, but she seemed to be satisfied by a sense of relief at not having caused my latest troubles.

Susan reached over and held Colby's hand. At first, Colby seemed uncomfortable with this, as if it was a breach of professional decorum, but then squeezed her lover's hand and relaxed.

"It's a small town," I said. "Did you two know each other when you were younger."

Susan smiled and glanced at Colby and then back to me. "Not really. My father sent me to a boarding school, so I wasn't around here very often. We didn't meet until my father's death."

I noticed my hands were shaking, so I crossed my arms and tucked them away. I decided the only way I was going to get my mind of a fix was to keep talking.

"Is this considered your permanent address? I mean, do you split time at another location?"

"Honestly, I've been too busy with the company to think about where I'll eventually settle," Susan said. "I never intended to move back here in the first place."

At this, Colby's face tightened and I realized that, as with many couples, the subject of relocation might be a source of stress.

"Were you involved with MRS prior to your father's murder?"

Susan shifted in her seat and Colby's eyes found mine.

"No," Susan said. "As I mentioned before, I was still finishing up at Dartmouth."

"I just didn't know if your father kept you in the loop on business matters. For instance, if he talked to you about trying to buy The Camp because of the Goshen stone deposit."

Susan's posture changed as the atmosphere changed from friendly to something akin to official.

"I was aware he had interest in purchasing the land."

"But you never followed up on it? You never made Seth an offer?"

"Trevor, what are you—" Colby started to interject.

With her free hand, Susan reached over and patted Colby on the forearm. "It's okay," she said. "It's a logical question. That's why I hired you, right?"

I didn't reply.

"I didn't make Seth an offer on the land because I love Sally here," she said, while tilting her head toward Colby.

I was confused and, judging by her expression, so was Colby.

"Sally believes Seth killed my father. I don't know for sure if that's true, but I believe in her instincts enough that there is no way I'm giving one dollar to the man she thinks may be responsible for my father's death. I don't give a damn how profitable the land may be. If there is any chance Seth, or anyone associated with him, killed my father then he gets nothing from me. The hard truth is I can probably live with myself if my father's killer is never caught, but I'd die if I ever found out I'd helped make his murderer a millionaire."

"Fair enough," I said. "I'm sorry I brought it up."

"I understand," she said in a way that made me think she really did. "Perhaps it would put your mind at ease a little more if you understood my vision for the company is much different from my father's."

I wasn't sure it would make one bit of difference, but my hands were shaking and my veins were pulsing, so I asked, "How so?"

She leaned forward and whispered, "Don't tell the shareholders, but I'm a tree-hugging idealist."

"I don't think that's going to jive with the MRS mission statement."

Leaning back, she said, "Exactly. I'm slowly getting us out of the mining and drilling business. I'm going to steer the company into solar and wind energy and help develop more efficient biofuels."

I pondered this and thought about all the environmental activists who protested MRS operations and imagined that protester population transitioning into one of angry, out-of-work coal miners, fracking specialists, and quarry workers.

"You're going to need more security," I said.

Then I realized, she had no security with her.

"If you don't mind me asking, where is Brady Mason? Doesn't he accompany you when you're out, like he did with our father?"

"He insisted on following me down here, but took off once I got inside. He'll come back when I call him."

"You're not staying?" Colby asked.

"Not tonight. I just wanted to check on you. If you get time, swing by the house tomorrow."

Susan Lanskard pulled out a phone and typed out a quick text message. I presumed she was letting Brady Mason know she would be leaving soon and that he needed to head this way if he wished to follow her."

"Why don't you have Brady or your driver take you around?" I asked.

"I like my independence," she said. "Once you start letting other people drive you, you get comfortable with giving up control."

Within five minutes, her phone chimed letting her know her security escort was ready. After giving Colby a quick kiss, Susan Lanskard left the house and left me with hands that continued to tremble.

Three hours of tumultuous sleep was all I managed on Colby's lumpy couch. We had stayed up talking in her living room until four in the morning when she disappeared into her bedroom and I succumbed to enervation. I woke when a snowplow passed by the house and its flashing and rotating yellow lights turned the darkened living room into a sea of shapes and shadows. I watched the lights dance across the ceiling, then fade away into the winter quiet.

My head ached and my hands felt weak and unsure. I told myself I should never have come to this place. I should have stayed in Pittsburgh and refused Chase's request for me to meet Susan Lanskard. I understood the landscape in the city. My footing was solid in an urban environment and I could anticipate the moves of my adversaries. In this rural backdrop, I was nothing more than a distance runner who couldn't gain traction. My usual strengths were negated by an unfamiliar and unforgiving topography. Now, I was being hunted like a game

animal in the middle of nowhere and my feelings of disorient-
tation were as biting as the season.

Everything here seemed upside-down and backwards. A
former cop was the prey, while a criminal was the predator. A
powerful businessman who destroyed the environment was a
victim, while a well-respected Olympian was the police chief's
main suspect. Even the few leads I had generated seemed wrong.
The drugs I found in Faust's room may have been a small component of this case, but something was telling me they weren't
an essential part of the mechanism. Then there was my initial
conversation with Faust, which still didn't make any sense to
me. Several hours ago, I had been onto something in my mind
before reaching under my pillow and finding...that.

What if Faust wasn't trying to steer me away from someone,
but rather *to* someone? He had to know his words could only
make me look harder at Seth and David, but what if he knew
there was nothing there to find? Then, I could end up pursuing
the real killer and clearing the names of his friends. But why not
just point me in the right direction without all the game playing? Why the reverse psychology?

Because of the drugs, I realized.

If the killer knew Faust was doping, then the cocky German
had to expect he would be exposed as a cheat if it got around he
had helped the investigation. By attempting to get me to look in
the right direction while pointing me the wrong way, Faust was
again trying to cheat the system and come away with a clean
image. Maybe, I thought. Possibly, I hoped. In my current state
of weariness and my growing urge to get high, maybe my
thoughts were the only things backwards.

I heard water running somewhere in the house and realized
Colby was waking up. I went into a guest bathroom where
Colby had left some towels and quickly showered in steaming

water. After dressing in my usual garb, I found a can of coffee and a pot in the kitchen and got the process going. I heard a quiet voice and moved toward the kitchen door. I started to push it open to tell Colby I was making coffee, but stopped and stayed out of sight when I heard another voice.

"I'm just saying it's strange," whispered a man.

"You're being ridiculous," Colby said, matching the man's volume.

"Then, why is it nobody can find this guy? How is it nobody has even seen him?"

"Earl Maddox sure as hell saw him," Colby said.

"No, he didn't. He says he never got a look at the attacker. But maybe he did. How do you know Galloway didn't do it and then threatened the old man?" said the voice that I was starting to recognize.

"Come on, Lemons," Colby said in a louder voice. "You know Maddox and he doesn't scare easily."

"Maddox had a gun right next to him when he got assaulted and he never reached for the thing. Why would he let a stranger, especially one that meets the description Galloway has given us, get close to him?"

"Look, this Lithuanian guy tried to hit Galloway with a car and shot at him. Now he's left eyeballs and fingers under the man's pillow. Are you trying to say Galloway is making up this entire thing and he put body parts in his own bed?"

There was a pause before Lemons said, "I'm saying that I checked out the area where Galloway claims he was nearly run down and I didn't find any shell casings or any other evidence of an attack. And let's not forget that nobody has reported any cars stolen or recovered."

Colby started to say something, but Lemons interrupted her.

"There's something else, Chief. Last night, I made a call to a friend of mine who works for Pittsburgh PD. I got him out of bed, but I thought it was important. How much do you really know about Galloway?"

Behind the door, I tensed. The conversation wasn't going in a good direction for me.

"I know a little," Colby said. "And, yes," she continued, anticipating what was coming, "I know he's had some problems."

"Not just problems, Chief. Their Office of Municipal Investigations—that's their internal affairs people—they were looking at him for some serious stuff."

"I know he's had some drug problems," Colby said. "He's been open about that fact. The man worked undercover for years and went through a rough time. It's not all that surprising."

"It's not only the fact he was an addict," Lemons said. "Did you know he was investigated for possibly executing one of the drug dealers who abducted him?"

Colby didn't answer. I held my post behind the door and didn't dare breathe.

"He tracked a man and shot him dead in a hotel room," Lemons said.

"It must have been a clean shoot or Galloway wouldn't be out walking around. That's the thing," Lemons said, lowering his voice again. "Nobody knows for sure. Galloway located the guy, but didn't wait for backup. I mean, he claimed he heard the dealer opening a window and thought he might be getting away. Galloway told investigators that's why he kicked in the door before backup could arrive..."

"But..." Colby said.

"But the whole scene was shady. Galloway claimed the guy had a knife and a knife *was* found at the scene and it *did* have Lukas Derela's—that was the dealer's name—it did have his

177

prints on the handle. But Derela's associates were questioned later and none of them ever remembered seeing him carry that particular knife."

Colby asked, "By 'associates,' I assume you mean his fellow drug dealers? They can't be considered credible and you know that."

"Probably not," Lemons said. "But during a subsequent internal investigation, Galloway admitted he was still using drugs and that he had experienced some blackouts and the occasional hallucination even when he wasn't high. Do you understand? He was *hallucinating* while sober.

There was a pause and I waited for Colby to defend me. Instead, she seemed to wait for more.

Lemons continued. "Galloway was already talking to department shrinks when the shooting occurred, but he had told them whatever they needed to hear so they would sign off on putting him back on duty. He didn't admit to everything until after he killed Derela and he had started questioning his own actions.

"Apparently, Galloway started doubting if he had really heard Derela trying to get out a window and if Derela had even been holding the knife. Galloway told the shrinks he felt he was starting to doubt reality. The next thing anyone knows, Galloway has quietly disappeared from the force and some of the Pittsburgh PD brass pulled some strings to get him a job as an investigator with the DA's office. During that time, these rumors of some mythical Lithuanian assassin start popping up, but nobody knows from where and nothing can be confirmed. Then for some reason, Galloway assaulted a prosecutor and got bounced out of his investigator position. The word is that the whole hit man thing is a bunch of crap and that Galloway has lost his marbles."

"There is no way your friend could know all of this," Colby

said. "The department psychiatrists wouldn't be permitted to talk about any specifics beyond if Galloway was fit for duty."

"I'm simply telling you what I heard. Those may be rumors, but here are some facts. First, nobody except Galloway has seen this mysterious Lithuanian. Maddox is still claiming he can't give a description and that the assailant talked in a raspy, unidentifiable voice. Second, there's no physical evidence that an attempt was made on Galloway's life and no tan Chevy Impalas have been reported stolen or recovered within a hundred miles of here. Third, a set of eyeballs and fingers were found by Galloway in an inn that was locked up with no sign of forced entry. Forth, I saw the look in Galloway's eyes when you two were on the couch in the lobby at the inn. He's hurting and looking to use. He's an addict with a history of psychological issues and it's possible The Lithuanian is something his conscience conjured up all on its own."

I had to admit Lemons was more insightful than I had assumed. I couldn't say I would have come to any different conclusions if I were in his shoes. The coffee pot behind me hissed, and for a minute I thought Colby might come to check behind the kitchen door. However, after a few beats she spoke.

"Do you realize what you are saying?"

"I do."

"If there is no Lithuanian enforcer..." Colby's words trailed off.

"Then a killer just slept under your roof," Lemons said.

I heard feet shuffle and then, ever-so-softly, Colby said, "Okay. Thank you."

The sound of the front door closing made its way to me and I moved away from my listening post and back to the coffee pot. I busied myself grabbing coffee mugs out of a cabinet and pouring two cups. By the time Colby entered the kitchen, I was setting the mugs on a table and doing my best to appear innocent.

I took a seat and said, "I made coffee. I hope you don't mind."

"No, of course not," she said politely while opening the refrigerator and grabbing a carton of milk.

She poured milk into her coffee, pulled up a chair, and slid the carton my way. I could see the internal debate going on inside of her. *Do I confront the potential psychopath, or enjoy my dark roast?* Ultimately, she opted for the coffee and avoided the subject of my mental well-being or lack thereof.

"Did you sleep any?" I asked.

"A little."

The coffee pot gave off one last exacerbated sizzle and we sat enveloped by quiet contemplation and anticipation. A heavy tension filled the room, as often happens when two people are uncomfortable with having more questions than answers. The tension is even worse when each person wonders if the answers would more disturbing than the original questions.

"I don't know where to go from here," Colby said, and for a second I thought she knew I had overheard the conversation in the living room. "The Fredricks aren't going to talk and I doubt Seth and David are feeling cooperative. Faust is dead. By now most of the biathletes are leaving town, either because they aren't competing in any more events or they were spooked by Faust's death." She rubbed her eyes and added, "Not to mention, your other situation."

I noted that my Lithuanian killer had become a *situation*. Killers are real. However, *situations...*

"We've accomplished absolutely nothing other than possibly getting a man murdered." She buried her head in her hands and slowly said, "Absolutely nothing."

The last of the steam drifted off my coffee and for the first time I read the words on the side of the mug. The words, *Centre County Crimestoppers Tip Line* were printed in block letters along with a 1-800 number. A sentence below the phone number stretched around the mug. *Be an eyewitness to a better community.*

I lowered my head and mentally sifted through the ashes of the investigation. When you pushed aside all the speculation and hypothesis, only a few facts remained. Fact one: Peter Lanskard had been killed by a sniper and the sniper went undetected. Fact two: The security employee, Mark Letterman, was the closest thing we had to an eyewitness and he had passed a polygraph last year. How was it possible that he hadn't seen anyone or anything? Fact three: Peter Lanskard was a sick man nearing the end. Fact four: He had a life insurance policy that paid out three million dollars to his daughter Susan. I blurred out and continued to let the stream of information flow past me.

"Hey, are you with me?" Colby asked.

Colby was eyeing me like she thought I might be crazy and delusional. At this point, I couldn't be sure if that particular train of thought wasn't right on track. Had I really seen a figure on the street when I looked out my window that night at the inn? He had simply vanished with the blowing snow the same way Seth had disappeared into the crowd at The Camp. I had seen Seth staring at me, right? It was true I had some serious problems with reality after my ordeal in Pittsburgh, but that Chevy causing me to dive off the country road—a road that nobody knew I was running on—was not a figment of my imagination. Was it? What about the bear? Even my closest friend, Chase Vinson, had let doubt creep into his voice after I told him about the encounter. I had been thinking about a bear bluffing a charge and then the creature had done that very thing. It was a coincidence, right?

"We have two last things to address," I said, ignoring her question about my state of mind. "Mark Letterman is the one individual who was in the vicinity of the shooter. He must have seen something, but doesn't realize it's important. I want to talk to him again."

"Okay," Colby said after taking a sip of her coffee. "I'll call up to the Lanskard house to see if he's on duty." She stood up and pushed her chair back under the table. "What is the second thing?"

"Can you find Lanskard's driver, Jason Leonard?"

"Sure," Colby said. "He drives Susan now, but if he's not needed he'll be at home or somewhere close by. Why?"

"Because he's the wild card everybody keeps forgetting about. If the security detail is trustworthy and they wouldn't have signaled the shooter about Lanskard's approach to the estate, then maybe Leonard somehow signaled the impending arrival."

"I interviewed him at length a year ago." Colby's gaze toward me was icy. "I was meticulous."

Although I had previously explained my wanting to address the case as if it had never been touched before, she was questioning my methods. Normally, I would have interviewed the driver myself, but with the shooter possibly leaving the area in the next twenty-four hours, time was short. This needed to be wrapped up now.

The flicker of anger I saw in Colby's face made me realize she no longer trusted me. The things Deputy Lemons had said had gotten to her and I couldn't do anything to alleviate her concerns. Most everything the man had said was true.

Colby stormed out of the kitchen and returned with a phone

up to her ear. "Hi, Brady, it's Sally Colby. I hate to bother you, but is Mark Letterman working right now? Okay, and is Jason Leonard around? Thanks."

Colby clicked off her phone and turned to me. "Mark Letterman is off-duty and so is Jason Leonard. I know where each of them lives. Brady lives a few miles from the estate, but Mark has a place about fifteen miles away. Who do you want us to go see first? Mark or Brady?"

Her tone confirmed that her attitude toward me was shifting drastically. My participation in this investigation now had a shelf life, and a short one at that. Colby needed some time away from the always personable Tin Man.

I suggested, "Why don't you drop me off at the inn so I can get my car? Then, you can go talk to Jason Leonard and I'll go talk to Letterman."

This idea seemed to appeal to her and her pose softened. She put the phone on the table and picked up her coffee.

"I realize I'm being short-tempered and defensive. Sorry about that. I'm tired and I'm suddenly reliving my failures from the first time this case went unsolved. I'll be okay, we can conduct the interviews together."

I shook my head and said, "No, you go without me. We're running out of time and it makes sense for you to talk to the driver. You know Leonard and have a rapport with them. I can go talk to Letterman since he doesn't seem to care for either of us anyway. We aren't losing any advantage by having me show up since he's already on the defensive regardless of who is asking the questions. Besides," I said. "I'm used to people being abrasive when I talk to them."

Colby said, "No shit," but a smile was creeping across her tired face. "Come on," she said while exiting the kitchen. "I'll take you to your car and give you his address."

I took one last drink of my now-cold coffee and read the words on the mug one more time. *Be an eyewitness to a better community.* "What did you see, Mr. Letterman?" I said quietly. "What did you see?"

CHAPTER 18

Mark Letterman's residence was a secluded two-story, single-family structure located at the end of an extensive gravel drive-way. Due to the ever-present snow on the ground I couldn't actually see much of the gravel, but I could hear some of it clinking off the bottom of my SUV. A pickup truck was parked off to one side and some tire tracks let me know that another car had been here recently. Beside the front porch, a child's sled and a small pair of Spider-Man boots were propped against a wall. Puffs of smoke rose from a chimney and floated into a brightening sky.

I parked behind the pickup and saw a college sticker stretched across the top of the back window. *Virginia Military Institute.* Fantastic. The hulking security operative, who already didn't like me, made it through a school I had been kicked out of due to my temper. I bet Letterman would love to know that little tidbit. Colby had guessed right about anger issues being a problem for me at VMI, but I wasn't going to confirm her suspicions. Besides, that was all in the past and I had mellowed.

Snow dumped into my inadequate shoes as I stepped out of the car. I hadn't made it halfway to the front door before I heard it open. Letterman was wearing beat-up jeans and a thick red and black flannel shirt. He looked a lot like the man on the packaging for the paper towels I buy at the grocery store.

"Hell no! You can't possibly be showing up at my house unannounced," he bellowed while rushing down the porch steps. "This is my home. This is where I live with my wife and son. There is no way you are coming out here to harass me!"

His fists were clenched, which I took to be a bad sign. He was also closing on me rapidly, which I took to be a threatening sign. He had at least thirty pounds of muscle on me, which I took to be a big neon *danger ahead* sign. I held up my hands in a passive gesture.

"I'm not here to harass you and I certainly don't want to disturb your family. You're right, I should have called first. Maybe we can head to a coffee shop or something so we don't bother your wife or kid."

Letterman stopped but kept his fists balled.

"My boy is at school and my wife went to the store. But I still don't have anything else to tell you. I'm tired of having my word doubted about what happened that day."

"I do not doubt your word," I said. "I'm simply thinking you may have seen something important and you don't realize its significance. You said it yourself—you were right there when the shooter escaped. You were positioned between where the shot originated and where the outer perimeter alarm was tripped. There is no way the shooter could have gotten past you..." I paused and tried to say the next part in the nicest possible way. I calmly said, "Unless maybe you didn't respond quite as fast as you told everyone."

"Goddamn it," he said as he took another step in my direction. His face flushed red and he barked, "I've had it with you, Chief Colby, and every cop in this area."

I slowly dug the toe of my left shoe into the snow surrounding my feet and said, "Relax, Mark. We're just talking. We actually have a lot in common. We may have even been together at the same college."

"I've talked enough," he said as he raised a fist and stepped forward to put me within striking distance.

Snapping my left foot forward, I managed to kick a heap of snow into the larger man's eyes. He instinctively raised his hands to his face and I took one long stride and used my right arm to deliver a solid straight punch to his diaphragm. People engaged in hand-to-hand combat often make a mistake by focusing on hitting an opponent in the head. But if you ask any experienced fighter, he'll tell you that he'd rather take ten punches to the head than one good shot to the body.

The human torso contains all sorts of important organs and most of them are protected by little more than thin rib bones. But most importantly, every fighter needs one very important thing to keep fighting: oxygen. If you take your opponent's oxygen, you take your opponent. I took Mark Letterman's oxygen and it was going to take him a while to get it back.

He knelt in the snow and struggled to breathe. I thought now he would calm down and we could talk like adults, then he raised one hand gave me the middle finger. I don't know if it was my racing adrenaline or the fact I had recently conveyed the same sentiment to a real or imagined Lithuanian assassin, but something in me snapped. With my left hand, I grabbed Letterman's right middle finger and snapped it backwards. He yelped, and moved his other hand to his now broken finger and gave me an opening I used to deliver a hard punch to his nose. Yeah, I had certainly mellowed. No doubt.

Letterman fell back in the snow and moaned. I'm not proud that I took another step toward him intending to kick him in the sides until I heard bones crack, but I was stopped by the sound of an approaching car.

"Mark! Mark!" yelled a woman who had jumped out of a green Subaru. I detected an Appalachian dialect when she yelled, "What are you doing? Who are you?" while running our direction. I felt shame overtaking me as the delicate woman held her hands to her face and knelt beside her bleeding spouse. I've always taken a great deal of pride in the fact that I could handle myself better than most in a fight. But seeing this slight, brunette, lady tending to a man she obviously cared about left me feeling hollow at best.

"I'm okay," said Letterman between labored breaths.

The thin woman stood and said, "You son of a bitch!"

She was understandably upset. She'd arrived home to find her loved one on the losing end of a fight with a stranger. The last thing I wanted to do was to further upset this lady who I was sure wanted nothing more than to have a peaceful existence with her nice little family.

I started to speak to the distraught woman. I was formulating an apology of a sort when out of nowhere she landed a right jab to my face, another right jab, and a left hook to my right kidney. I'm not sure what hit me after that, but feet—not mine—were involved and somehow I ended up on the ground in an arm bar. I'd like to say that I didn't hit the woman out of some since of chivalry, but the truth is she simply kicked my ass. I was really going to have to reassess my skills as a fighter, or at least find out when Appalachian ninjas started driving sensible family cars.

As I lay pinned in the snow with my left arm stressed to the breaking point, I saw a large pair of men's boots come up alongside the boots of the woman who was no doubt considering snapping me like a dry pretzel.

"Who is this knucklehead?" said the woman in a tone that was anything but distressed.

"His name's Trevor Galloway," Letterman said. "He's the former Pittsburgh cop who you read about in the paper."

"The one snooping around Peter Lanskard's death?"

"That's the one."

"Do you two know each other?" she asked.

"We met the other day," he said. Then remembering what I had said before we had started fighting, Letterman said, "A minute ago, he said we may have gone to college together."

"Why on earth was this man beating on you?" she asked. "And he's not very big, is he?" she asked the second question in a peculiar way. Was she mocking him?

"Well...I...I guess I started it," he said meekly.

"Uh-huh. Mr. Galloway, are you conscious? Can you hear me?"

I tried to say, "I am," but my mouth was mostly buried in the snow.

She must have interpreted the muffled sounds correctly, because she asked, "If I let you up are you going to cause any problems?"

"No, ma'am," I promised as more snow dumped into my mouth.

She released my arm and then helped me to my feet.

"If you try anything, I'm going to pummel you real good. Do you understand?" she asked.

I nodded while my hands probed my face and body, assessing the damage.

The woman scrutinized my ravaged face and said, "Whoa. Did I do all of that?"

"No," I said. "They're a side effect."

"Of what?"

"Charisma."

My attacker, who was all of five-foot-six and one-hundred-twenty pounds, stretched out a hand and said, "I'm Elizabeth Letterman. Mark is my husband."

I nervously took her hand, expecting to be put on the ground

189

again but we shook and she released me.

"For an old college buddy, you have an odd way of reuniting with your classmates."

"I don't actually know if we were at VMI at the same time," I admitted.

"Ha!" laughed Elizabeth Letterman at a joke I didn't know I was making. "Mark at VMI? Imagine that! He wouldn't have made it through the first semester!"

My eyes shifted to her husband who was both bleeding and blushing.

Elizabeth Letterman smiled broadly and she said, "Mr. Galloway, I'm the one who went to VMI and I'm quite certain I don't remember seeing you there. Of course, you look much older than me."

"I'm actually only—"

Oh, screw it.

"I didn't actually finish up there," I said.

The woman rolled her eyes and said, "A washout. It figures."

My frozen face stiffened with embarrassment as she pivoted on a foot and headed over to her car. She grabbed a sack of groceries from the back seat, closed the door with her foot, and started walking toward the house. Mark Letterman and I, both of us covered with snow, blood, and humiliation, watched her gallop toward the front door.

Without turning her head, she called back to us, "You two Nancies better get in this house before you get the sniffles!"

I looked at Mark Letterman who glanced back at me, then avoided my eyes like an insecure puppy.

"Do you...do you want to come inside?" he asked weakly.

I checked to make sure my gun was still in its holster. Then, I put my hands in my jacket pockets and shrugged like a middle-school boy being asked to dance for the first time.

"Should I?" I finally asked.

He crossed his arms and looked to the sky. "I suppose. She'll say I was rude if you don't come in for a while."

With my head down, I mumbled, "Well, I guess we better go inside."

"Yup," he agreed.

I stood next to a fireplace in the living room and tried to find the most advantageous way to turn so my clothes would dry out. Once again, I'd have to disassemble and check my gun to make sure it didn't get wet. After realizing I was soaked on all sides and one angle was as good as the next, I turned my back to the glorious heat. Mark Letterman came into the room pressing a bag of frozen peas to his face. Having only the use of only one hand, he had another bag tucked under his arm. He walked over to me and nodded down, indicating I should grab the bag of frozen carrots. The last thing I wanted right then was something cold, but I pressed the bag to the side of my mouth where my lip was split. The security man fell into a cushioned chair and used his good hand to cover his nose with the peas.

His wife took quick and deliberate steps into the room and leaned over her spouse. She had been carrying an assortment of items in her hands, which I couldn't see when she turned toward her husband. From behind, I saw her elbows rapidly move in small circles and I heard what sounded like paper and cloth tearing. A slight whimper came from the chair and she said, "Oh, hush."

When she straightened up and moved away, Mark Letterman's broken finger had been bandaged and splinted as well as any doctor could have performed the task. Before I realized she had left the room, Elizabeth Letterman returned and was shoving a glass of water in my direction.

"Now...what the hell do you want?" she asked me.

I took a sip of water and moved the glass away from my face in case she decided to punch me again.

"Whatever happened the day Peter Lanskard died, Mark was the closest to the shooter. I spoke to Mark before and he doesn't strike me as being the type to miss the obvious. So I was hoping he might remember something that was not so obvious."

The woman glanced at her husband who moved the frozen peas from his nose and placed them on top of his wounded finger.

"Well, you're right. Whatever his faults may be, he's good at his job. We've talked about the entire incident at length and he didn't see anything."

Speaking mostly to Mark, but not taking my eyes of his wife, I said, "Maybe there was something he wasn't comfortable telling you about. Something that he's embarrassed he missed at the time."

She took a half-step closer to me. "Mr. Galloway, you said my husband doesn't strike you as the type to miss the obvious. How do I strike you?"

I drew back as far as the fireplace behind me would allow and said, "Hard and quick."

She gave a hearty chuckle and backed out of my personal space.

"I mean do I strike you as the passive type who would not ask him a thousand questions and want to know every detail?"

I shook my head.

"And don't think for a second that he would lie to me," she said.

Over on the chair, Mark Letterman was leaning his head

back to keep his nose from bleeding. Even in the awkward position, he managed to shake his head from side to side to confirm the truth to his wife's words. Elizabeth Letterman moved to her own chair and I took a seat on a ledge protruding from the bottom of the fireplace.

Facing Mark Letterman, I said, "I'm no expert in the tactics of personal protection, but if a threat to the subject being protected becomes apparent, am I right to assume that all resources are sent to the subject, and not necessarily to the threat?

"That's right," said the security man. "Maximum to the protectee. Pursuing and apprehending a threat is of secondary importance."

"So when the shot rang out," I said. "What was the first radio traffic that went over the air?"

He thought for a moment before saying, "Shooter in the woods. Castle is down."

"Castle?"

"It was our code name for Mr. Lanskard."

"Who was doing the speaking?"

"Brady Mason, of course."

"Now, I'm going to ask you to try to remember back to the moment you heard the radio traffic. I know you were already out patrolling on the ATV at the time. Did you hear the shot?"

Letterman nodded.

"What did you do when you heard it?"

Letterman said, "I stopped the ATV so I could listen, but I wasn't alarmed. Hearing shots out here isn't uncommon even when it's not hunting season."

"But then you heard the radio traffic."

"Right."

I asked, "When Mason said there was a shooter in the

woods, did you head back toward the house to help protect Peter Lanskard? Wouldn't that be what your training tells you to do?"

"It would be, but I didn't," Letterman said as he set his makeshift icepack on a table.

"Why not?" I said, wondering why a trained protection operative would not react as his countless hours of training had taught him to do.

"Because like I said, I heard the shot."

My expression conveyed my confusion, so he explained.

"I knew Mr. Lanskard had arrived in front of the house and was nowhere near the wood line. I knew what I had heard was a shot from a powerful rifle. I knew that there was no way Brady or any of the team would have let a threat with a rifle get anywhere near Mr. Lanskard. Therefore, I knew that Lanskard was either safe or dead and that the assailant took the shot from a distance. Since there were no other follow-up shots, I had to assume the move against the boss wasn't an all-out assault and that this was a sniper attack. Therefore, I stayed in the woods and positioned myself between the house and the previous alarm activation."

I was speechless. From the outset I had misread the man in front of me. After he finished his explanation, I realized that nearly one year ago Mark Letterman had brilliantly analyzed the situation and did something that is incredibly difficult to do. He ignored his training after weighing all he knew about weapons, strategies used by assassins, and the terrain. His response—or lack of response to the protectee—was perfect. This man was good at his job and took pride in his profession. No wonder he was so offended by all the questions. Who could blame him?

I glanced over at his wife who was looking at her husband.

As clearly as she had been mocking him earlier, she was now beaming with pride at her husband's analytic skills.

"Okay," I said to Mark. "You sold me. I believe you one hundred percent and I'm sorry if I offended you. Bear with me while I ask a few more questions. I don't mean any offense by them and I'm simply trying to make the illogical logical."

I waited until the man gave me a nod to proceed.

"Is there any way the shooter made a wide half-circle away from your position and still managed to break the outer perimeter alarm without you seeing him?"

He rubbed his eyes, which were still watering from the blow to his nose. "Not in the time frame we're looking at. You've seen the area around the main house. The trees are spaced out pretty well and there are good lines of sight in all directions. That part of the property has rolling hills, but nothing so steep that someone could duck down and stay out of view for very long."

"Then every theory that has been presented must be incorrect," I said while moving my own homemade ice pack to a different part of my face. I stood and started to pace, but stopped when something occurred to me. I couldn't believe I hadn't thought about it before.

"What about a tunnel?" I asked with a hint of excitement. "This area has to have old mines and wherever you find mines you find networks of tunnels. Maybe there's a tunnel that starts somewhere just inside the perimeter and comes out near the point where we think the shot was fired. If the tunnel is large enough, the shooter could even have used some sort of vehicle to travel underground."

Hearing the words come out of my mouth gave me a momentary dash of hope, but both the Lettermans were already shaking their heads before I had finished speaking.

Mark Letterman said, "We thought about that last year. We checked for tunnels as best we could throughout the rest of that winter and then again after the thaw. There isn't anything there."

He stood and I could sense his frustration as he moved to a window. His wife's expression no longer showed pride. She was feeling empathy for a man who had spent the past year racked with guilt for having not protected his employer.

"Is it possible the alarms malfunctioned and we are operating off bad data?" I asked. "Or is it possible there's human error involved? Perhaps somebody thought an alarm activated that didn't?" I was reaching and I knew it.

The security man said, "False alarms are always a possibility, but our system is one of the best and it automatically records any activations in an electronic log. We went back and looked at the log and the timing and sequence are correct. Look, the shortest distance between two points is a straight line and I was right in between Point A and Point B. There was nothing there," he said staring at the floor and taking a deep breath. "Nothing."

I considered his last word and my eyes blurred as I once again tried to identify the known facts from the guesswork. A hazy theme was developing somewhere in my mind. The case was starting to be defined by absence, rather than presence. There was "nothing" in Letterman's vision on the fateful day. The physical evidence was "nowhere." Colby referred to the shooter as a "ghost." Even Maddox referred to The Lithuanian as a "phantom." Why had no one else seen the Lithuanian? What about that bear? Why did so much of this seem unreal? *Please. Please don't let me be losing my mind. Not again.*

A wave of anger crashed into me as I thought of the bad breaks I'd been dealt. I didn't ask to get abducted and abused. I didn't willingly become an addict. The prosecutor I punched didn't have to push me to the edge. Hell, I didn't even ask to work this case. But now I was freezing my ass off in a place where people were dying and even Colby was losing faith in me. Bullshit.

My mind went deep into the landscape of the Lanskard property and placed my body next to Letterman's ATV. I could see him responding to a routine alarm and stopping when the shot rang out. I watched carefully as he pressed an earpiece deeper into his ear and listed to Ray Mason announce that Peter Lanskard was hit. His eyes widened and a brief battle ensued between his training and his intuition. Even in those seconds, his mind was on high alert and his eyes vigilantly scanned his surroundings. He missed nothing. There was nothing to miss. A skilled sniper had fired a weapon and escaped and nobody knew how. To make matters worse, here I was a year after following up on a previously investigated dead end. The case was still cold and I was failing at my job—again.

Peter Lanskard was dead. Markus Faust was dead. Earl Maddox was in the hospital. Fingers and eyes had been placed under my damn pillow—and I certainly didn't think I was capable of doing that to a human being.

Screw this "crazy addict" crap. Death was here, people were lying, nobody trusted me, my room at the inn didn't have a fucking TV, and I had just had my ass handed to me by a woman I outweighed by seventy pounds.

Somebody had to pay.

The intruding voice was quiet and sincere, but my head snapped up when Elizabeth Letterman said, "Oh, my. I've seen that look before."

Damn. How long had I been gone this time? I wasn't sure, but I thought the blur-outs were getting more intense.

She stood and walked toward me. "I saw it a lot when I was serving in Afghanistan. Those are the eyes of a man who's at the end of his rope and is planning on unleashing something fierce."

"I'm fine," I assured her as I tried to unclench my jaw.

She sized me up as if I hadn't been standing in her house for the past ten minutes and said, "I know I got the best of you out there, but Mark is no pushover. When I pulled up you were looking as if you weren't nearly finished inflicting pain. Not by a long shot."

I looked away.

"Oh, my God," she blurted. "Galloway! VMI."

I tensed and stared out a window.

"You're the rat who put that upperclassman into a coma! You're a legend."

It was amazing how all these years later I still hated the word rat, although it simply referred to a first year VMI cadet.

I looked her in the eyes and said defensively, "I didn't put him in a coma. He woke up a few hours after the fight."

Elizabeth Letterman's eyes were as big as saucers. It was like she'd confirmed the existence of Bigfoot. I think she found it even more entertaining since this particular Bigfoot had been kicked out of Sasquatch school.

She said, "A lot of people don't think that story is real. But now that I've seen an example of you losing your temper..."

"It was a long time ago," I mumbled. "I had a short fuse back then."

She turned to her husband who was nursing his bandaged hand and nose.

"Mr. Galloway, I worked explosive ordinance disposal in the Army. You learn a lot about explosives when you are an EOD tech. There are several ways a device can be set off. Some explosives are set off by remote control, some by a timer, some by manually pressing a button on the device, and some by lighting a fuse. Most explosives are stable. Some you could toss off a building, let them smack the pavement, and nothing would happen. But other types of explosives are so unstable they can detonate if they are subject to the slightest disturbance. With all due respect, sir, you do not appear to be of the stable variety."

CHAPTER 19

I ended up back at Nick's Diner where I ordered a late breakfast. I sat in the same booth I had occupied after nearly being run over by my possibly imaginary nemeses. The same waitress I'd had before came to my table. I ordered the number 4 special, which wasn't very special since it strongly resembled the preceding three. The waitress grimaced when she looked at me and I wondered what my face would look like by the time I got out of this town. *If* I got out of this town.

"Skiing accident," I said unconvincingly before she scampered off to eyeball me from a distance like everyone else in the diner.

Now that I was looking around, I recognized a lot of the faces. Many of the customers were senior citizens and had been sitting here the last time I visited. This time, their stares were even more pronounced toward the leather jacket wearing, wrecked outsider sitting by himself. Most of the citizenry of this quiet town had to have been shell-shocked from being in close proximity to more than one homicide in the past thirteen months. Washaway probably hadn't even had to deal with the commission of a crime between those two tragic events. Well, not counting Seth thinking someone had tried to break into the shed in his back yard. But Seth had told me there wasn't even any damage to the shed.

Actually, I realized. That wasn't exactly what Seth told me. I mentally kicked myself for not seeing that he had never answered my question. Then, I kicked myself harder for making a terrible assumption about attempted break-ins. When someone tries to break into a structure, the assumption is that someone wanted something that was already inside. But what if the attempt to enter the shed was like everything else in this place? What if it was about *absence*? This was about what was *not* in the shed.

After a few minutes of being lost in thought, my food arrived and I ate while my entire way of contemplating this case turned upside-down. I needed a few more facts and I wondered if Colby had learned anything new during her visit with Jason Leonard. I wasn't too surprised she hadn't called me yet, as I was probably hours away from being designated persona-non-grata in this county. I took a bite of toast and inevitably, the waitress appeared at my side and asked if I needed anything else. I have no idea how waiters and waitresses magically materialize and ask a question exactly when the customer has a mouth full of food. I shook my head and she gladly departed. I took a drink of coffee.

I guess it's all about having perfect timing.

Something clicked in my brain and I put my coffee mug down a little too hard, drawing more stares.

It's all in the timing.

I dug in a pocket, found my phone, and punched the buttons. Colby answered after two rings.

"Are you still with Jason Leonard?" I asked excitedly.

Several seconds passed before she said, "Yes."

Something was wrong. She must have decided to pull the welcome mat from under my feet. Hell, she'd probably heard about me beating on Mark Letterman. We didn't have time for this. In less than a day, The Camp would be wrapping-up operations.

Rapidly, I said "I'm on to something. We need to—"

"He's dead."

My mouth tightened and my eyes narrowed. "Who's dead?"

"Jason Leonard is dead," she told me. "I'm guessing it happened a few hours ago, but I won't know for sure until the M.E. gets the body temp. He was shot through the back of the head while walking through his own back yard. It looks a lot like the Lanskard murder."

"What's the address?"

My stomach churned as I drove across a bridge named for a fallen soldier. The sign bearing the soldier's name looked new and I realized how refreshing it was to be in a place where people still respected not only soldiers, but also police officers. Colby had ruffled a lot of feathers with her handling of the Lanskard investigation, but nobody was questioning her authority. Even when someone was calling her a "bitch," I got the sense that there was an underlying respect for the uniform.

In recent months, law enforcement all over the country had come under great scrutiny due to the deaths of some suspects. The fallout spun out of control thanks to the media, the activist groups, and the way some police departments responded to the controversies. The resulting polarization had made life difficult for everyone involved and uninformed screams from both sides had drowned out rational discussion. But here, in this place, I could see officers were treated with a measure of respect. I realized if this second run at the Lanskard investigation fell short and ended up needlessly costing the lives of more people, all that could change.

The bridge ended and I slowed the SUV as the road twisted around a mountain. My phone beeped, telling me it needed to be recharged. I leaned over and opened my glove box to grab my car charger. Keeping my eyes fixed on the treacherous road, I fumbled around feeling for the coiled cord. My hand grasped something soft and I peeked to my right as I withdrew the item. The human ear fell from my fingertips as I hit the brakes causing the car to enter a sideways skid. Desperately trying to regain control of the car, and myself, I overcorrected and some-how reversed the spin and the car shot off the road. The tires caught something on the shoulder of the road and the SUV flipped and rolled down a hill. Sounds of broken glass and bending metal flooded the interior as a world I already didn't understand spun out of control. The seatbelt kept me in place as the car tumbled down a hill for several seconds before striking a tree.

I opened my eyes and stared though the cracked windshield. I was right side up, so that was good. I was covered in broken glass from most of windows and cold air filled the car, so that was bad. I was alive, so that was unexpected. After a couple of attempts, I managed to remove my seatbelt and get out of the car. Every part of me ached and I groaned when I took a step. I groaned again when I looked at the car. It appeared both the SUV and I were nearly totaled. I returned to my open door and searched for my phone. Amazingly, it was on the floorboard near the gas pedal and it still had power. I twisted my upper-body and my left shoulder shrieked with pain. This was more than a bruise and it was going to be a problem I didn't have time for.

I fought against the stabbing sensation, stood and started to dial 9-1-1, but stopped myself. Scooting back into the car, I started looking for the ear. My mind raced as I searched. I knew the ear likely belonged to the same person who used to own the fingers and eyes that had been left in my room. Of course, there was no question who had left the ear for me to find in the SUV. My problem was that Colby and Deputy Lemons were questioning my sanity and I feared what would happen if it was discovered I had a human ear in my possession. I'd go from investigator to suspect in a flash. In fact, I'd be lucky if I wasn't forcibly issued a nice white straightjacket to match the fallen snow.

As it turned out, my concern about what to do with the ear was unnecessary. After searching every inch of the SUV, I wasn't able to find it anywhere. I searched the area around the car and retraced the path I'd taken down the embankment, but there was nothing but glass, plastic, and metal. The ear had fallen out one of the shattered windows at some point during the descent. It wasn't there. It wasn't anywhere. But I had held it in my hand. My own thoughts did their best to convince me of that truth.

I could still feel it between my fingertips.

I saw it.

It was real.

It had to be real.

Having found nothing else questionable in the trashed SUV, I climbed up to the road and called 9-1-1. Thirty minutes later, I was joined by Deputy Lemons. The gruff police officer didn't make any pretense of being concerned for my welfare.

He looked down the hill toward the SUV and addressed me with a sandpaper voice. "How did you manage to do that?"

"I was careless," I said as I shrugged. The shrug sent a bolt of lightning through my shoulder and I gasped audibly while grabbing my shoulder.

"What's wrong with you?"

"My left shoulder got banged up," I said.

The deputy adjusted his Stetson. "I'll call for a flatbed to come out here. It will be tough in these conditions, but they can try to use a winch and retrieve your car. I'll take you to the hospital to get checked out."

I informed him I had been on my way to Jason Leonard's house to see the crime scene.

"Yeah, I was too," he said with agitation. "But Colby heard the radio traffic from the dispatcher after you called nine-one-one and sent me out here. She also told me to make sure you went straight to the hospital if you were injured in the slightest. She said that if you argue with me, I'm to put you in cuffs and drag you there for your own good." The deputy spat on the ground. "I guess she's tired of seeing you get your ass kicked."

I wanted to argue but I didn't have a leg to stand on, metaphorically speaking. This was ironic since these days my legs were the only parts of me not crushed, bruised, cut, or scraped.

"Do you need to get anything out of your car?"

I thought about that damned ear and the meaning it conveyed.

Yeah, I heard your first message. I heard it loud and clear.

I had my phone, my charger, my gun, and most of my mind. My laptop and the rest of my clothing were still at the inn and I had a few personal items at Colby's house. Somewhere in my suitcase was a pill bottle containing meds that prevent hallucinations. However, I had stopped taking those a couple of days ago because of the way they clouded my mind. What good is it to have a razor-sharp intellect if it's always sheathed?

"I don't need anything," I said to Lemons.

The man grunted and gestured to his cruiser.

* * *

The examination area at the hospital was like every other one I'd ever seen. Unnaturally chilly, silver instruments sat on sterile counters while anxious patients sat on tables covered with paper that crinkled with every move. The room was nothing more than a compartment off the side of the emergency room where I had been deposited by Lemons. A nurse asked me a series of questions and then checked my temperature. Then, she placed two fingers over the inside of my wrist while looking at her watch.

She readjusted the position of her fingers twice before playfully saying, "It's tough to find a pulse on you. You sure you got a heart in there?"

"It's been debated."

Eventually she confirmed my right to walk among the living and went on her way. I sat uncomfortably on the exam table and made a few attempts at rotating my left arm. I thought I was improving, then again, I think I'm fairly good at lying to myself. I was halfway through a disagreeable joint rotation when none other than Dr. Raylene Westerly pulled back a curtain and entered the room. I shouldn't have been surprised. How many ER doctors would a small rural hospital have on duty during any given week?

"Mr. Galloway," she said with a smile. "I see the testosterone overdose epidemic has claimed yet another victim."

"It was just a car accident," I said.

Using a finger to lift my chin, she said, "It looks like your face took another beating. I don't think the air bag did all that."

"Somehow, the air bag never deployed," I said. Pointing to my face, I said, "This...is from something else."

"Uh-huh," she said while jotting something on a clipboard. Her black ponytail was draped over her shoulder. She looked up and swung it out of the way.

"I'm not exactly clear on what you do for a living," she said.

"Me neither."

"Whatever it is, maybe you should choose a new line of work. Did you ever want to do anything else?"

"When I was younger, I wanted to be an engineer."

"Electrical?"

"Train."

She laughed, and not one of those *I'm being polite because you just got pulverized in a significant car accident* laughs.

"So now your shoulder is hurting?"

I described the pain and she had me test the shoulder's mobility. I can't even say I demonstrated a range of motion. It was more like a struggling through a few degrees on a rusted protractor.

"We'll do an x-ray here and schedule an MRI for later this week. You may have damaged the rotator cuff and possibly some other tendons. I'll refer you to a specialist back in Pittsburgh unless you have someone specific in mind who accepts your insurance."

She scribbled some more and said, "I may be able to get you in for the MRI as soon as—"

"I'll have to get that done in Pittsburgh too."

"Oh, you're leaving soon?" she asked.

Maybe I did hit my head pretty hard in the accident, because she I thought she actually sounded disappointed.

"Yes," I said. "I may be finished here by tomorrow."

"I see."

I listened to her pen scratch paper.

"Maybe I could drive back here for the follow-up appointments with the specialist," I said. "I'm sure there is someone here you could recommend."

She tilted her head. "You're going to drive over two hundred miles to see a specialist for your shoulder? That's a long way."

"I guess you're right."

This time I was sure I saw disappointment in her demeanor. So I added, "Then, I suppose I'll have to get dinner while I'm here. Maybe more than once."

The smile returned. "Yes, you would."

"I don't know the area that well. Maybe you could help me find a nice restaurant?"

There you go, Galloway. Charisma.

She laughed. "I'm sure you've eaten dinner since you've been here."

"I've only been to a handful of places. Nick's Diner, some bar in Washaway, and the other was an Olive Garden north of town. I'm sure there are other options, but I could use some personal guidance."

For a moment, I thought I had said something wrong, because her expression grew serious and she pulled a different notepad out of her pocket. The pen danced across the paper and she tore three sheets off the tiny booklet.

Handing me the first, she said, "This is a prescription for painkillers. Vicodin." Handing me the second, she said, "This is an anti-inflammatory." Handing me the third she said, "This is my personal phone number."

You're doing fine, Galloway. Smooth.

"I'll be sure to use it," I said, meaning the third one. Hopefully, I'd have the strength not to fill the prescriptions, especially the Vicodin.

The doctor added, "I'll have someone come in and take you down the hall for x-rays. If they show any breaks or other serious damage, we'll have to put you in a sling and I'll reevaluate those prescriptions. If we don't see anything that needs immediate treatment, a nurse will take you back to the lobby and you can check out of here."

She walked away and drew back the curtain while saying, "About dinner—can I make one request?"

"Of course," I said confidently.

With a quick look back, she mentioned, "If it's not too much to ask, don't grab anyone's penis during our date." With a rustle of plastic and a few scrapes of metal rings against the curtain rod, she was gone.

I heard Chase Vinson's mockery in my head. *The legend of Trevor Galloway knows no bounds.*

Fantastic.

I signed some paperwork at the desk on my way out of the ER and made my way toward the entrance where I had arrived. The x-rays had shown no breaks, but the hospital staff had issued me a cloth sling for my arm and shoulder anyway. Like a true Central Pennsylvania testosterone junkie, I'd balled up the cloth and Velcro contraption and tucked it into my jacket. No reason to start taking intelligent advice now. I'd been doing so well on my own thus far.

My aforementioned razor sharp intellect must have been slightly dulled from the wreck, because it wasn't until I reached the revolving door that I realized I had no car, no ride, and nobody to call. I was certain Colby was finishing up with the Jason Leonard crime scene and Lemons was likely with her. Any other deputies working would either be helping secure the scene, searching for shell casings and other evidence, or attending to Washaway's citizens. I thought about hanging around the hospital to visit Maddox, but the thought that I might have had one of my "moments" and hurt him, persuaded me to stay away.

My phone was dead, and I didn't see an easily accessible power outlet, so I decided to go old-school. I found a registration desk and asked a kid who might have been old enough to buy a lottery ticket for a phone and a phone book. The boy who wore a name tag reading *Derrick* was no obviously no stranger to hair gel and woven bracelets. He had no trouble pointing me to a phone, but he had no idea what I was talking about when I had requested a phone book. Exhibiting an ocean of patience, I explained to Derrick the existence of, and the purpose for, the celebrated telephone directory.

"Whoa. So you can find out people's phone numbers and addresses in a book?" he asked with sincerity.

I dipped my head and tried not to get upset. "Not everybody, but a lot of people are in there."

"But how do you know what page to look at?" He leaned back as if I was a guru revealing the secret of life. The top of his button-down shirt opened up and I noticed a diminutive few burn holes in his white T-shirt.

I straightened up as high as I could. "I told you. It's in alphabetical order by last name."

"Right. Yeah...right."

"So do you see one back there behind your desk?" I asked while hunching over and putting my elbows on the desk so his eyes would follow me. "Maybe on a shelf or in a drawer. This isn't a heavily populated area, so it's probably not very thick."

His eyes lit up. "You mean the ones in the city are bigger? Do people have longer names?"

You'd better hope the thing is thin, because I'm going to whack you—

I stood tall again. "Two things, kid. First, I need to you look for anything back there that has the words *phone book*, *telephone directory*, or *white pages* on the cover."

"Are they called *white pages* because—"

Oh, my God.

"Second thing. You need to lay off the weed. Seriously."

He started to protest.

I blurted, "You have burn holes on your T-shirt where you've been smoking up and some of the seeds have fallen and eaten through your shirt. Also, your eyes have been following me each time I heightened or lowered myself. Whenever you look up, your eyes involuntarily jerk and dance around. The same thing happens when you direct your gaze down, which happened each time I lowered myself. It's called vertical gaze nystagmus and while it's always present to some extent, it becomes exaggerated when a person is impaired. Your eyes weren't only jerking around, they were break dancing."

"What's—"

"Kid, I swear if you ask me what break dancing is I'm going to tie those hemp bracelets together and use them to strangle you."

He regarded my bludgeoned face and my tone of voice. With rushed motions he tore through the papers and files in and around his desk. Hesitantly, he glanced up and he had difficulty finding the words, so I helped him.

"You don't have a phone book."

He shook his head. Then, he seemed to have an idea and held up a finger. He dug into the pocket of his jeans and pulled out an iPhone.

"Do you want to use this?"

I pinched the bridge of my nose and said, "Yeah. I would love to use your phone. Thank you."

He handed it to me and I started to type in a search for Mark Letterman's home phone number. If Mark Letterman couldn't give me a ride, maybe his wife would be willing. At least I knew she wasn't threatened by me.

From behind the desk, Derrick said proudly, "I can show you how to use Google if you want!"

I tossed him a hand grenade stare. *Seriously, I'm not that old.*

Maybe I needed to Google the A-Team and leave this mess to them.

CHAPTER 20

Mark Letterman had started his shift at the Lanskard estate, so it was Elizabeth Letterman who was kind enough to give me a ride back to town. I wondered how her husband had explained his bruises and broken finger to his colleagues. If he told them the truth, there undoubtedly would be a few more people who would gladly buy me a bus ticket out of town. Elizabeth Letterman gave me what I'm sure she thought was good-natured ribbing about my winter driving skills while I let my phone charge.

I'd thought about asking Elizabeth to take me to Jason Leonard's home, but decided my presence might create animosity with Colby, Lemons, and whoever else might be there. Besides, they would soon be finished with evidence collection and the scene would be secured as much as an outdoor kill zone could be. Elizabeth dropped me off in front of the inn and I thanked her for the ride. She gave me the name of a rental car place several miles away and I made a mental note to make a reservation.

I had intended on going into the inn to clean up, but decided I'd be better off surrounded by people. The pounding my body and mind had taken, along with the lack of sleep, were taking me to the edge of someplace dark. Solitude was not my friend and I longed for a familiar setting where people exuded normalcy. Figuring this would be my last visit, I entered Nick's Diner. This was a mistake. Rather than whispers and sideways glances like before, something here had turned openly hostile.

It seemed that word of Jason Leonard's death had rushed through the town's streets like a reservoir after a dam break. Idle chatter had replaced by hard glares, as the townspeople scowled at the pincushion stranger who was no longer associated only with an old case, but new deaths. As I made my way to a booth, the clinking of silverware and plates ground to a halt and was replaced by involuntary sniffs and coughs. I took refuge behind a menu and the waitress—the same waitress from the previous visits—brought me water with a wedge of lemon. She must have figured out I hate lemon.

"Do you have beer?"

The waitress slid the water glass a few inches in my direction and said a little too loudly, "We don't serve alcohol here."

An elderly woman and her husband stood to leave and she made a production of taking a path past my booth. Somehow I hadn't noticed them sitting at the neighboring table although they had been only a few feet away. The woman did her best to keep her expression pleasant, but her tone was lecturing.

"This is a nice town with nice people. You should let us be. Everyone has heard about the trouble you've brought. Maddox has run that inn for forty years and he's never had a lick of trouble. Then you show up asking ridiculous questions, getting people hurt, and getting into bar fights."

Bar fights?

Oh, the thing with Faust at the Tavern. *Yeah, my bad.*

I looked around, but none of the other customers seemed to be paying any attention to me being lectured by one of their own.

"I can take one look at you and see you're a hard-drinking man," she scolded.

Not really. But I have goals.

"It's not too late to change your ways," she said with flourish. "And be not drunk with wine, wherein is excess; but be filled with the Spirit! Ephesians, chapter five, verse eighteen.

I rubbed my fingers through my hair. Felt a snag when I hit some crusted blood—probably my own. I was tired. So, so tired. My shoulder was killing me and my thoughts were beginning to jumble again. Worse, I was feeling bitter and when I feel bitter I can get mean.

She crooned, "You have not eaten bread, and you have not drunk wine or strong drink, that you—"

I slammed my hands onto the table. "If men get into a fight with one another, and the wife of one intervenes to rescue her husband from the grip of his opponent by reaching out and seizing his genitals, you shall cut off her hand; show no pity! Deuteronomy, chapter twenty-five, verses eleven and twelve."

Well, *now* everybody was looking at me. Their expressions were of bewilderment, condescension, and resentment. The woman was taken aback and regarded me as if I had been speaking Aramaic.

"Oh, I'm sorry," I said. "I thought we were spouting off random Bible verses. I've got a doozy that addresses all the bacon people eat around here. Would you like to hear it?"

More stares from the crowd. A few shifted uncomfortably in their chairs.

Apparently the woman didn't want to hear anymore, because she hissed something and left with her husband who now knew he was on his own during a fight. She likely wasn't going to lend him a hand.

As I watched the couple leave, I noticed the waitress standing beside a table on the other side of the room. She was having a lively conversation with some customers and all of them were taking quick peeks in my direction. Realizing I wasn't going to get the chance to order anytime soon, I pulled out my phone and called Colby.

"Are you still at Jason Leonard's house?"

In the background, her police radio squawked. "I just left. I'm headed back to the station."

"Can you tell me more about the scene?"

Colby ignored my question. "What did they say at the hospital? How are you?"

"I'm fine. A few bumps and bruises."

"Trevor," she chided. "HIPAA or no HIPAA, I'll find out."

I had no doubt that the hospital being outside of town wouldn't do much to impede the informal Washaway Gossip Network.

"Nothing is broken," I said. "My shoulder is messed up, but I'll live."

Silence for a moment. With hesitance she said, "Maybe you've done enough."

"No way," I snapped. "We've still got tonight and most of tomorrow to solve this thing before our suspect pool takes off."

I tried to remember what I had been thinking about before Colby first told me about Jason Leonard's murder. Seth. I had been thinking about what Seth had told me about the attempted break-in of his shed.

I said, "I think I figured something out. We need—"

Colby said, "We're out of time."

"What?"

"When I discovered Jason Leonard's body, I sent one of my deputies to The Camp. Trevor, they're packing up. In fact, some of the competitors already left town."

"No," I said defiantly.

"Yes. They cancelled today's event because of Faust's death.

Everybody thought it would be more respectful to shut it down."

Of course. I should have seen it coming as I watched the somber procession pass by after Faust had been found dead. To hold a competition the next day would have been callous. Besides, the main event had already occurred. All that was left was the...

My head dipped and my vision blurred. This time I wasn't standing next to Brady Mason while he watched his boss die. This time I was standing at the edge of the Lanskard property watching the preparation for a killing. As clear as anything I had ever seen, I saw how it happened. I stood helplessly as the perimeter alarm was tripped. Then I moved to the shooter's nest and watched as the sniper lay prone and unfolded a portable tripod to steady the barrel. I heard the sounds as the executioner drew in a slow, steady breath of cold air and exhaled hot carbon dioxide. A finger squeezed the trigger in an unhurried motion and the .308 round spat out the end of the rifle. Then I watched what happened next. I heard Letterman's ATV and the shouts of a security detail going into response mode. I saw it all. I felt it all.

This entire time, I'd been doing everything in my power to not think of the crime like I would a drug operation. However, the components of criminal enterprises are often the same. You have the logistical component, the surveillance component, and the operational component. Whether you're talking about terrorism or a street-level drug deal, those are the gears in the machine. The teeth of the gears join and separate and work in conjunction with each other. Until one of them doesn't.

"Trevor? Do you think you can do that?"

My world came back into focus. "I'm sorry, what?"

"I asked if you could walk away from this. It's not my place to say this, but I don't think you're well. I didn't want to bring this up, but I know about your—"

No time for this.

"Are you near the Lanskard house?" I asked.

"Trevor…"

"Can you drive over there? Right now."

Seconds ticked by. "Why?"

"I need you to ask Brady Mason a few questions. I need to know if there was an alarm activation anywhere on the premises in the hours before Peter Lanskard arrived home."

"You know there was," she said. "There was an activation less than five minutes before he arrived. That's when the shooter headed toward the tree line."

"No," I said. "I'm betting there was an activation *before* that one—even if it was two or three hours before the shooting. The activation could have been anywhere on the perimeter."

"Okay," she said warily.

"And find out if the second activation was in *exactly* the same spot as the one where the shooter entered the property."

"It was. It was the same part of the perimeter."

"No, I mean *exactly*. There is no way they positioned those microwave sensors between every tree."

Colby hesitated, but then said she would ask the question.

"One more thing. Ask him if the alarms were turned off after the second activation."

"After the activation from when the shooter left?"

"Right."

"What are you thinking?"

"I'm thinking that after you talk to Brady Mason, you should locate the Wrangle brothers and ask them to come to your station to answer some questions."

Colby said, "What questions?"

"Anything," I fired back. "Make up something. Tell them you're going to be reviewing the original statements and confirming the information."

"I might be able to convince David to come in, but there's no way Seth is going to talk to me."

"Yes, he will," I said. "Tell him you have some information about the sounds he heard outside his house the night of the shooting. Tell him you have a good idea who was trying to get into his shed."

Colby was so quiet I could hear her car engine in the background.

"Did I botch this thing a year ago?" she said softly.

"The crime you were investigating was botched from the start," I said. "*That* was the missing piece."

I told Colby I'd make my way to the police station and ended the call while continuing to arrange all the pieces in my mind. My finger tapped against the table and I mumbled to myself. Nothing I had could be considered solid evidence, but David Wrangle was the key. I knew he was a man on the brink and the right questions might be enough to break him. He was a top-notch athlete who supposedly started drinking after he had hurt his knee. But elite athletes don't respond to physical adversity by heading to the liquor store—especially not military veterans who know the battle of competition is nothing compared to real war.

An injury didn't put David Wrangle on a path toward self-destruction, but I knew what did. I knew, because I'd been in a similar spot. Even after most of my physical injuries had healed, one thing had remained and was ever-present. One never becomes deaf to the voice of guilt. I was willing to bet that David Wrangle could relate all too well.

I stopped tapping my finger and mumbling when the waitress appeared at my side.

"Do you want to order something?"

I looked down at the glass of water I hadn't touched.

My mood was on the upswing again. "No, thank you. If you don't mind me asking, what's your name?"

She eyed me with apprehension. "Wilma."

"Wilma," I said. "I'm sorry if I've caused you or your customers any distress. I don't think I'll be coming back here again."

She half-snorted and half-sneered so everyone could hear. "It would suit everybody fine if you didn't visit us anymore."

Approving nods all around. On my way to the door, phrases like "Good riddance" and "Don't come back" were grumbled. I didn't care. My adrenaline gets going when I think I've broken a case and I get a little high. I pushed on the glass door and felt the crisp air hit my bruised face. I turned back to the diner and saw I was still being observed from all angles.

I let the door rest against the shoulder of my black leather jacket and put two thumbs in the air as I said, "Heyyyy!"

I didn't stick around to find out if anyone thought it was funny.

TARGET 5
WEIGHT

CHAPTER 21

The Washaway Township Police Department was unimposing, squeezed between the office of a local magistrate and an antique store. Wooden shingles swayed in front of every structure on Main Street, including the one that housed the small police force. The front door was open and I rang a bell at the reception desk. Deputy Lemons came around a corner, then shook his head upon seeing me. With an air of disdain and a series of grumbles, he let me know Colby had called ahead and wanted me to wait in the conference room. He guided me through a narrow hallway, opened a door, and gestured to a table. The door slammed behind me as I took a seat and I decided to make a call.

The voice on the phone announced, "Vinson."

"Tell me you found something," I said.

Chase Vinson said, "You're expecting a lot in a short period of time."

"If you want me to solve a year-old case in less than a week, you need to give me your A game."

He laughed and said, "Actually, I was about to call you. I do have something for you. You were right to have me start with the Army. My friend with CID tells me that both Jaden and Linda Fredrick served. Nothing in Jaden's file was particularly interesting, but your hunch about Linda was dead on."

"Tell me."

"She was an MP. And while she was with the Military Police she was known for two things."

I tapped my finger on the table and waited.

"Biathlon and shooting competitions," he said.

"You mean shooting competitions using weapons other than biathlon rifles?"

"Exactly," he said. "She was apparently quite the sharp-shooter and was part of something called the Army Marksman-ship Unit for a while before she got into biathlon."

I leaned forward and asked, "Any idea what kind of weapon she used for the shooting competitions?"

"It was a bolt-action rifle that's used in something called a Palma competition. One of the requirements for those competi-tions is that the rifles have to be able to fire specific types of rounds."

"Like a .308 round?"

"That's one of the more common ones."

"Are the weapons used in Palma competitions specialized?"

Something bothered me about where this was going and Chase was right there with me.

"They are," he said. Then he added, "I know what you're thinking. You wouldn't imagine someone would be dumb enough to use a weapon like that for a homicide. It wouldn't be as unique as a fingerprint, but it would certainly be damning if that rifle was ever found. Besides, those things are too expensive to toss away. Figuring Linda Fredrick probably owns more than one weapon, I did some more checking. *Technically*, there are a couple of high-powered semi-automatic rifles registered to her, but nothing that fires a .308 round."

"Technically," I repeated hopefully.

"Basic hunting rifles aren't easily traced to a person, just the heavier stuff. She could own a dozen hunting rifles and we would never know unless we tracked the weapon back to a particular gun shop. Additionally, with her expertise in firearms, she probably knows how to modify rifles. Hell, she could probably build one from spare parts."

"True. But again, she wouldn't want to leave a specific signature of any kind. Every other person around here owns a hunting rifle. If you were going to kill a man and stay under the radar, you would use something more basic."

I thanked my friend and disconnected the call. Thoughts were spinning around my head, but this time I grabbed onto the vital pieces of intel and deciphered the information. I considered I might be completely off-base with my hypothesis, but I didn't think so. The case had gone unsolved because the initial plot had never been fully carried out. Colby and the rest of the cops never stood a chance because they assumed the killer's plan had been realized when Peter Lanskard's blood soaked the fresh snow. It was that preconception that led to false deductions, and those deductions led nowhere.

My eyes blurred and the comfort of the office was shattered by the wind whipping through the Pennsylvania hills. This time the Lanskard shooting had already occurred and all that was left was to carry out the final steps of the plan. I stood in front of the shed on Seth's property and I saw my hand reach for the handle. The hinges protested as the door swung open. My eyes swept forward and there on the floor was a knife positioned next to an unrecognizable form.

This is wrong.

The build of the figure was familiar. I knew the hair. The tattoos.

What is this?

The walls of the shed mutated into those of a hotel room. The plywood floor became covered with cheap carpet. The room brightened and the figure on the floor came into focus. Not just a figure—a body. The body lay motionless with hair covering his face. Blood seeped from a chest that did not move with respiration.

Get back to the case. Focus on the Lanskard investigation.

I leaned down over the body and brushed hair away from his face. Lukas Derela's eyes were shut tight. Dropping to one knee, I checked his neck for pulse. Finding nothing, I twisted to find the knife. Not just *a* knife, but *his* knife. A knife that had a shield imprinted on its black handle. The knife was gone. My breathing became rapid and I could feel sweat forming on my face. This was impossible. There was no knife. But if there was no knife then Derela must be alive because I wouldn't have killed him in cold blood.

In a panic, I swiveled back to Derela to check again for a pulse. I leapt back as the criminal's eyelids flipped open and one of his hands flew up and squeezed my arm. The index finger on his other hand pointed into my chest, right over my heart. The pressure increased and the pain became sharp and insufferable.

Stop it. This isn't real.

I couldn't will my body to move as he sat up and placed his nose inches from mine. His penetrating, unblinking, pitch black eyes never left my face. The finger pressed harder into my heart.

His mouth opened and he yelled one word. "Absence!"

No.

The door of the police station conference room popped as it began to open. I jarred back to reality and wiped my brow. Through the partially open door, Colby finished a conversation she had been having with Lemons and I used the time to compose myself. Instinctively, I placed a hand over my heart and felt for the beating.

Absence.

My mouth was dry and hands were shaking. The blurring out—inserting myself into a scene—was how I worked. It was my strength. Now, the past was creeping in and I wasn't even sure how much of that past was real. I was beginning to understand that an imagined past might be every bit as dangerous as a genuine one.

Colby entered the room and stopped dead in her tracks when she saw me at the table.

"Trevor, you're as white as a ghost. Jesus. Are you sweating? You should have stayed at the hospital."

I was glad she was attributing my current condition to the car wreck.

"I'll be okay," I said weakly. "I'm tired, but I'll bounce back."

"Oh, what the hell?" She flashed across the room and grabbed a box of tissues. Balling several up in her hands, she sprinted back and held them up to my nose.

"Your nose is bleeding. Here, hold this in place."

I did as I was told and she took a seat beside me.

"Trevor, I need to get you back to the ER now. You might have internal bleeding."

"Did you find the Wrangles? Are they coming?"

She was incredulous. "This case isn't worth your life." She debated for a moment before continuing. "It's not worth you getting sick...again. I know about the hallucinations. I think you need help."

She seemed to brace herself for a counterattack, but I had nothing to give. Instead, I tried to explain.

"Do you remember how you mentioned that trouble has a way of finding me?"

She nodded.

"It's not entirely true. I have this ability to mentally insert myself into a hypothetical situation and see how things play out. You know how I seem to zone out from time to time? Well, those are my blur-outs. I lose myself in thought and sometimes I find myself watching a crime unfold."

"All of us do that sometimes," said Colby. "Cops try to put themselves into the shoes of a criminal."

I shook my head. My shoulder wailed, but I buried the pain.

"I don't put myself into the shoes of the criminal. It's more like I'm an observer on the sidelines and I can see all the angles. But more than that I can feel temperature, smell the air, and have to shield my eyes from the sun. It's like I'm actually there."

Colby leaned back and crossed her legs. "I know hallucinations can seem real."

"Those aren't hallucinations," I snapped and took the tissues away from my face. I softened my tone and explained, "Those moments when I zone out are how I get things done. The medication for the hallucinations won't let me get to that place. I can't blur-out if I'm taking those pills. If I can't blur-out, then I can't solve cases. If I can't solve cases, then I really don't know what I'll do for the rest of my life."

"You don't have to solve cases," she said kindly. "There are lots of things you can do. Didn't you ever want to do anything else?"

I was spent. My mind and my body were running on fumes. I was running out of time to solve the case and I was ticking down to a personal apocalypse. I could practically hear the countdown clock in my head. As high as I felt when I was leaving the diner, the downswing was even more pronounced.

Drawing in a heavy breath, I said, "I thought about being an engineer once."

Colby smiled. "Trains, I would presume."

Sharp as a tack.

"How bad are they now?" she asked.

"How bad are what?"

"Your hallucinations."

I raised my uninjured shoulder in a semi-shrug. "I haven't had any in months."

She didn't speak and looked at me with a sorrowful expression. I froze and felt my spine give. The look on her face was something I'd seen too many times. It was the look one gets before telling someone about the death of a loved one. It was the look you give someone you care about right before you destroy their world.

"What is it?" I said quietly.

"Trevor, I got a call from Wilma."

The waitress. Oh, so that was it. Well, that wasn't too bad.

"I apologized to her. I shouldn't have snapped at the old lady like that. I just get ticked when people get judgmental and selectively pick Bible—"

"Trevor," she interrupted.

"What?"

"Wilma said you were sitting in a booth talking about the Bible and seemed to be arguing with somebody."

"Right," I said. "The old woman. She'd come over..."

Absence.

Colby lowered her eyes as I fell silent.

Silence for a full minute. Then in a near whisper, I said, "There was no woman. Was there?"

She shook her head.

I knew then that Chief Sally Colby had made absolutely

certain she was nothing like Chief Monty Caskins, who had called her family and unsympathetically delivered tragic news all those years ago. In fact, Sally Colby was extremely good at giving death notifications. In the kindest way possible, she had just informed me that my hopes for sanity, which had been on life support, were no longer with us.

"I can get it under control," I said.

She took my hand in hers. "An addict's promise."

I swallowed hard.

She asked, "So, I guess the question is: What are you addicted to now?"

Answers. I knew I was addicted to finding answers. Perhaps there is no more potent—or dangerous—drug than an answer to deadly riddle.

"I can finish this," I said.

"If *we* finish this, will you get help?"

More time passed than I had intended before I replied. "Yes."

She didn't believe me, but she let it go. I didn't believe me, because I couldn't let things go.

I beckoned whatever concentration I had left and said, "Are they coming?"

Colby released my hand and did her best to resume her professional demeanor. "Seth was a few minutes behind me. He agreed to come, but insisted on driving himself. He initially told me to get lost, but then I did what you suggested and mentioned that we had information about his shed break-in and his tone changed. He agreed to give us a half-hour and he raised David on the radio and to ask him to come too. David said he had to check something on the course and would drive over here in a few minutes."

She tossed a notebook on the table. "What's this all about, Trevor?"

I started to answer, but then Seth Wrangle was escorted into the room by Deputy Lemons. The former Olympian took a seat and scowled.

"I'm here, although I don't know why I agreed to this. What do you want?" he said.

"Let's wait a few minutes for your brother to arrive," I said. I half-expected for Seth to ask why we needed to wait on David, but when he didn't it helped to confirm my suspicions.

I asked Colby where they kept the coffee, left the room, threw away the tissues I'd been holding on my nose, and took my time before returning and placing four cups on the table. For once, I was the one who kept checking my watch as we waited for David Wrangle to appear.

"Did he say he was going to stop somewhere on the way?" Colby asked.

"No," Seth said. "He said he needed to finish up a couple things and would be right behind me."

We sipped hot tar from cheap cups and let the time pass until it was apparent Seth's brother had been delayed or decided not to come.

"I don't think Peter Lanskard killed himself," I said.

Seth locked eyes with me and didn't flinch.

"I don't think you killed him either. But I know who was supposed to take the fall."

He didn't speak and his eyes dropped to the Styrofoam cradled in his hand.

"When we talked about you hearing noises by your shed on the night after the murder, I asked you if there was any damage to the shed."

"So?" he said defensively.

"I didn't catch it at the time, but you never answered my question."

"Yes, I did," he said. "Look, I'm leaving town tomorrow and headed to another camp in Maine. I don't have a lot of time to waste. Chief Colby made it sound like you had new information to give me. If you do, then get to it."

"I asked you about damage to the shed and you told me that 'nothing was missing.' That's not the same thing. So let me ask you an entirely different question."

Seth turned slightly and picked fuzz off his fleece.

I leaned forward and asked, "What kind of rifle did you find in your shed?"

He swallowed hard and put his hands together on the table. I could feel Colby's eyes darting back and forth between us.

Finally, he said, "A Remington 700."

I leaned back and asked, "Can that fire a .308 round?"

He nodded once.

"Had you ever seen it before?"

"Absolutely not!" he shouted. Then, more softly he said, "I've never owned a rifle like that in my life. But when I opened up the shed and my flashlight beam hit that gun, I knew it meant trouble. I took a good look at it, saw the serial number had been filed off and right then I knew that it was the gun that killed Pete."

"And you didn't think to call me?" Colby asked loudly.

Seth shot her a menacing look. "You had been questioning me all afternoon and it was clear you thought I had something to do with the shooting. I had already watched you search my camp and I figured you would be searching my home soon enough. If I handed you the murder weapon, I knew you'd have me in cuffs in no time."

232

"But that's not the only reason you didn't call her, is it?" I said.

He lowered his head and something gave way behind his gaze.

"Did you know for sure David was somehow involved, or were you guessing?" I asked.

He sighed. "I didn't know for sure. I still don't. Maybe he had nothing to do with any of this, but…"

"But what?"

"David has a drinking problem and his behavior can be erratic, but it had gotten worse in the days before the shooting. He had become more frustrated with me for not selling the property and he thought I was being selfish. We had huge fights about it, but I insisted on holding onto the land for another year or two."

Seth rubbed his forehead and closed his eyes.

"None of it makes any sense," he said. "I don't know why I thought David might have killed Pete and I certainly don't know why he would hide the rifle in my shed. Pete wanted to buy the place eventually and David never had anything against the man, but I couldn't shake the feeling that he was somehow mixed up in this."

"Did you keep the rifle?" I asked.

"No," he said. "I disassembled it and tossed the pieces out all over the county roads."

I turned to Colby. "I assume you never searched Seth's home or the shed."

She shook her head. "Just his camp. I admit I wanted to search everything, but the judge wouldn't issue a search warrant for Seth's home. He didn't think I had enough probable cause and I knew Seth wouldn't consent since I he was already furious with me."

I asked Seth, "Did you ever confront your brother?"

His voice cracked as he spoke. "No. I guess I was afraid of what he'd say. If he shot Pete, I have to believe he had a reason. He wouldn't kill a man in cold blood. I know he wouldn't."

He wouldn't kill a man in cold blood. A flash of Lukas Derela's limp body flashed in front of my eyes. *Cold blood. I'd seen his knife before. He'd threatened me with it dozens of times while I'd been strapped to that chair. Weeks after I'd been rescued, I'd returned alone to the house and sifted through the gang's belongings. I hadn't seen the knife that day. I hadn't pocketed it. Right?*

"Mr. Galloway?" Seth Wrangle's voice had gone from defensive to one of concern. "If you don't mind me saying so, you look terrible. Are you feeling all right?"

Wiping a hand over my face, I said, "If it's any consolation, David didn't pull the trigger."

He watched me expectantly.

"However, he was an accomplice. In fact, I suspect he was the spotter who made the call when Peter Lanskard's car approached the property."

Any remaining hopefulness drained from Seth Wrangle's face. He asked, "Why? Why would he want to hurt Pete?"

"Peter Lanskard wasn't the ultimate target," I said. "You were."

"I don't understand. I wasn't at Pete's house. I was right where I said I was, at The Camp."

"Mr. Wrangle, I know this is a personal question but are you wealthy?" I asked. "I mean, I know you will be wealthy when you sell the land, but what is the state of your finances at this moment?"

He tried to chuckle and said, "I'm anything but wealthy. Do you see a lot of former Olympic biathletes doing television commercials? In this country, you can outrun linebackers or hit a bunch of homeruns and sponsors come running. But nobody cares if you're one of the best endurance athletes on the planet." Pointing at me, he said, "You mentioned you've done some distance running."

"I have."

"Right now, can you name the top five marathoners in the U.S.?"

I admitted I couldn't.

He crossed his arms and I could tell he'd had this conversation with others more than once.

Getting him back on point, I asked, "So if you were charged with murder and needed to retain a quality attorney, would you have difficulty coming up with a legal fund?"

"I suppose," he said.

Colby broke in with, "Where are you going with this, Trevor?"

"My point is, if you needed money—I mean *really* needed money for something like hiring a formidable defense team, you would have to sell the land you share with your brother and the Fredricks, right?"

"I don't think there would be any other option," he agreed.

I looked at Colby and said, "The reason none of this made sense a year ago is that this was a bungled setup from the beginning. The intent was to have Seth arrested for the murder of Peter Lanskard. As both of you told me, there were rumors around town that Seth and Peter were at odds with each other over selling the land where The Camp is situated. I think those rumors were planted. As I've learned over the past few days, it's easy for gossip to spread in this town, whether it's true or not."

Colby cleared her throat.

"Fine," I said. "Most of it about me was true."

Colby smiled with satisfaction.

I ignored her and moved on with explaining my theory. "If Peter was killed and the murder weapon was found on Seth's property, at a minimum he would be arrested. A conviction might be less likely, but by then he would have been forced to sell the land to fund his defense."

Colby said, "But I didn't have enough probable cause to search Seth's home or property. How would the rifle have ever been discovered?"

"I think that's where David failed," I said. "My guess is that stashing the rifle was only part of the plan. Not knowing for certain if Seth's shed would be searched, David would have also had to find a way of ensuring the police had cause to look there. I think the next step was to plant some .308 ammo, or something else incriminating, in the main office of The Camp or elsewhere. Maybe David calls in an anonymous tip and the police ask for consent to again search the office. Any of the property owners could grant consent to a search of The Camp even if Seth objected because he was pissed about being harassed by the police all day.

"The plan went haywire when Seth heard noises around his shed and popped out of his house. David couldn't have been certain that Seth hadn't spotted him. If he planted more evidence and called in the tip, then Seth would have known for certain what David was up to."

Seth was hanging on my every word and he didn't like any of them.

I continued, "It's possible that David returned later and saw that the rifle was missing, or maybe he lost his nerve. Either way, the police were never tipped off and nothing else was planted. Of course, I could be wrong and David may not have been the one to plant the gun, but I'm guessing that it was his assignment since he would be expected to carry his weight in the plan and he would have had the least risky parts.

"His primary duties were to gather intel and serve as the spotter. Chief Colby told me David was friends with Jason Leonard, who was Peter Lanskard's driver. It would have been easy for David to ask casual questions about Lanskard's alarm system and to find out when Peter was due to arrive back into town. Again, it's not like there are too many secrets in Washaway. Of course, now we can't ask Jason Leonard questions because he was a loose end that needed to be handled."

"There's no way David would have killed Jason," Seth said.

"He probably didn't," I said. "He wouldn't have been trusted to pull the trigger on anyone. With his shaky hands, it's easy to assume that David would be the best option to serve as a stationary spotter for Peter's murder and I doubt he would have been willing or able to shoot Jason Leonard."

Colby said, "Okay, there is still the issue of the timing. If Seth didn't pull the trigger, then who did? Nobody else I know of can ski fast enough and shoot well enough to have pulled this off."

"What did Brady Mason have to say when you asked him the questions I gave you?"

"You were right. He said there was a perimeter alarm activation on the north side an hour before Peter arrived. It was checked and cleared."

"And what about the alarm activation that we assumed signaled the shooter's escape? Was it actually in the same spot as the one where we presumed the shooter entered?"

Colby shrugged. "Mason said the technology doesn't allow them to be certain, but the difference could have been up to thirty yards."

I asked, "And after the shooting when it had been

determined the shooter had escaped, did they turn off the system?"

The chief of police said, "They didn't turn it off, but they stopped monitoring the system altogether since I was roaming around with my deputies and the state police. We were triggering every sensor along the perimeter and lighting up their monitors. Essentially, the system was useless at that point."

I pondered this and decided my hypothesis was proving to be reasonable.

Colby said, "Trevor?"

"It was a relay," I said.

Seth and Colby looked at me like I had lost my mind.

"We cancelled the relay," Seth said. "It didn't seem right with—"

"Not your relay—although thinking about that event is what made me realize how it was done," I said. "The killers'. It wasn't exactly a relay, but it was a team effort."

Seth and Colby looked at each other and there seemed to be a silent confirmation that I had lost my mind.

"The first leg of the relay actually started when the northern perimeter was broken an hour before Lanskard arrived. That was your shooter."

"The grounds were checked and nobody was found," Colby reminded me.

I said, "When we were talking a while back, you said that the shooter knew how to get in and out of the woods like a ghost. I think you were more right than you know. We have to be realistic. If someone skied onto the property and rapidly moved away from the point of entry then went silent and used camouflage, what's the likelihood that the person would be detected?"

"Not good," Colby said.

I turned my attention back to Seth Wrangle.

"When I visited your camp and talked to the Fredricks, they were wearing white snowsuits underneath brightly colored vests. I assume white suits like that are common."

"Sure," he said.

I surmised, "With a suit like that, it would be easy to vanish into a snowy landscape and lay low until it was time to get into a shooting position. That's exactly what Linda Fredrick did that day. She was an expert shot during her time in the military with weapons a lot more powerful than a .22 biathlon rifle. In fact, she used to participate in competitions with a different kind of bolt-action rifle. I'm guessing that a Remington 700, like the one you found in your shed, is a bolt-action, and not a semi-automatic that would be easier to trace in any firearms database."

Seth nodded.

I said, "Linda Fredrick evaded detection and once she was well within the perimeter and the alarm had been written off as being caused by wildlife, she made her way to her firing position and waited for Peter Lanskard to arrive."

"What about the next two alarms?" Colby asked. "The ones we assumed were the sniper entering and escaping."

"Misdirection," I said. "David was set up somewhere along the road leading up to the Lanskard estate. He called and let Jaden Fredrick know when Peter Lanskard's car was approaching. Jaden triggered the alarm and left the property. A few minutes later, Linda put Peter Lanskard in the crosshairs and ended his life. Four minutes after that, Jaden found a spot where he couldn't be seen by Letterman, and once again tripped the alarm before scurrying away. The logical conclusion was that the second alarm activation was the shooter leaving the property. Linda would have already hidden herself somewhere else on the outskirts of the grounds until the police started their search of the woods. Then she left while the numerous alarm activations were being ignored. This was organized like your average urban drug dealing operation. With those you have your logistical coordinator—Jaden. You have your lookout—David. And you have your street operator—Linda. Each had a role to play and the success of the transaction depended on everyone following through.

"The scheme was complex, but served two purposes. It made it appear that there was one person setting off the alarm right before and after the shot was fired, and the timing of the alarms indicated that the shooter was an incredible skier. The timing, plus the eventual discovery of the Remington in Seth's shed, would implicate Seth in the killing. He would then have little choice but to agree to the sale of the land and David and the Fredricks would have their millions."

"No," Seth said. "David and I have had our differences and he has his problems, but I can't believe he would be involved with a murder or want me to go to prison."

I thought about that and checked my watch again. A sense of dread crept under my skin. I looked down started to blur-out. I stopped myself, fearing where it would take me. Doing my best to keep one foot in the real world, I talked my way through it.

"Maybe you're right. Perhaps the Fredricks conned David by telling him they were only going to take a shot in Lanskard's direction, but that they weren't going to kill him. He could have thought that the worst that you would get hit with was an attempted murder charge that would probably get pled down to a lesser charge in the hands of a competent attorney. But when David got more than he bargained for, he was trapped and the amount of guilt he's been carrying has to be immense. That's why he's still drinking and appears to be on shaky ground."

Again, I lowered my head and gazed at my watch. "David isn't coming," I said.

Seth pulled out a phone and dialed a number.

"No answer on his cell," he said.

He dialed another number. "Gracie, have you seen David?"

Seth listened intently before he pressed a button and put the phone in his pocket.

"Gracie says that David was in his office and had some sort of argument with Linda and Jaden. There was a struggle and David stormed outside and hopped on our only tracked four-wheeler. According to Gracie, Linda and Jaden were talking in low voices before they grabbed some skis and took off after him."

Seth's eyes were wide and the color drained from his face. "Gracie said she went back to the office where they were fighting and there was a lockbox open on the floor. It was empty."

"What was in the lockbox?" Colby asked.

"David kept a pistol in there," Seth said with great concern.

"What do you think?" Colby asked.

A wave of guilt hit me. "Seth, when you raised David on the radio to tell him to come over here, did you mention to him that we had new information about your shed break-in?"

Seth said he had.

"He must have figured out that we had a good idea about his involvement and saw this as a trap. I wanted to rattle his cage, but this may have pushed him over the edge. If he told the Fredricks that he was thinking of coming clean..."

I didn't have to finish my sentence.

Colby stood. "We better get out there. I'll drive."

I stood as well. "Seth, I saw some of the course, but how big is your camp?"

"Big enough that I need to go with you. I know where he

likes to go to be alone, and I can guide you."

Seth ran out of the room ahead of us. Colby turned to me. "Do you think David is going to hurt himself?"

"If he doesn't, the Fredricks will."

CHAPTER 22

Seth threw the car door open before Colby could bring the cruiser to a stop. He ran into the main office of The Camp and emerged seconds later with skis, poles, and boots.

I stared dumbly at Colby. "Can you go with him?"

She returned my look. "I don't know how to ski. Do you?"

We both blinked at each other. I walked over to Seth who was busy equipping himself. "Seth, we don't ski. Which way do we go and how do we get there?"

He didn't even look up from his feet as he pointed in a direction opposite from the part of the course I had seen the previous day.

"There's a pond about a mile in that direction," he said. "David generally goes out there and either sits by the water or goes up on the hill that overlooks the valley. I'm heading up the hill, then I'll check the pond."

Colby and I exchanged glances and I once again asked, "But how do we get there if we don't ski and if there is no four-wheeler? I assume Colby's car isn't going to do the job."

Seth Wrangle shook his head, pushed off with his ski poles, and was gone.

"Crap," Colby said as she looked out over rolling hills blanketed with snow. "There's no way my car is going to make it ten yards off the road."

My eyes searched for a solution that wasn't going to present itself. Finally I said, "We have to run."

Colby opened her mouth to argue, but resigned herself to the job ahead of us. "Let's go."

For several minutes the two of us plodded along in snow that was suitable for skis but certainly too deep to develop a consistent running stride. My breath was heavy and the moisture was immediately freezing on my face. Colby stumbled along in her boots, while I tried my best to ignore the snow and ice that had sunk into my shoes. I wasn't sure how much time had passed when we reached a steep hill and noticed ski marks heading around it in each direction. Both of us were breathless and I struggled to articulate my thoughts.

"You go to the right and I'll head left," I gasped before the sound of a gunshot echoed through the valley.

"That was no biathlon rifle," I said.

Colby, also out of breath, couldn't speak, but proceeded to move around to the right. I did my best to resume my previous pace and followed the tracks in front of me until they started overlapping with what appeared to be tire impressions. The ski marks and tire tracks wove through a cluster of evergreens that formed a canopy over the land. Green and brown needles bit at my ankles as I plodded through snow and pinecones. *Needles. I'm always haunted by needles.* My lungs begged for more air, my wounded shoulder burned, and my eyes watered as I pushed through the trees and found myself in a clearing within view of a frozen pond.

Linda and Jaden Fredrick were on skis and had their backs to me. The couple was a hundred yards away and oblivious to my presence. On the ground beside them lay a screaming and bleeding Seth Wrangle holding a bloody leg. Linda Fredrick kept a pistol pointed at Seth, while her eyes remained trained on another man a few feet away. At the edge of the pond, which I could now tell was not completely frozen over, stood a mortified David Wrangle. David held his own pistol in a trembling hand. I listened as well as I could while I kept running.

"Drop the gun or I kill him right now," yelled Linda who kept her pistol trained on Seth.

David did as he was told and held his hands out to his side.

"Now, start backing up," she said. "You know it's for the best, anyway."

David looked over his shoulder at the cracked ice. He glanced back to the Fredricks and shook his head. Another shot rang out and Seth grabbed his other leg and howled. I drew my weapon and started a long sprint toward the pond.

"Please don't!" David begged. "Please!"

"Do it!" Jaden commanded. "Now!"

Through wet eyes I saw David take a step back toward an icy demise.

"Keep going, David," yelled Jaden.

Seth said something I couldn't understand and was immediately kicked by the woman pointing a gun at him. David took two more steps backward and I could tell he was getting close to the thinner portion of the ice.

I could barely make out David's voice. "I'm sorry, Seth," he said. "They told me that nobody would get hurt. They told me you wouldn't even get convicted, but that your reputation around here would be ruined and you would have no reason to hold on to the property. I'm so sorry." He took another step.

I was still nearly thirty yards away from the Fredricks when Linda heard my approach and turned. My breathing was out of control and my heart was beating out of my chest. My vision was hazy and my fingers numb with the cold. Somewhere in my head, memories of my police training and voices of old instructors found their way to the present day. I raised my shooting hand, mostly to see if I still held the weapon with my unfeeling grasp. I feebly tried to issue a verbal command for her to drop her pistol, but before I could speak with any volume Linda started to lift pistol. I stopped dead in my tracks.

My finger tightened on the trigger, or at least I thought it did. In an impossibly rapid slideshow flash, a series of images raced through my mind. Pittsburgh. That attic. Lukas Derela. Needles. A knife. My badge sliding across a captain's desk—surrendered. Maddox on the floor. Markus Faust. The bear. The car crash.

The Lithuanian.

Finally, I saw a fuzzy sight picture beyond my weapon. Then I heard the sound of primal rage as a cataclysmic explosion sounded through the barrel of my Sig Sauer 250. The nine-millimeter bullet from the pistol struck her above the right eyebrow.

Linda Fredrick's legs held her in position, not wanting to accept the signature on her death warrant. Seconds passed before Jaden reached out for his wife only to grasp air as she fell in snow that slowly transitioned from white to crimson.

Wiping my eyes, I advanced on Jaden. The shock that consumed his face quickly turned to rage. He ducked down beside his wife's body, reached into the snow, and came up holding a pistol. Dropping to one knee I did my best to focus on my sights, but the wind caused tears to once again flood my eyes. In that frozen moment, I understood I was a dead man.

Colby's voice boomed, "Drop it and don't move, Jaden!"

I blinked heavily as I heard a gun erupt. My eyes cleared enough to see Jaden fall onto his wife's corpse while at the same time grabbing his right arm. The gun he had been holding, flew through the air and landed several feet away, buried once again. Before Jaden could get his bearings, Colby had the man in cuffs.

My hands were shaking from the cold, fatigue, and the rush of adrenaline as I made my way to the pond. David cautiously let his feet slide him back to solid ground and he tended to his brother who was now sitting upright. Colby glanced up and noticed me staring at the hole in Linda Fredrick's head.

"Hell of a shot," Colby said.

I couldn't speak. Even if I could have, it wouldn't have felt right to say anything with a woman's dead eyes looking up at me.

"Damn, Galloway," Seth said through the pain. "If you can learn to do that with skis and a rifle, you're going to take my job away from me."

I still couldn't take in enough air to find my voice, so I shook my head.

He continued, "Biathlon is a little harder to learn for guys like you who are in your fifties, but it's possible."

I looked at Colby and she fought back a smile.

Shaking my head, I managed to gasp, "I'm only...I'm—"

"He's the Tin Man," Colby interrupted. "He's timeless."

CHAPTER 23

Cops don't like it when non-cops shoot people. Therefore, after half the officers in central Pennsylvania descended upon The Camp, I was pulled away by a group of state troopers and interviewed at length. They had taken my gun, which I hoped I would get back at some point, and confirmed that it was legally registered in my name. In spite of being cold, tired, and irritated that I had been forced to kill someone, my story never changed and I was eventually cut loose as the day turned into night. I felt naked without my gun and my phone had died again. It would have to stay dead a while since I'd lost the charger as well as my shoulder brace while running around The Camp. So I had no weapons and no usable phone. Hell, I didn't even have a pocketknife. If my hallucination showed up to kill me, I'd have to rely on a useless set of car keys to save me. Maybe I could throw them at any enemies that presented themselves. Perfect.

Colby insisted I stay one more night on her couch rather than find a hotel or try to drive back to Pittsburgh in my exhausted condition. I started to argue, but as I was coming down from an adrenaline high and had been having some strong doubts about my mental stability, I quickly gave in to the chief of police who probably thought I was nuts. Not wanting to be an imposition any longer than necessary, I told Colby I wanted to get on the road first thing in the morning and asked if someone could take me back to the inn so I could retrieve the rest of my belongings.

She understood and, since she was going to be tied up for a while longer, asked a deputy from a neighboring jurisdiction to drive me into Washaway. The deputy started leading me to his car when Colby called out to me.

"Do you still have that key I gave you?"

I dug into the pockets of my jeans and was surprised to find the key to the inn. I held it up for her to see.

"Don't lose it," she said. "We don't have another one. And please lock up when you're finished."

Fearing I'd lose a stray key, I put it on my keychain with my car keys.

"I'll lock up," I said.

"In and out and then back to my house, okay?" she asked, but it really wasn't a question. "Have the deputy go inside with you."

I nodded and pointed toward the deputy who was out of earshot. "Does he know where you live in case I can't remember how to get out there?"

"He knows," she answered.

It's Washaway. Of course he knows.

I caught up to the deputy who was nice enough to let me sit in the front seat of the cruiser. The car warmed up after a few miles and I leaned my head back and let the heat wash over me. I was enjoying the quiet but then the young deputy tried a little too hard to get a conversation going. At first, I wasn't sure if he was really that friendly or he just wanted the scoop on what had happened at The Camp. I considered that he might be as suspicious of me as the rest of the cops who had been at the scene and he was trying to build rapport in the hopes I'd reveal some earthshattering new fact.

The affable deputy, who may have been three years removed from high school, pulled into a space on the street halfway between the inn and Nick's Diner. The hue of the streetlights reflected off sections of the blackened road and gave the town an eerie noir feel.

Pointing at the diner, he said, "I'm going to get some hot chocolate for the road, do you want to go with me? Maybe you'd feel better talking about what happened today."

I decided he was definitely trying to win Adolescent-Deputy-Of-The-Year points by trying to engage me in a heartfelt discussion about the day's events. I knew he was having visions of getting pats on the back for getting me to spill my guts and admit to doing something illegal. Part of me wanted to lecture him on his clumsy, bush-league approach, but I'd aggravated enough people for the winter. Besides, even though the local cops were understandably suspicious of me, I really didn't have anything to hide. I politely declined the deputy's invitation by saying I'd seen enough of Nick's Diner and the diner had certainly seen enough of me.

He looked at me questioningly and asked, "Do you want me to get something for you?" Remembering what happened the last time I was alone in the inn, I thought about asking the baby-faced cop to accompany me inside. I suddenly felt silly asking this kid who wanted hot chocolate to come inside in case the Big Bad Wolf was waiting in the dark. I told him I'd be fine and that I'd meet him back at the car in a few minutes. In the recesses of my mind, I heard Dr. Raylene Westerly's disapproving voice saying two words: *testosterone overdose.*

I approached the front door of the inn, reached down and picked up a newspaper that was mostly covered with snow. I'd made the mistake of trying to grab it with my left hand and my shoulder violently revolted. I knew I'd have to get that MRI done sooner than later, although I was dreading having to deal with what were sure to be substantial medical expenses. I felt a glimmer of hope when it occurred to me that Susan Lanskard might be willing to take care of the medical bills. Even though I'd never officially negotiated a fee with her, I assumed requesting reasonable expenses would be appropriate. You know...like a new car, repaired shoulder, and hotel bills. I didn't want to take advantage of the lady, but this little trip to the sticks was going to make my credit card company very happy.

Taking the key, I turned the cheap deadbolt, pushed the door open, and took a step inside the dark lobby. I felt along a wall, banged into a coat stand, and eventually found the light switch. Other than not being filled with law enforcement officers, the lobby appeared no different than the night I'd found a horrible surprise in my bed.

I glanced over to the front desk, remembering Maddox lying on the floor. *I couldn't have done that to him*, I told myself. However, I remembered the vividness of the hallucinations I had experienced not that long ago. I recounted a time I'd suddenly become aware of standing in my kitchen, but not remembering how I had gotten there. I could still feel the panic in my chest when people I'd been talking to suddenly disappeared, having never been real at all. A sickening feeling hit me as I thought the earlier incident in the diner.

I shivered as I had visions of hitting Maddox from behind and whispering into his ear with a harsh voice. Were these cruel daydreams, or memories? There had been times before when I'd been unable to distinguish the line between fantasy and reality. It had gotten worse after I'd shot Derela in that hotel room, but I'd become confused before that night. At the time, I was certain I'd heard him trying to escape out a window just as I was sure he'd been holding a knife. Now, I wasn't even sure if I had beaten an old man who had done nothing but show me kindness. Colby was right. Being alone was a very bad idea, and I needed to get out of this place.

The staircase darkened as it rose and I followed the path until the light ended. I searched a wall in the upstairs hallway and was able to flick on another light. The door to my room was closed and I reached out with the same key I'd used on the front entrance. I grasped the iron knob and prepared to unlock the door, but the knob turned smoothly and the door opened. I wondered why the crime scene techs hadn't locked it after processing the scene. *Because the evidence had been collected and the inn's exterior doors were locked.* There was no reason to lock up the room.

I entered the room and turned on the inadequate lights. I could see that the forensic guys had taken not only the sheets and pillows from the bed, but the entire top mattress. I was sure that some blood had soaked down into the bed and the techs didn't want to be accused of being sloppy in what amounted to a high-profile crime.

Searching the room, I instinctively felt for my gun, which of course was not on me. By now it was in an evidence locker so it could later be fired and undergo ballistic analysis. Even with Colby being a witness, the state police investigators weren't going to take any chances at being embarrassed after I'd come in and solved a case they'd never cracked. I looked at the keys in my other hand and sarcastically mumbled, "Gee, at least I have this deadly weapon."

I finished checking the room, found my laptop in the spot I'd left it, and slid it into its case. I started to pick it up and leave, when I heard a voice coming from somewhere outside the window. I pulled the curtain back in time to see Maddox getting out of a pickup truck and waving to the driver. He had apparently badgered his way out of the hospital and caught a ride home from somebody. He walked toward the front door, which was directly under my window, and disappeared from my line of sight. The truck pulled away and I watched the its taillights dim as it left. All was quiet as I noticed it was starting to snow again.

Snow piling up on top of snow. More weight being added to an existing burden. In some history class long ago, I had been told a story about a man who had been caught up in the Salem witch trials. The town's powerful figures had laid the man out, set boards on top of his chest and stomach, and started placing heavy stones on the boards. The point of this slow suffocation, called pressing, was to force the man to make a plea to the charge of witchcraft. The man repeatedly refused to make a plea, and instead of begging for the torture to stop, he was quoted as speaking the phrase "more weight" hoping that death would stop his pain. Eventually it did, but not soon enough.

I watched the snow freefall faster. *How much weight can the mind carry before we start asking for mercy? How much more until I completely snap? I can take the meds, but then what am I? Is the gain greater than the loss?* My mind began to settle into calm self-inspection and deep contemplation.

"You did not appreciate my message?"

My heart jammed into my throat and I whirled around toward the jagged, accented voice.

More accented words slithered through the room. "I do hope you kept a souvenir before the police officers took everything away."

I blinked and waited for him to vanish again like he had done on the street. Instead, the figure took three heavy steps into the room.

"What is the matter?" he asked. "You do not seem so anxious to make rude gestures toward me anymore."

I noted his appearance was exactly the same as when he had

253

stood on top of the hill and taken a shot at me. Then, I realized the possible importance of that fact. His appearance was *exactly* the same. He was wearing the same clothes, same jacket, his hair looked identical, and he had the same gun in his hand—everything. Had my previous hallucinations ever changed clothes? I wasn't sure.

"You look terrible, Detective Galloway," said The Lithuanian. He made a *tsk tsk* noise. "But you are not a detective anymore, no? You stayed a detective long enough to kill my cousin and then you quit."

I didn't speak. I didn't move.

"I wanted to kill you in Pittsburgh," said the figure. "I could have killed you in Pittsburgh. I watched you many, many times and could have taken your life whenever I wished."

My voice failed, but then I asked, "Why didn't you?"

He shrugged, the gun still in his right hand. "The people I work for thought it would bring about unwanted attention if I killed you in the city."

"The people you work with are all locked up or dead," I said with a bit more force.

He shook his head and smiled as I wondered if I was having a conversation with myself.

"No, no. Those men were only part of the organization. In some ways, my Pittsburgh associates being taken away ended up being a good thing. The police believe our organization is no longer operating in the city and now we have much more freedom. My employers were concerned that if it was discovered that something unfortunate happened to you, everything would be locked down and our people would be hunted."

With his left hand, he reached behind his back and withdrew a long knife. He twirled it around with his fingers and took another step forward. Instinctively I tried to step back, but I was already against the window.

"So, I had to wait," he continued. "I was very patient and did what was best for my people. But I never forgot about you, Mr. Galloway. Not for one second did I forget about you."

With my right foot, I gently tapped one time, as I said, "If you were able to wait, you must not have cared that much about your cousin."

I tapped my foot again.

The Lithuanian sighed. "Lukas was not a good businessman and to be truthful, he was—how do you say it in America—a jackass?"

"I agree," I said while softly tapping my foot one time. I then realized agreeing may not be the brightest move. However, the man didn't react.

"But he was my cousin. If I were to let his death go unavenged," he said shaking his head, "then I would be no man at all." He smirked again. "An eye for an eye and all that."

"Yeah, I got the message," I said while tapping one time. "The eyes and fingers," I continued with another quick tap. "Who did they belong to?" I finished the question with a tap.

"A nice man named Elvin, I believe. I found him in a hunting cabin far from here. He told me his wife was not expecting him back for several days, so I knew he would not be missed. His four-wheel drive truck is parked down the street. That other car was no good in this snow."

He pointed the gun at me while starting to walk toward me. Fearing the conversation was winding down I quickly found more words.

I tapped my foot while I said, "Did Lukas carry a knife like yours?"

He stopped in the middle of the room and looked at the knife in his hand.

"Lukas always carried his favorite knife, but you know this. I read in the newspapers that he attacked you with a knife when you shot him."

I tapped again and blurted, "The one that he carried—did it have a shield imprinted in a black handle?"

"Ah, yes. The shield you speak of is a Vytis. It is a symbol of my country—"

The knife belonged to Lukas Derela. I didn't imagine it. I opened my right hand and let go of the keys I had been clutching. The metal hit the floor creating a pronounced final tap. The Lithuanian's eyes dropped and he stared at the keys. He looked back up at me and started laughing.

"What is this?" he said with a grin. "You wish to bribe me with your car?" He laughed again and took another step forward. Then, as quickly as it arrived, the smile vanished from his face and something menacing and evil appeared in his expression. Raising the knife, he hissed, "I don't want your car, I want your eyes."

I used my foot to slide the keys on the floor until they came to rest against his boots. The moment the keys came to thud, two thoughts entered my mind.

The first was: *Thank God. He's real.*

The second was: *Damn. He's real.*

Our eyes locked and time stood still as I felt that old rage come to life. Neither of us breathed. I stood tall and any fear I had vanished into the night.

Then, I decided to show this killer exactly how bad my temper could be.

"They keys aren't a bribe," I told him. "They're a message of my own."

He paused, confused. Then his eyes widened and he leaned forward to take another step.

I yelled, "Now, Maddox! Light him up!"

The wooden floor underneath The Lithuanian's feet exploded and his body jerked violently from side to side as I tried to shield my eyes from shards of wood. Not all the 9mm rounds being fired from Earl Maddox's very modern H&K MP5 submachine gun made it through the floor, but plenty did. I had left the semiautomatic weapon in the former sailor's bedroom and he had understood my Morse code distress signal while distinguishing between the two sets of footsteps coming from my room. Locations of voices in a home can be hard to pinpoint, but the keys sliding across Maddox's ceiling and coming to a halt in a position several feet away from my SOS had been all the man needed for confirmation.

When the gunfire ceased, the assassin was dumbfounded and still standing. His eyes were wide and he was looking at me, but not at me. Blood came out of his mouth and his legs gave way. He fell to the floor with a thud.

I heard Maddox yell, "Did I get him?"

"You got him," I said as I knelt next to the hit man.

The killer tried to speak, but nothing would come out the first time. He gasped again and the look on his face fell somewhere between frightened and vacant. Whatever he had been expecting on this trip, his own death hadn't been part of the agenda. Now a monster, who had felt so little compassion for others, was facing his mortality. There was genuine fear in his eyes, and I wondered if he was sensing something akin to a conscience. What goes through your mind when you're in excruciating pain and the only two outcomes facing you are imprisonment or death?

The sounds were barely audible, but he said something in

Lithuanian. Although I didn't speak the language, I think I could have made the translation.

More weight.

EPILOGUE

A shadow fell over the drink I had been nursing for ten minutes. The muscle-bound, tattooed tank rumbled into the booth and sat facing me. A thin man at another table seemed to take notice of the new arrival, who struck fear into the less-scrupulous citizens of Pittsburgh. Color drained from the man's face and he pulled a toothpick from between his lips, left some money on his table, and headed for the door. The entire way out the restaurant, toothpick guy kept checking to see if trouble was following him from the diner and into the bustling streets of patchwork asphalt and blacktop characteristic of this section of the city.

"You never lose your charm with the citizenry," I said, hoping toothpick guy was real.

"I don't consider him a citizen," Chase Vinson said. "He recently took over that pawn shop over on Liberty and the word is he's fencing items from a string of burglaries in Squirrel Hill. I'll get him. It's a matter of time."

The waitress approached and asked, "What can I get for you, Chase?"

He looked at me and I said, "I already ordered."

Chase said, "I'll take the Sloppy Joe platter and a Coke, Janice."

She turned to me. "Do you want another iced tea, sweetie?"

"I'm good, thanks."

She scurried away and shouted the order back into the

kitchen. Chase unwrapped utensils from a napkin, flattened the thin white paper out onto the table, and lined up the silverware. He turned slightly to allow his heavy arm to rest on the back of the booth.

"Are you doing okay?" he asked.

"I am."

"Any problems with the shooting?"

"No," I said. "I caught a little grief from the state police about not being a registered PI, but they eventually accepted the fact that I had a concealed weapons permit and fired in self-defense. Chief Colby ran some interference for me."

"That's not what I meant, and you know it."

I did know.

"You killed someone," he said. "An easy thing to do, but not an easy thing to do. You know what I mean?"

"I'm doing fine. No unusual nightmares, hallucinations, or urges."

His face soured. "As opposed to the usual ones?"

"Damn it, Chase. You're a pain in the ass."

The sour look vanished and he smiled. "That's true."

A Coke appeared in front of my friend and he took a sizable gulp.

"I thought that case would keep you busy for a few weeks," he said.

I shrugged. "All it needed was a fresh set of eyes. The crime was screwed up, so the investigation followed suit."

He put down his drink and smiled broadly.

"What?" I asked.

"I called Colby. She said you sprinted across an open field after running at least a mile in the snow then fired a round into the head of that Fredrick woman."

"Yeah. And?"

"Colby said you hit her from at least twenty-five yards away. She said it was the most amazing piece of shooting she had ever seen. She said that after the shooting you were still panting and shaking and that the head shot was one for the history books."

I unwrapped my silverware so I would have something to do with my hands.

"She's young," I said coyly. "She hasn't seen much."

"Uh-huh," my friend said. "I don't suppose you happened to mention that you were aiming at the woman's chest—which I'm assuming you were since you're not dumb enough to attempt a head shot at any great distance."

"It never came up," I said with an expression I hoped was innocent.

Chase snickered, then turned serious.

"I assume you haven't heard anything new about your Lithuanian friend?"

I shook my head. Amazingly, the killer who it turned out was absolutely not a boogieman my mind had conjured up, survived the shooting. Out of the thirty bullets Maddox had fired from the MP5, only a few had struck the sociopath. He was currently under heavy guard at the local hospital and was due to be transported to a more secure facility any day now.

Chase laid one of his arms on the table and he clenched his fist. A quarter-inch of ink peeked out from the cuff of his dress shirt. I tried to recall which tattoo it was, but couldn't.

"How the hell did that son of a bitch take six bullets and live?"

I shrugged. "Two lodged in his legs, and three in his torso. Then there was the other one."

I didn't feel the need to once again elaborate on the path of the final bullet that struck The Lithuanian since I had already told Chase on the phone that the psycho now had one less testicle. Colby had attempted to interview The Lithuanian, whose prints weren't on file, and she told me he was very unhappy about the loss and placed the blame squarely on me. As Chase recalled our previous conversation, he cringed slightly as his arm slid from the table and he subconsciously protected his own assets.

We had a lengthy awkward male moment of injured-genitalia silence. Chase squirmed and I could tell he wasn't sure if, given what I had been through, it was all right to use the black humor so common among cops and other first respon-ders. I could see he was debating making some sort of crude lost-testicle joke and while I enjoyed watching the tough guy squirm in that booth, I decided to throw him a lifeline.

I cleared my throat. "Imagine what I'll find under my pillow next time."

Chase laughed loudly and said, "And the legend of Trevor Galloway continues to know no bounds."

"They still haven't been able to ID him."

Chase's expression turned serious. "They will. Everybody is somebody."

"He told me his organization is active in Pittsburgh. He implied the police aren't on to them and they've managed to stay under the radar since..." I searched for the right words.

Chase finished my thought. "Since the crew that took you was eliminated."

"If it's true," I said. "It means my original investigation only scratched the surface. What if there's an entire drug pipeline that has gone completely undetected? It means everything I went through was for nothing."

Chase's expression turned sour. "Don't even think that way. No matter what, some very bad people got locked up."

"Or killed," I said, thinking of Lukas Derela.

He leaned forward and growled, "Damn right. You tracked that piece of shit down and you put a bullet in his chest. He had it coming and that's that." Chase leaned back and continued. "I'm not going to say that you should forget the past, because we both know it's not that simple. But forget about what this guy said about his organization and all that. Even if it's true, it's not your problem."

Yet I knew it was my problem. At the very least I was now responsible for not only Lukas Derela's death, but also the fact that the organization's top enforcer was out of circulation. When a criminal enterprise loses key members, the people running the show are going to be pissed. Regardless of what Chase said, the problem was very much mine.

Chase said, "It's too bad about that guy he cut up. What was his name?"

"Elvin," I said. "Elvin Simple. He was in the wrong place at the wrong time."

We sat somberly and thought about the poor man's fate. I'd already told Chase about how the body had been found at his hunting cabin, minus the fingers and eyes. I told him about the grieving widow. I told him about the police finding beige Chevy that had nearly killed me parked behind the cabin. What I didn't tell Chase was that I'd been stunned when Elvin Simple, age fifty-two, of Altoona, PA was found with both his ears. I also didn't tell Chase how I'd gone to a salvage yard to take one last look at my SUV and had found no blood or evidence of any kind that indicated my fingers had held anything more than thin air prior to the crash. I didn't tell him any of this and I wouldn't tell him.

As if he could read my thoughts, he asked, "Are you back on the meds?"

I nodded.

"For good?"

I nodded. *For now.*

He feigned satisfaction with my response and slid that topic off the table. He scanned the street through the window beside us. "I may have another job for you, when you're ready."

I opened my mouth, but he held up a giant paw. "Not now. When you're ready. You're not."

Our food arrived and Chase asked me if I knew what Seth Wrangle was going to do now that most of his staff was either dead or headed to prison.

"He said he's going to sell the land, or at least lease the mineral rights, and allow a company to dig it up," I said. "He wants to pay for his brother's defense attorneys. Since he needs the money immediately, and there are some portions of the property that haven't been explored for Goshen, he's going to end up taking a reduced price but he'll still make out well."

"Seriously?" Chase said. "So David Wrangle wanted to frame his own brother so that Seth would have to sell the land in order to support his own defense. Now the money from the transaction will go toward David Wrangle's defense fund instead?"

"Right."

"That's messed up," he said shaking his enormous head. "It's a good thing David and the Fredricks jacked-up the frame job."

"The plan might have worked, if David wouldn't have gotten spooked," I said. "According to David, Linda Fredrick used a pair of Seth's gloves when she shot Peter Lanskard. She wore latex gloves under Seth's gloves—which he always labeled with his initials—to make sure that she didn't leave any of her own DNA inside of them. After using the Remington, the gloves obviously would have been covered with gunshot residue. David was supposed to plant the rifle in Seth's shed and the gloves in a dumpster near a grocery store in Washaway Township. Then, he would call in an anonymous tip to the police stating that someone had been acting suspiciously around the dumpster and had tossed something in there. The tip would include a partial license plate number, which would happen to match Seth's car. With that evidence, Colby would certainly have enough for a warrant and would have found the rifle in the shed.

"David bailed out on the plan once he thought Seth may have spotted him. He was already on the fence since he'd found out Peter Lanskard was dead. The Fredricks had lied to him and told him they intended on staging an attempt on Lanskard's life, but they weren't going to actually shoot him. But once Lanskard was killed, David was in as deep as the other two. The Fredricks were furious when David failed to plant the gun, but there wasn't much they could do about it at that point. They were willing to cut their losses until David told them he was going to meet with Colby and me and tell us the whole story. David was falling apart and couldn't take the stress anymore."

"How did Faust fit in?"

"According to David, when I popped up and started asking questions, he got nervous and had a heated discussion with the Fredricks. Faust overhead the conversation and they spotted him before he could slink away. The Fredricks knew that Faust was using HGH and blackmailed him to keep his mouth shut. I think Faust approached me in order to passively steer me towards the Fredricks by provoking me to look at Seth Wrangle closely enough that I'd eventually clear him. He knew that word would get back to the Fredricks that he was trying to scare me off, but his real agenda was to put me on to the Fredricks."

"So he was trying to do the right thing," Chase said.

I shrugged a shoulder and said, "Maybe. His motives may

have been selfish and he simply wanted to eliminate his black-mailers. Regardless, after they saw me talking to him at The Camp, they took an opportunity to silence him permanently. Jaden Fredrick isn't talking, but David said the Fredricks told him that Jaden forced Faust off the course and Linda followed Faust after he crashed down the hill. Then Linda smashed his head against a rock and jumped back in the race before anyone was looking. That was why the Fredrick's finish times were slower than usual. Even with Jaden refusing to speak, I'm sure David Wrangle will testify and that may be enough to at least convict Jaden for Peter Lanskard's murder. David needs as much help from the DA as possible, so he's not holding any-thing back."

"What about the driver? Jason Leonard?"

"He was totally innocent in the whole thing," I said. "In the days before the shooting at the estate, David had managed to use Leonard to get Peter Lanskard's expected arrival time. The Fredricks didn't consider him a liability until…"

My friend completed my sentence. "Until you showed up."

"Right." *More weight.*

A few moments passed before Vinson asked, "So who pulled the trigger on the driver?"

"David said he doesn't know, but thinks it was Jaden Fredrick. But like I said, Jaden's not talking."

"Well, I don't feel sorry for David and neither should his brother. Seth should let him swing."

"Maybe," I said. "I think Seth feels guilty for not selling the land sooner and getting his brother some help for his addiction. Now, he's trying to make amends. It's what brothers do."

"Would you do that for me?" he asked.

"Would I do what for you?"

"Sell your land and come to my rescue if I get locked up for murder."

"We aren't brothers," I said to the man whose blond hair sharply contrasted by black waves and who towered over me by a good six inches.

"No kidding," he said with an eye roll. "But we're friends. If I were in David Wrangle's position, would you rush to bail me out?"

I looked up and down Chase's massive frame. "The question is irrelevant."

"Why is that?"

"Your heavy ass would have fallen through the ice on that pond."

One side of his face curled up. "Heartless, man. Totally heartless."

I couldn't help but smile.

ACKNOWLEDGMENTS

I would like to convey special thanks to Olympic biathlete Curt Schreiner for his valuable assistance in researching this book. Any inaccuracies regarding this amazingly technical sport are mine and mine alone. I would also like to thank Craig Fischer for lending me his expertise in the field of perimeter alarm systems. While I do have some knowledge of firearms, Sam Lerch helped me nail down some of the details regarding long range shooting. I cannot begin to properly express my gratitude toward Eric Campbell and Lance Wright at Down & Out Books for their support of a novel that is admittedly unusual. Over the years I have enjoyed a great amount of support from the International Thriller Writers organization, the Pittsburgh chapter of Sisters in Crime, Mystery Lovers Bookshop, and the entire Pittsburgh literary community for which I am extremely grateful. I appreciate the assistance of Chief Kevin Meyer and the entire Cranberry Township, PA Police Department in helping me better understand law enforcement operations in Pennsylvania. Finally, I am thankful to my family for being incredibly patient and supportive.

J.J. Hensley is a former police officer and former Special Agent with the U.S. Secret Service. He is the author of the novels *Resolve*, *Measure Twice*, and *Chalk's Outline*. J.J. graduated from Penn State University with a B.S. in Administration of Justice and has a M.S. degree in Criminal Justice Administration from Columbia Southern University.

Mr. Hensley's first novel *Resolve* was named one of the Best Books of 2013 by *Suspense Magazine* and was a Thriller Award finalist.

He is a member of the International Thriller Writers and Sisters in Crime.

http://www.hensley-books.com/

OTHER TITLES FROM DOWN AND OUT BOOKS

See www.DownAndOutBooks.com for complete list

By J.L. Abramo
Chasing Charlie Chan
Circling the Runway
Brooklyn Justice
Coney Island Avenue

By Trey R. Barker
Exit Blood
Death is Not Forever
No Harder Prison

By Eric Beetner
Unloaded (editor)
Criminal Elements
Rumrunners
Leadfoot

By Eric Beetner
and Frank Zafiro
The Backlist
The Shortlist

By G.J. Brown
Falling

By Angel Luis Colón
No Happy Endings
Meat City on Fire (*)

By Shawn Corridan
and Gary Waid
Gitmo

By Frank De Blase
Pine Box for a Pin-Up
Busted Valentines
A Cougar's Kiss

By Les Edgerton
The Genuine, Imitation,
Plastic Kidnapping
Lagniappe
Just Like That (*)

By Danny Gardner
A Negro and an Ofay

By Jack Getze
Big Mojo
Big Shoes
The Black Kachina

By Richard Godwin
Wrong Crowd
Buffalo and Sour Mash
Crystal on Electric Acetate

By Jeffery Hess
Beachhead
Cold War Canoe Club

By Matt Hilton
Rules of Honor
The Lawless Kind
The Devil's Anvil
No Safe Place

By Lawrence Kelter
and Frank Zafiro
The Last Collar

By Lawrence Kelter
Back to Brooklyn
My Cousin Vinny (*)

(*)—Coming Soon

OTHER TITLES FROM DOWN AND OUT BOOKS

See www.DownAndOutBooks.com for complete list

By Jerry Kennealy
Screen Test
Polo's Long Shot (*)

By Dana King
Worst Enemies
Grind Joint
Resurrection Mall

By Ross Klavan, Tim O'Mara
and Charles Salzberg
Triple Shot

By S.W. Lauden
Crosswise
Crossed Bones

By Paul D. Marks and
Andrew McAleer (editor)
Coast to Coast vol. 1
Coast to Coast vol. 2

By Gerald O'Connor
The Origins of Benjamin Hackett

By Gary Phillips
The Perpetrators
Scoundrels (Editor)
Treacherous
3 the Hard Way

By Thomas Pluck
Bad Boy Boogie

By Tom Pitts
Hustle
American Static

By Robert J. Randisi
Upon My Soul
Souls of the Dead
Envy the Dead

By Charles Salzberg
Devil in the Hole
Swann's Last Song
Swann Dives In
Swann's Way Out

By Scott Loring Sanders
Shooting Creek and Other Stories

By Ryan Sayles
The Subtle Art of Brutality
Warpath
Let Me Put My Stories In You

By John Shepphird
The Shill
Kill the Shill
Beware the Shill

By James R. Tuck (editor)
Mama Tried vol. 1
Mama Tried vol. 2 (*)

By Lono Waiwaiole
Wiley's Lament
Wiley's Shuffle
Wiley's Refrain
Dark Paradise
Leon's Legacy

By Nathan Walpow
The Logan Triad

(*)—Coming Soon

CPSIA information can be obtained
at www.ICGtesting.com
Printed in the USA
LVHW090152130120
643413LV00001B/25/P